LIFEMARK

OTHER NOVELS BY CHRIS FABRY

HOPE IS AT THE HEART
OF EVERY JOURNEY

Tyndale House Publishers
Carol Stream, Illinois

FROM THE CREATORS OF WAR ROOM

LIFEMARK

A NOVELIZATION BY
CHRIS FABRY

BASED ON THE MOTION PICTURE BY
THE KENDRICK BROTHERS

Visit Tyndale online at tyndale.com.

Visit Chris Fabry's website at chrisfabry.com.

For more information about *Lifemark*, visit kendrickbrothers.com.

Lifemark

Published in association with the literary agency Working Title Agency, WTA Services, LLC, Franklin, TN.

Lifemark is a work of fiction. Where real people, events, establishments, organizations, or locales appear, they are used fictitiously. All other elements of the novel are drawn from the authors' imaginations.

For information about special discounts for bulk purchases, please contact Tyndale House Publishers at csresponse@tyndale.com, or call 1-855-277-9400.

Library of Congress Cataloging-in-Publication Data

A catalog record for this book is available from the Library of Congress.

ISBN 978-1-4964-6126-1 (HC)
ISBN 978-1-4964-6127-8 (SC)

Printed in the United States of America

28 27 26 25 24 23 22
7   6   5   4   3   2   1

*Dedicated to Melissa Coles, whose courage and
selfless act brought inspiration to this beautiful story.
May your life, faith, and example bring hope and
healing to millions. God sees you and loves you!*

PART 1

CHAPTER 1

✦ ✦ ✦

The lake sat at the end of a winding dirt road on the outskirts of Columbus, Indiana, forty miles south of Indianapolis. Water rippled muddy brown this time of year because of spring rain runoff that collected and funneled into the lake from three directions. The deepest end of the lake was best for fishing and on this late afternoon, two teenage girls sat on the rock ledge looking down at their lines in the water.

Kelly White was doing more talking than fishing, as usual. She had long blonde hair and stood barely an inch over five feet tall. She'd weigh a hundred pounds if she jumped in the river and got weighed as soon as she climbed out. Because of her height and the way she moved, walking with the confidence of a top-level athlete, most boys in high school thought she was a gymnast or maybe a dancer. She was neither. She just liked boys and liked to walk as if they were watching every step. And the reason she'd agreed to meet her friend Melissa at the lake was not to fish but to talk about a boy she was interested in who was a year older.

Melissa Long, eighteen and a senior at Fleetwood High, stood on the rocks and cast her line about halfway across the lake. She was six inches taller than Kelly and nobody thought she was a dancer or a gymnast. In fact, most people didn't notice Melissa, or so she thought. She was the kind of girl you might miss in a yearbook, just pass her picture and keep turning pages. And her face had a quality to it that made her look different in each photo, like she was able to morph and change with whatever group was around her.

Melissa had long brown hair that curled from a recent perm she'd convinced a friend to give her—a hairdo in a box she'd bought at the drugstore on sale, buy one get one free. She couldn't afford a salon. Couldn't afford food, for that matter, which was why she was fishing. She'd saved up for the perm and it had turned out less frizzy than she'd feared. Her friend who had applied all the chemicals said she almost looked pretty.

Green eyes and an easy smile hid some of the pain beneath the layers of her life. Those who noticed her, who lingered on the picture or studied her in class, thought she was looking for something she hadn't found. And it was true—Melissa was on a search. You could see it in her eyes, though she wouldn't have been able to pinpoint exactly what she was looking for.

Her bobber settled and she watched it move on the undulating surface, the wind picking up. When Kelly reeled her line in, Melissa frowned and said, "Stop doing that every ten seconds. The goal is to catch a fish, not scare them away."

"You reeled yours in. Why can't I?"

"Just leave it in the water."

"I think something took my bait," Kelly said. She finished reeling and lifted the rod and the hook swung empty. "See. Told you. Put another minnow on for me."

Melissa shook her head. "Bait your own hook, Barbie."

"I can do it, but I don't like the smell. It never bothers you." Kelly dropped the rod and lay on a flat rock with her hands behind her head, staring at the clouds. The ones overhead were white and rounded, like vanilla ice cream in a cone. Others to the south were darker, a chocolaty-gray, and they seemed to be moving toward them.

"When you get out in the big bad world, you're going to wish you knew how to do things like this," Melissa said, picking up Kelly's rod. She baited the hook and cast the line to the right in a good spot, knowing this wasn't for Kelly, it was for her. She needed a fish or two to take home.

"What's baiting a hook going to do for me in the big bad world? Tell me that."

"It's not about baiting your hook. It's about being able to do something on your own instead of needing others. If you can't bait your own hook, you won't last long out there."

"Is that your philosophy of life?"

"That's the truth. Period."

Kelly studied the cloud formations as Melissa felt a strike on her line. She set the hook and reeled in an eighteen-inch crappie, holding it up with a thumb through the gill.

"Look how shiny he is. Like a silver dollar."

"How do you know it's not a she?"

Melissa ignored the question and put the fish on the stringer and put it back in the water with the two others she'd caught. She grabbed another minnow from the bucket and held it tightly as she passed the hook through the eyes. It pained her to hurt the tiny fish, but the hunger inside pushed her past that. She pulled the rod back and cast the line again, the bobber hitting with a plop, and checked the other line. The bobber floated steady.

"Tell me what he said again," Kelly said.

"Tell you what who said?"

"You know who. Lee. What did he say to Brian about me?"

"Lee's nothing but bad news. Why are you hanging around him?"

"You need me to explain?" She sat up. "He's cuter than Justin Timberlake, has bigger muscles, too. What's not to like?"

"I'm telling you he's bad news. You're a dog chasing a car. What are you going to do when you catch him?"

"I'll figure it out when it happens."

"Nothing good is going to come from you chasing him."

Kelly scoffed. "Like you're one to talk."

"What's that mean?"

"It means you ought to look in the mirror."

Melissa scowled and rolled her eyes, her back to her friend. "Brian's not like Lee. He's one of the good ones."

"Right. And you're not chasing after him at all, are you? Sharon said . . ." She stopped, evidently thinking better of finishing the thought.

Melissa turned. "Sharon said what?"

"Nothing."

Melissa put a hand on her hip. "What did she say?"

Kelly dipped her head like a second grader who had

been taught not to tattle. But Melissa saw a glint in her friend's eyes as she glanced up. She was enjoying this.

"Sharon said she saw you going into Brian's apartment. With a suitcase."

Melissa tried not to react. "So? I'm staying there for a while."

"Right. She said you two are practically married. Hanging all over each other in the hallway. Said you've moved in with him."

A glance at the bobber. "You know what it's like at my house."

"Yeah. But Sharon said you'd be staying there no matter how messed up your family is. Said you're head over heels."

Melissa kept her back turned and tried not to smile. She hated that others were talking about her, especially Sharon. What a pain. She was from the other side of the tracks, a better neighborhood—her dad was a lawyer or something. Sharon always had her nose in the air and looked down on others, but Melissa had to admit, at least to herself, that she wasn't far from the truth. Melissa was in love. She'd found the one. And it was the real thing, not some high school crush. She'd had those before. No, she and Brian had something special. Every time she heard that Whitney Houston song on the radio, she saw his face and that crooked smile of his and she sang along—*"I will always love you."* Well, she didn't actually sing, she mouthed the words, but it was the same. They had found each other, him with his family problems a mirror to hers. She wanted to spend the rest of her life with him. And he felt the same about her.

Thunder sounded in the distance. Melissa reeled in her line, the bobber skipping across the water and leaving a V in its wake. She picked up Kelly's and did the same.

"Come on, tell me," Kelly said. "What did Lee say to Brian about me?"

A big sigh. "Lee likes you. Thinks you're pretty. Gorgeous."

"He said that? He called me gorgeous?"

"Not with words, more with grunts. Like a caveman. He's not a good guy, Kelly. But I can tell I'm not going to be able to talk sense into you."

Kelly rose and stretched, yawning. Her shirt rose above her pierced navel. "He thinks I'm gorgeous."

Melissa grabbed the stringer of fish from the water and dumped the bucket of minnows into the lake. "Here, take the rods. We need to get back before the rain comes."

They walked the dirt road near a cornfield with plants that peeked out of the ground as if looking for the sky. In the summer the corn would be higher than Melissa's head, and she made a mental note to come back when she could grab a few ears for supper without being seen. Who would miss a few ears of corn?

"What's Brian going to do after graduation?" Kelly said, trudging behind. "He got that planned out?"

The question touched a nerve and made Melissa queasy. She answered a little too quickly, her voice sounding uncertain. "He'll find a job. He's just concentrating on finishing school first."

A flash of lightning in the distance and then a low rumble. They picked up their pace, approaching a hackberry tree that towered above them.

"They're closing down a section of the plant where my dad works," Kelly said. "He might have to drive to Indianapolis . . ."

Kelly's voice faded as her friend's face changed. Melissa put the stringer in the grass and dropped the minnow bucket. Running to the tree, she put her hand on the trunk and leaned forward. She hadn't had anything for lunch, so nothing came up but acid water, but her stomach clenched and she couldn't stop the churning.

When she could finally stand, her hand still on the tree and her head spinning, she saw Kelly studying her.

"Something you ate?" Kelly said.

"Probably."

Two hours later, as the downpour subsided, Melissa walked through the puddles along the street and into the pharmacy, shaking the water from her hair like a wet dog.

She pulled a plastic bag from under her shirt and waited by the makeup until there was no line at the cash register and put the bag before a man she didn't recognize. Then she stared at her hands and wondered if the man smelled the fish that lingered.

"What's this?"

"I want to return it."

He untied the bag and looked inside. "Got a receipt?"

She shook her head. "I just bought it a couple of weeks ago."

"If you don't have a receipt—"

"I don't want cash. I just want store credit. To exchange it for something else."

"Was there something wrong with it?"

"No. I never opened it."

Before he could respond, she hurried to an aisle in the back by the pharmacy, found what she needed, and returned to the front. A woman the age of her mother stood at the register, leafing through dollar bills, a plastic rain bonnet on her head. A greeting card sat on the counter, and the woman handed the bills to the man and turned, spotting what Melissa held in her hands before she could hide it.

The woman looked up at Melissa, pursed her lips and shook her head, and took the greeting card and the receipt and left.

"I want to exchange it for this," Melissa said, putting the pregnancy test kit beside the unused home perm box she'd bought. "I think they're about the same price."

The man stared at the two items before him as if he were trying to figure out some complicated mathematical theorem. Or was it a postulate? Melissa hadn't done well in geometry and had opted for consumer math instead of algebra. Unless some miracle happened, she wasn't going to college. And if you weren't going to college, who needed algebra or calculus?

The man looked up at her again and started to say something but held back. When he'd done his calculation, he said, "You're four dollars short."

She dug in both pockets of her cutoffs. She knew there were no bills there, just coins. She placed eighty-seven cents on the counter. "That's all I've got."

"You're still short."

Someone pushed a cart behind her. She looked at the cashier and could tell from his eyes she needed to fish or cut bait. She scraped the coins into her hand and grabbed the perm box, thrust it into the plastic bag, and walked out the door.

The rain came harder and sideways now, and she stood under the eave in the only dry spot on the sidewalk, in the white glow of fluorescence. She only needed three dollars and change but at the moment it felt like three million.

She could go back and ask Brian, but he'd want to know what it was for and besides, she knew he didn't have any money by the fact that he had no cigarettes left.

The door opened and a ding sounded behind her. Then someone said, "Excuse me."

Melissa turned.

"I couldn't help overhearing." A woman had her purse open, fishing for something. She pulled out a five-dollar bill and held it out. "I hope this will help you."

"You don't have to do that," Melissa said as she took the bill.

"I know. It's just something I feel the . . . well, I want you to have it. And I want you to know that He sees you."

Melissa looked behind her, then back at the woman. "Who sees me?"

She smiled and put a hand on Melissa's shoulder. Then she walked into the rain.

Melissa went back inside the store.

When Melissa came out of the bathroom, she found Brian watching wrestling on the TV he'd been given for Christmas when he was fourteen. She stood beside it, and when he didn't look at her, she turned it off.

"Hey, I was watching that!"

When he looked at her face, he stopped protesting and sat up. "What's wrong? You look like a muskrat, by the way."

"Thanks. That's a sweet thing to say."

"I just meant your hair. Where'd you go, anyway?"

"Drugstore." She sat beside him and held out the pregnancy test. "I bought this."

"Is it a thermometer?"

She handed it to him and he held it closer, studying the section where the test showed a plus sign.

"It's a thing you pee on to tell you if you're pregnant."

His mouth dropped and he couldn't take his eyes off of it. After what seemed like an ice age he said, "Why would you need to buy this?"

"Maybe if I give you a little more time, you'll figure it out?"

He looked at her, then back at the object in his hand. "You think you might be pregnant?"

"I've been sick to my stomach every morning for the past week."

"What does it say?"

"Says you're going to be a father."

The air seemed to leave the room for both of them.

"Whoa."

"Is that all you can think to say?"

He looked at her again. "I didn't . . . I mean . . . I don't know what to say. What do you want me to say?"

She saw him all blurry now, like in one of those hall-of-mirrors rooms at the county fair. She wiped her eyes and tried to stay in control, but her chin quivered and she couldn't stop it, and she hated that. She'd sat in the bathroom for a half hour after the test turned positive while a wave of emotion and fear swept over her. What she hadn't prepared for in all of that was the unexpected feeling that crept up on her. Something she couldn't tell Brian.

Brian put the pregnancy test on the TV tray by the couch. Both had been given to him by a friend who was going to haul them to the dump, along with a kitchen table and a broken refrigerator. Brian had taken them and had duct-taped the broken table leg and wedged it in the corner of the kitchen so it would stand.

"What are you going to do?" he said.

Melissa pulled her head back, then looked away. Her face felt hot all of a sudden and she clenched her fists. She'd had fights with Brian, but she'd never felt this way before. "What am I going to do? Is that your question?"

"Yeah, I mean, what do you want me to ask you?"

"How about, what are *we* going to do? You're part of this, you know."

"I know that." His eyes got soft and he reached out to touch her shoulder, but she moved away. The couch cushions sagged. She grabbed the edge and pulled herself up, leaning against the wall with her arms crossed.

"We're not ready, Melissa. I don't have a job. I'm behind on the rent. There's no food. I'm not going to my mom for help and I know you don't want to go to your dad."

He was right about all of that. And there were more reasons they weren't ready and shouldn't be having a baby. But Melissa couldn't shake the feeling she'd had in the bathroom. Mixed in with all the fear and shame and feeling stupid for not being more careful and a hundred other bad thoughts was a single word that rose to the surface like a rainbow trout in her heart.

Mother.

She was going to be a mother. And there was something about that word, something about the concept, that made her feel alive. That tingle inside surprised her. On one hand, she felt like a million bricks had collapsed on top of her. She couldn't breathe. And there was nobody she could tell because she knew what they'd think, what they'd say.

At the same time—and it was the strangest thing to feel this way—she sensed there was something good growing inside her. But every time she thought of that, another brick would fall and snap her back to reality.

"What do you think we should do, then?" Brian said.

"I don't know."

CHAPTER 2

✦　✦　✦

A week after Melissa placed the positive pregnancy test in his hands, Brian parked next to a dingy gray building that sat in the shadow of I-65. Above was a half-lit sign that should have read *Pawn-a-Palooza*, but at night you could only see one *a*, one *P*, and the *looz*. The business didn't need a sign for its clientele. Anybody who wanted fast cash or a little offtrack betting or the perpetual poker game in one of the back rooms knew this was the place.

Brian winced from neck pain that had been nagging him all day. He'd slept on it wrong or maybe strained a muscle trying to fix some of their furniture. He kept tilting his head and stretching to try to work it out.

Maybe it was the stress of Melissa's news. He shook that thought away and carried a boom box into the store. It was only a month ago that he'd bought it. He'd had extra cash back then and it seemed like a good idea.

He placed the boom box on the counter in front of a burly man with a beard and bloodshot eyes the color of an Indiana sunset.

The man glanced at it, then looked up at him. "We don't deal with stolen items."

"I didn't steal it. I bought it a month ago."

"What's wrong with it?"

"Nothing. It works great."

"Why don't you take it back to the store where you bought it, then?"

"I did. They said I needed a receipt. They only offered a store credit, and I need cash."

"How much did you pay for it?"

"Three hundred."

The man scowled. He pointed to an overflowing shelf of car radios and older boom boxes. When Brian turned his head, a pain shot through his neck and he grabbed it.

"I already got radios like that."

"But this one's almost new."

The man stared at the boom box, then picked it up and looked it over. "How much you want?"

"Two eighty."

"No way. I'll give you two hundred. Take it or leave it."

Brian looked down and rubbed his neck again. The woman who answered the phone at the abortion clinic in Indianapolis had said they needed $220. He'd called three in the area, and theirs was the lowest price. He hadn't told Melissa any of that. He didn't want her to say they didn't have enough money for the procedure.

He also needed ten bucks for something to eat.

Brian leaned forward and spoke with a humble tone, hoping the man would read between the lines. "I need it for my girlfriend."

The man's eyebrows went up. "You want to trade for an engagement ring? We got some nice ones down here in—"

"I'm not looking for a ring. I need the cash. I need $230." He swallowed hard and locked eyes. "She's in trouble. We're in trouble."

The man studied him a moment, then stepped toward the register and took out $230.

In Brian's mind there was only one answer to their predicament. When your car was headed toward a cliff, you turned the wheel and slammed on the brakes. You let your instincts take over. Simple as that.

But he could tell there was something going on in

Melissa. Her instincts were telling her something else, and he felt it was up to him to guide her instead of forcing her. So on the way home he spent ten bucks to pick up dinner from Melissa's favorite fast-food restaurant, Taco Bell.

In the apartment, he put the brown bag on the table and called for her. No answer. He pecked on the closed bathroom door.

"Hey, I brought you something."

She groaned and her voice echoed like her head was in a bucket. "Be there in a minute."

The food was cold by the time she came out. Her face was one shade less than marshmallow, and she had one hand on her stomach and the other wiping sweat from her forehead. When she saw the food, she scrunched her face in disbelief.

"Where'd you get the money for this?"

"It's a surprise. Come on and eat."

She shook her head and made another face. "That's not very appetizing right now."

"You love Taco Bell. I got you nachos."

She swallowed hard. "The smell turns my stomach. Why didn't you ask me? I would have told you to get me some saltines."

"Fine." Brian tossed her box of nachos in the refrigerator and slammed the door. "I try to do something nice for you and this is what I get."

"Why are you getting mad? I'm sick as a dog. This is not personal."

Brian sat at the table thinking of the boom box he'd just sold. It felt like everything he touched went south. He took a deep breath. "I just wanted to make you feel better. Have things get back to normal. I thought the food would help."

She wandered to the couch and sat, her back to him, sinking deep into the cushions.

"Look, I think we need to talk," he said. It was easier to say that without looking her in the face.

"About what?"

"You know what."

"Then go on and talk."

"I hate seeing you go through this."

"Well, there's nothing either of us can do about it now."

Yes, there is, he thought. But he didn't say that.

"Have you told anybody?" he said.

"No. Who am I going to tell? My family? You know what they'd say. 'We told you so.'"

The words stung, but they were the truth. It was one of the things that had drawn them together, her family's dislike of him. He nodded and the pain shot up his neck again and he rubbed it. He waited for the courage to speak.

"You know, you don't have to go through this. You could take care of it."

Her head didn't move. Finally she said, "You think I don't know that?"

He swallowed hard. "I called a clinic today. There's one close to Indy. Nobody would know you there. I could drive you."

She turned and glared at him.

"Melissa, it's not fair to have a kid right now."

"Fair for who?"

"For you. For either of us."

She touched her stomach. "And what about the baby?"

He thought a moment. "It's not fair for the kid either. What kind of chance is it going to have? Right now's not the time to start a family. We need more time. Get our feet under us."

He stood and sat beside her, the cushions sinking lower. Then he put his arm around her shoulders and she didn't move away.

"One day you're going to have kids. And you're going to be a great mom."

Melissa looked at him and there was a tremble in her voice when she said, "I'm scared, Brian."

"It's going to be okay."

"You promise?"

"I promise. We'll get this done and make a new start."

"And you'll go with me?"

"Of course. I said I would. I'm here for the long haul."

"I've got some money coming for graduation, I think."

"That's great. See, things are coming together. You'll see. It's going to work out. It'll be like it never happened."

✦   ✦   ✦

"Like it never happened."

Those words echoed inside Melissa's head the next morning as she knelt in the bathroom, her stomach clenching. She wondered if all pregnant women went through this same nausea. Had her mother gone through this with her?

She felt so tired and alone—and yet she wasn't alone. Brian was there for her and he seemed to care. But was he right? Would she be able to simply move past this and forget it? Would it feel like it never happened?

At a school health fair, she'd picked up a clinic brochure. She'd almost tossed it away. She would never need an abortion. Other people had those. But she read that the "procedure" (the flyer always used a different word than *abortion* for some reason) was safe and painless. The unplanned pregnancy was not something that needed to put your life on hold. There was a safe way to get on with your life and empower yourself.

Beside the word *safe* was an asterisk, and in the fine print at the bottom she read something about side effects. They were rare, but some women experienced complications and even hospitalization. But the overwhelming message of the pamphlet was that abortion helped women take control of their own bodies and their futures.

If that were true, why was she having a problem with it? Why did she have a nagging feeling, like the nausea that followed her through the day, that this wasn't just a blob of tissue growing inside, but a human being? Her child.

She sat back, still on her knees, and remembered a girl who'd been two years ahead of her in school. What was her name? Andrea? Annie? She couldn't remember. There'd been a bonfire the night before the homecoming football game and the girl, whatever her name was, had sat on a log in a hoodie and spoken to those near her. Melissa had listened to their conversation.

"What was it like?" someone asked.

"It's not that big of a deal. It's like any other doctor's appointment. It's like having your teeth cleaned."

The other girls laughed.

"But doesn't it hurt?" someone said. "I heard you bleed a lot afterward."

The girl rolled her eyes. "I'd do anything to not have a kid. Why should I be punished? The peace of mind was worth a little bleeding and cramping. That's all that happened to me. And now things are back to normal. I made a mistake and I dealt with it."

"What about inside the clinic? My mom said it's dark and dirty in there."

"Your mom is probably the kind that protests. It was like any other doctor's office. The nurses were nice. The doctor told me what was going to happen. It's the best decision I ever made."

"No second thoughts?" another girl said.

"The only thing I'd do different is find a place where those crazies weren't out front. They were holding signs with grisly pictures. I wish I hadn't seen those. But I guess they're everywhere. It ought to be illegal to protest like that."

Melissa had seen the girl in the hallway the next week. She was tall and good-looking, and a guy from the football team had his arm around her. Was he the one who had arranged the procedure like Brian was arranging hers? Would the clinic near Indianapolis have protesters?

She stood and looked in the mirror, her face pale. She suddenly felt ravenous, so she stumbled to the refrigerator and found the nachos from the night before. She was so hungry she didn't even heat them up.

The memory of that fireside chat about abortion comforted Melissa, and she wondered how many other friends or acquaintances—even teachers—had gone through the procedure and simply hadn't talked about it. But the memory also troubled her. Maybe it was the matter-of-fact way the girl had spoken. It seemed more important, more weighty, than having your teeth cleaned.

Then an even more somber thought came. Why did those people stand outside the clinic with signs and try to convince the women to change their minds? What right did they have to judge? Wasn't this something a woman ought to decide on her own without pressure from others? *Unless . . .*

She didn't want to think of the *unless*. Her mother's friend, Addie, was a big churchgoer, one of those with bumper stickers on the back of her car. *It's a child, not a choice. Abortion stops a beating heart.* Melissa had gone to her church's youth group a few times when she was younger. There were some cute guys there, but she didn't understand all the talk about the Bible. When she was invited again, Melissa politely refused and said she was busy, and the woman seemed sad as she drove away.

Was Addie one of those people who yelled at girls walking into a clinic? What would happen if Melissa called and asked her opinion? She shook her head at the thought. Whether she talked to her parents or any of their friends, it would just be one big I-told-you-so.

No, the only person she could trust was Brian. He was the only one who really cared. She took another bite of cold nachos and then ran to the bathroom.

CHAPTER 3

✦ ✦ ✦

Pain often provides an opportunity we don't desire. And on that day in 1999, the pain in the heart of Susan Colton provided another opportunity for her husband to love her well.

The two rode in silence, passing the Louisiana country-side as Jimmy drove their Jeep as if steered by some inner compass.

Susan was thirty-six, with blonde, shoulder-length hair and a pleasant smile. She and Jimmy made the perfect pair, everyone said. He was two years older but they both could pass for much younger. He had neatly trimmed brown hair and a boyish smile that had attracted her at first glance, though she had tried not to seem too interested. Now all he had to do was flash that smile and her heart melted.

Jimmy, a constant listener to talk radio anytime he was in the car, talking back to whoever's voice he heard, sensed that Susan needed the quiet. That was part of his inner compass too. He had an ability to know what she needed without asking, at least a lot of the time.

She would have smiled at the thought, and maybe it would have driven her to give thanks for the idea that passed through her mind, but at this moment on this stretch of lonely road, she was preoccupied by other things. Memories flashed. Events of the past that led them to the hard ground ahead.

It was frightening how easy it was to be back there again. All it took was a sound, a scent, an image, and her heart was right there in the hospital hallway with the family gathered around the large nursery windows, standing on tiptoe for a better look. She'd been ecstatic about her firstborn. It had been a difficult pregnancy, but since it was her first, she could only compare it to those of other moms who shared their experience.

She closed her eyes as the tires hummed on the pavement. She saw the doctor's face, the ashen look he gave her. The way he walked into the room, tentative, and crossed his arms. She heard the way he said her name, like he was a judge about to read a sentence handed down by a jury.

"Susan, there's something wrong."

Michael was born on the ninth of November and died on the nineteenth, and she had poured out as much love in those ten days as she could, speaking comfort to him and herself at the same time. She read from the Psalms, particularly the twenty-third, and though it was the darkest valley she had ever walked through, it was also the most peaceful. So still and quiet she could hear each breath he took, every heartbeat. Somehow she had felt God's presence through that crucible like never before.

Michael looked perfect. He was perfect. Except that he wasn't. But she believed enough in the goodness of God that even a brief life, one that crushed her with grief, had a purpose. And as his body grew frail and his heartbeat faint, she comforted herself with the thought that her son had drawn her closer to her heavenly Father. What more could a mother ask of a son?

In the midst of her lament came questions. A life lived fully always came with questions. And as she watched Jimmy hold Michael for the last time before the nurse came for his little body, through tears she prayed something she felt incapable of praying on her own.

I choose to thank You for ten days rather than question

*why You didn't give ten months or ten years. I don't under-
stand, Lord. Hold on to me.*

Jimmy handed his son to the nurse without tears,
and at first it upset Susan. It felt like she was carrying
more than her fair share of the grief. But the longer they
walked together, the more she understood that Jimmy was
carrying as much of the load as she was, if not more. He
just carried it differently. Fewer tears, at least that she saw,
and more staring out the window and going for walks
and sitting quietly alone. But he was there for her in her
tears, right beside her. Her tears seemed to draw him, and
he became more comfortable with them. She began to
believe that there were things you could never know about
others until you walked through the deep water together.
Through Michael's death, she realized Jimmy's silence
wasn't indifference but simply another way of moving
through the flood. Some swam. Some waded. Some went
under and didn't surface until they were downstream.

Less than a year later, Susan learned she was pregnant
again, and they both believed God was giving them joy
amid the sorrow, beauty for ashes. She would never forget
Michael and the things she learned through that stinging
loss, but life would be different with John David. And she
determined she would raise John with a knowledge of his
brother.

However, the diagnosis of a genetic defect was the same

for their second son. Doctors expected John's life to be as brief as his brother's, a handful of days. But Susan held him and rocked him and sang to him and kissed him for a whole week that turned into two and then three. She had long enough with him in her arms to see a little of his personality coming through. The way he crooked his mouth and looked into her eyes, like he could see her soul. By the time he had lived two dozen days, she believed God was going to give more time, that something miraculous was going to happen.

But there was no miracle. And when they gathered at the freshly dug grave with the tiny white casket, it felt like she would never escape the valley of the shadow of death.

Jimmy had said something to her a few weeks after John died that stuck with her. He had again stared out the window and taken long walks alone, processing his grief privately. The empty crib stood as a memorial now and she couldn't look at it but she also couldn't stand to get rid of it.

One day Jimmy came up behind her at the breakfast table and put a hand on her shoulder and just stood there as if he were gathering the courage to say what he held inside.

"You know, I think God must trust us a lot to give a double burden like this."

He patted her shoulder but as he walked away, she said, "I don't want Him to trust us like that. I want my sons."

He turned and studied her face and nodded. "I understand."

Susan got out of the car and they walked together across the freshly mowed grass. She carried a bouquet of yellow lilies and baby's breath and knelt in front of the stones. Between the markers was a vase, and she removed the withered and spent bouquet and handed it to Jimmy, replacing it with fresh flowers between her two sons.

The marker on the left said:

MICHAEL JOHN COLTON
Infant son of Jimmy and Susan
Nov. 9, 1993–Nov. 19, 1993

The marker on the right said:

JOHN DAVID COLTON
Infant son of Jimmy and Susan
June 15, 1995–July 15, 1995

"John would be three now," Susan said. "Michael would be five."

As she stared at the stones, she could see the boys in her arms. She could feel the warmth of their skin and what it felt like to kiss their foreheads and watch them open their eyes and look into hers. And she wondered what heaven might be like for them, if they were doing all the things they were never able to do on earth—run and play and laugh. Sometimes she dreamed of them wearing matching backpacks and getting on the school bus. She always awoke from those dreams smiling, knowing it was the only place she saw them.

She took Jimmy's hand in her own and they walked back to the car, stopping once at a new headstone. Fresh grief for a family they didn't know. She whispered a prayer for them.

Jimmy didn't start the car when he got in. She glanced at him. He seemed deep in thought. Finally he spoke.

"What if we contacted the adoption agency one more time?"

She turned and looked out the windshield, trying not to react too quickly to the suggestion. Her gaze focused on the little stones in the distance, the ones with baby shoes and lilies between them. The question opened another wound in a series of losses they had experienced between John's death and today.

Susan shook her head. "No. I know that I should be happy when a birth mom changes her mind and keeps her baby." Her chin quavered and she felt like she would come apart. "But my heart just can't take it again."

She saw the love in Jimmy's eyes. It worked itself out

in a commitment that didn't give up. But she could tell even with his placid face that somewhere inside he was hurt.

"I'm sorry," she said. "It's just hard for me."

He smiled at her. "I understand."

CHAPTER 4

✦ ✦ ✦

The two-story brick building known as Parker Avenue
Family Planning sat on the south side of Indianapolis on
a tree-lined street with modest homes nearby. It could
have housed lawyers or Realtors or several dentists. The
only out-of-the-ordinary thing Melissa noticed as they
pulled to the back of the parking lot was the number of
people on the sidewalk. As they drove by, she shielded her
face and tried not to look at them.

The drive up had been quiet. Like a funeral. Brian
turned on his favorite rock station, but there was a loose

connection he had missed when he installed the radio, and the speakers crackled and popped and finally died.

Brian handed her the cash she'd need and Melissa put the bills in her purse. She couldn't look at him. She felt cold and numb.

"Melissa, we agreed," Brian said.

"I know," she said quickly, stopping him before he could say anything else. She stared at the protesters holding signs and singing. Some looked like they were praying.

"I'm sorry," she said. "This is just hard for me."

Brian looked in the rearview mirror. "Do they come to the car or . . . ?"

"I don't know. I've never done this before," she said, snapping at him.

Two women in light-green scrubs approached the passenger-side door and Melissa got out, the women quickly draping a blanket over her, leaving just enough room for Melissa to see.

"We're going to put this over your head to protect you."

They both held radios close to Melissa's ears, blaring rock music. She assumed they wanted to drown out the protesters. The music did cut out some voices, but as she neared the entrance, in the confusion and hurry, one voice cut through the mayhem.

"Your baby has ten fingers and ten toes," a woman called out. "Please don't kill it."

The noise subsided as they made it to the front desk. The two women in scrubs took the blanket and gestured toward the lady behind the counter.

"Name, please."

"Umm . . . Melissa Long."

She placed her driver's license on the counter, but the woman shook her head. "We don't need that."

Melissa thought that was odd. No proof needed of her identity. She put it back in her purse and turned to see Brian standing just inside the door, looking around the plain white waiting room as if he didn't know whether to sit or go back to the car.

"It's two hundred twenty."

Melissa turned back toward the lady, who looked as if she'd already had a bad day. She quickly opened her purse and handed her the cash.

The woman took the money and placed two forms in front of Melissa. "Fill these out and someone will be with you shortly."

After she turned in her information, she sat quietly next to Brian. There were two other men in the waiting room and neither of them seemed comfortable. One of them, an African American man in his forties, kept picking up magazines, glancing at them, and putting them back down. Another man, Caucasian, maybe thirty, glanced at his watch, then the floor.

A few minutes later a door opened. A woman called Melissa's name and she stood.

"I'll see you when you come out," Brian said.

She glanced at him, then followed the woman through a door and down the hallway to a room where she undressed and put on a hospital gown. It seemed just like other appointments she'd been to at the doctor's office, but she knew this was going to be different. She felt it in her stomach.

The nurse handed her a paper cup with a blue pill inside. "You'll need to take this."

Melissa didn't ask what it was for, just took it and wadded up the cup and tossed it in the trash. Beside the wastebasket sat a silver tray with tools that glistened in the fluorescent light. Some looked like scissors on one end, but on the other they had odd shapes with teeth that would fit into a gear of some sort. She studied the tray and wondered if those were for her. She glanced around the room and noticed that everything seemed like silver metal. The cabinet, a table, and a round silver stool on wheels made the room feel hard and cold. Other than that, the room had white walls with nothing on them.

She sat on the exam table, her feet not touching the floor, and crossed her arms, suddenly feeling a chill. Then she heard footsteps. The doctor knocked lightly, then came inside, and as soon as she saw his face, she knew she'd remember it the rest of her life. He nodded to her and turned and washed his hands in the sink, soaping up to his elbows and rinsing off like she'd seen on TV shows. He dried his hands with paper towels and tossed them in the trash.

He avoided her eyes as he slid on a pair of blue surgical gloves. Then he sat on the silver stool and scooted across the room as if he'd done that a thousand times before and could navigate the room with his eyes closed.

He tapped the stirrups and motioned for her to put her feet in them, still avoiding eye contact.

Melissa obeyed and leaned back, laying her head on the table as the doctor turned toward the tray of instruments. Her heart raced faster, and she could feel her pulse throbbing in her neck.

Thoughts began racing through her mind, and the words she had just heard outside echoed in her head.

"Your baby has ten fingers and ten toes."

Melissa grimaced and tried to dismiss the thought. She had promised Brian she would do this. She just wanted to get it over with. Yet the quiet in the room felt eerie and unsettling. Why did this feel so wrong?

Get up. There's still time.

Melissa froze. The words had been spoken clearly but were not audible. The doctor still had not spoken a word to her as he positioned himself for the procedure.

Her eyes widened. She stared at the white-tiled ceiling, still waiting for the doctor to start. Then the words came again, this time with more urgency.

Get up! There's still time.

Melissa turned her head to the right as if trying to find the person speaking to her. Then she saw him.

There, in a blurry reflection on the side of the silver cabinet, she saw herself on the table. She could see the doctor's reflection too. But she also saw someone standing beside her. A young man, maybe twenty, with short brown hair. Yet no one else was in the room.

Melissa felt the doctor touch her leg as he began the procedure, but she jerked her feet out of the stirrups and sat up.

"Stop. I can't do this!"

The doctor paused, looking her in the eyes for the first time. Then he looked down and sighed in frustration.

Without a word, he stood, ripped his gloves off, threw them in the trash, and walked out the door.

Melissa sat still a moment, trying to calm herself. The only sound she heard was her own heart pounding.

God, was that You speaking to me? Who was that young man in the reflection?

She stood and took her clothes from the hanger by the door and quickly dressed, then walked out. As she headed down the hall, she passed another young girl sitting outside a different procedure room. She was pale and slumped over, still wearing her medical gown. Melissa turned her gaze toward the waiting room door.

✦ ✦ ✦

Brian tried not to imagine what was happening beyond the walls of the waiting room. He rubbed his hands and tried not to hear the voices of the people outside. They pleaded with each person who walked in.

"Stop!"

"You don't have to do this to your baby."

"People will help you!"

He glanced at the clock. How long would she be in there? He'd sensed on the drive up that she was having a hard time with the decision. But this was the best choice. Just a few more minutes and it would all be over.

The door opened and Melissa walked out and put a gown in a hamper by the door. She slung her purse over her shoulder and quickly walked past the reception desk. He stood and followed her outside but didn't catch up to her until she was at the car.

"You didn't have to do it!" someone yelled.

"God can forgive you!"

Brian and Melissa got in the car and started to buckle up. Brian felt somewhat relieved that the whole ordeal was over.

"Well, that didn't take long."

Melissa was quiet and turned her face toward the window as he pulled out of the parking lot.

What was he supposed to say? He wanted to know if it hurt, if the people were nice to her, what they said about how she'd feel in the next few days. But from her silence and the way she stared out the window, he decided to focus on finding his way back to the interstate.

Twenty minutes later he gripped the steering wheel and mustered the courage to speak.

"You okay?"

Still staring out the window, she began to shake her head.

"Are you hurting? What's going on? Talk to me."

Silence. Then a little girl's voice. "I didn't do it."

Brian shifted in his seat, his heart rate increasing. "What are you talking about? What do you mean?"

Melissa put a hand to her face, and he heard her soft sobs. Finally she said, "I couldn't do it, Brian."

"Are you kidding me?" he said, then said it again louder when she kept crying and didn't respond. "Melissa, I gave you $220!"

She was crying harder now, tears and sobs and no holding back, her body shuddering.

"Melissa, I can't get that money back! I sold my radio so we could do this. What were you thinking?"

He had sacrificed so much for this. He had given her a chance at a future and what had she done? She'd thrown it away.

"Come on, answer me! What were you thinking?"

"I want to go home, Brian," she whispered.

"Well, do you want to have a kid in high school? Is that what you want?"

"Can we please just go home?"

"Is that what you want?" he yelled. "What are you going to do?" He couldn't hold back his anger and the sense of betrayal he felt. How many times had they gone over the plan? She had agreed. He had given her all that money. They were united as "we," and now she had done something on her own, on a whim, an impetuous decision. She'd just walked out of the clinic.

He turned to her and banged the steering wheel. "Melissa, what are you going to do?"

She shook her head and sobbed. Finally she whispered, "I don't know."

Back at the apartment, Melissa collapsed on the couch, wrung out like a dishrag. All the emotion had leaked from her on the drive home, and she felt she'd let Brian down. He was cold and distant as they walked into the apartment, and as she watched him open the refrigerator and stare inside, she just felt numb.

She couldn't get the doctor's face out of her mind or the way he had rolled his eyes before he walked out of the room. The other painful image from the morning was the people outside, the ones holding signs. When she'd gone into the building, women had protected her—put a blanket over her head and tried to drown out the voices with music. Those women were not there when she clutched her purse and walked to Brian's car. And when she glanced at those who lined the wrought iron fence with their signs, she saw the looks on their faces. Like she was a murderer. They thought she had gone through with the abortion and she couldn't shake the judgment she felt.

Brian crouched before the refrigerator and Melissa lifted her head to see inside. A plastic water jug. A bottle of ketchup. Mustard. Ranch dressing.

"Well, is this how you want your baby to live?" he said.

"Our baby," she said.

He closed the door and put his back to the counter and stared at her. She ran through different scenarios of what they might do. How would they make it now that she had closed this door?

"We could move back in with my dad." Even saying that left a bad taste in her mouth.

"Then you're going to have to tell him," Brian said.

She could tell by how quick he answered and the tone of his voice that he had run through the scenario.

"And you already know he's not going to let you keep it," he added. "We got this place to get away from him and now you want to go back?"

He waited for an answer, but Melissa turned her head and stared at the back of the couch. Brian was right. She was stuck. And it felt like she'd turned down the best answer to their problems when she got off that table and walked out of that room. But something inside told her there was another path to take.

"Is that what you want?" Brian said, bringing her back to reality.

Then his voice grew soft and gentle. Instead of the biting questions, he said, almost tenderly, "Melissa, we haven't even eaten today."

"You think I don't know that?" she said.

He walked out of the room, and the feeling of being left alone overpowered her. She had believed from the moment she met Brian that he was the one. When he put his arm around her, when he smiled at her, she felt tingly inside, like there was nothing in the world that could matter as much as the two of them being together. There didn't seem to be any problem they could encounter that would take that feeling away.

She considered him her soul mate, which meant they

were destined for each other and her life would not have been complete unless they met and fell in love. But the pregnancy had caused her to see a different side of Brian. What if he wasn't the one? What were the chances of her soul mate being in the same town she had grown up in? The thought troubled her and she pushed it away.

Brian grabbed their fishing rods and headed to the car. He was backing out when Melissa approached, and he stopped. She got in the passenger side and they rode in silence. There was a lake Brian liked a few miles from their apartment. She liked to walk to the rocky waters near the cornfields, but he preferred a reservoir near a park. It was peaceful here with grassy slopes and quiet water.

After stopping at a bait shop, they sat on the bank and Melissa baited her hook with a minnow, putting the hook through the eyes. Brian would rather use worms, but the minnows were cheaper. Yet he struggled to work his hook into the minnow.

"What are you doing? You've got to hook it through the eye."

"I know how to bait my own hook," Brian said.

Fishing not only provided food, it helped him think. Casting the line and reeling it in. The back and forth and the waiting made his mind slow instead of spinning with all the questions and pressure he felt. Without all the anger and disappointment and whatever else was stirring, he got the courage to speak.

"Look, I can't be a father right now. I can't. Maybe one day, but I . . . we've got to finish school, I've got to get a job . . ."

"I can't just turn this off, Brian. It may feel like you can because you're not the one carrying it, but I can't do that."

"I'm just trying to do what's best for us, Melissa."

"I know." Her voice was soft and it felt like she understood him. Then she said, "I just want to do what's best for the baby."

CHAPTER 5

✦ ✦ ✦

Susan Colton opened the envelope, resigned to the feelings that rose once she saw the return address. She knew inside was an invitation to a baby shower. She took a deep breath, the same deep breath she took every year in May when Mother's Day rolled around. That was a date she dreaded, an open wound that never healed. A baby shower invitation created the same pain.

It wasn't that she didn't appreciate her mother or other women who were recognized at church with flowers and encouraging words from the pulpit. She wanted moms to be recognized and appreciated. But for her, the day was a reminder of what she wasn't experiencing—what she'd lost and would never have. So on that Sunday in May she always stayed home from church and found something else to do, protecting her heart.

A proverb came to mind. "Each heart knows its own bitterness, and no one else can fully share its joy." Only she knew the struggle she felt as she opened the invitation, printed in blue and pink. The shower was for Evelyn Miller, a good friend. She'd been there through the losses of Michael and John. Susan stared at the hand-drawn stork, and instead of crumpling the paper and throwing it away, instead of feeling the stabbing pain of all she'd lost, she smiled. She had prayed for the ability to rejoice with others at their good news, and this was the first time she'd felt like she might actually be able to attend such an event.

She took note of the list of requested items at the bottom of the page. There was also a phone number for the coordinator of the event so that more expensive gifts weren't duplicated.

Jimmy was at the sink cleaning dishes when she put the mail on the desk in the kitchen. She walked down the hallway to the first door and when it swung open, she felt like she was looking at a gravestone to all her hopes and dreams. Her eyes settled on the white crib.

She walked into the room and closed her eyes, imagining the space filled with the voices of children. She ran her hands along the crib frame, feeling the smooth wood, admiring the craftsmanship. She touched a stuffed bear in the corner behind several pillows and imagined what it would have been like to see her son dragging the toy to the breakfast table, yawning and wiping sleep from his eyes.

As she left, she lingered at the door, looking at the unused rocking chair in the corner. Everything in the room was unused. Why was she holding on?

She closed the door and walked to the kitchen, grabbing her purse and shopping list.

Jimmy dried his hands on a dish towel and turned to her, a serious look on his face. "Did you think I wouldn't notice?"

Susan innocently said, "What are you talking about?"

He swung the towel over his shoulder and turned dramatically, reaching for something behind the toaster. He pulled out an open box of Caramel deLites Girl Scout cookies and held them up as if they were evidence at a trial. "You promised to leave me half."

"Did I . . . not?" she said, straight-faced, playing along with the accusation.

Jimmy pulled out the plastic container and held it up for the jury of one. "Two," he said.

Susan acted unfazed by the proceedings, her face a blank slate.

"There are two cookies in this box, which, for some reason, was hidden behind the toaster." He put the container in the box and placed it before her on the counter. Without a hint of a smile he said, "What do you have to say for yourself?"

"Only that . . . I meant to eat those, too," she said.

Finally Jimmy bobbed his head, raising his eyebrows. "Oh, there will be consequences."

She lifted her hands and waved her fingers at him. "Consequences? What kind of consequences?"

He took the wet dish towel from his shoulder and flicked it at her, the end cracking like a whip.

"No, Jimmy! Seriously, stop it!"

He moved around the island and she ran from him, laughing. "No!"

"You promised!" Jimmy said, snapping the towel again. "Listen, you owe me an entire box of cookies all for myself and you can't have any of them."

She stopped in her original position and Jimmy went back to holding the towel normally. "I'm going to get you a box of cookies right now. I'm going right this minute!"

Smiling, he said, "You don't have to go right now. I can be patient."

She added cookies to her list. "That's okay. I have to pick up some diapers and some wipes and a few other things."

Jimmy had gone back to drying. He held a yellow

dinner plate in his hands but stopped and turned slowly, looking for an explanation.

Susan smiled. "Umm, for the Millers' baby shower. It's on Saturday."

"Oh," Jimmy said, resuming his drying. He put the dish in the drying rack and turned to the sink.

Susan had practiced how to bring up what she was about to say. She'd run through the scenarios in her mind of when might be best to broach the topic. Now seemed as good a time as any.

"That kind of reminds me. They don't have a crib yet. And I was thinking that maybe we could give them ours."

When Jimmy finally turned and looked at her, the same proverb came to mind.

"Each heart knows its own bitterness . . ."

He took a deep breath. "Could we take a little time to think about that?"

She saw the pain in his eyes. She could hear it in his voice too. "Of course," she said, smiling. "Because I would only want to do that if you wanted to do that."

He nodded and folded the dish towel for no reason.

"Okay, I'm going to go to the store and get you a very large box of cookies," she said, pausing. "And thank you for doing the dishes."

"Love you," he said as she walked away.

"Love you," she said.

✦ ✦ ✦

To Jimmy, Susan's words about the crib were a punch in the gut. He tried not to let her see his reaction. He had forced a smile and given her a gentle pushback. She had left smiling. She'd said she loved him. And it made him wonder if perhaps her request was a test. He hadn't given up on using that crib and that room. Sure, they had gone through the wringer with Michael and John, and his heart was just as broken as hers. But instead of giving up, he felt more committed to fatherhood than ever, though he wasn't sure why.

Perhaps Susan had mentioned the crib to see if his resolve was still steady. They had applied for adoption and had gone through the entire process, even to the point of hearing a baby might be available. Then came the silence and the eventual call.

"We're so sorry."

Susan slipped into a depression, but it wasn't so much a slip as a free fall. Jimmy helped as much as he could, but it was only when they pulled their application that she was able to find a semblance of peace.

He thought about their playful exchange over the cookies. That was one way he could tell they were getting back to themselves—to be able to laugh and have fun with each other was a sign they had progressed. And the laughter felt good.

So what does it look like to love your wife in this situation?

He saw the phone on the desk and walked to it and opened the directory. At the front was the number for the adoption agency he and Susan had chosen. What would happen if he called? What would happen if they gave this one more try? But he couldn't do that without Susan's okay. If another adoption fell through . . .

He picked up the phone and dialed the number. A pleasant voice answered.

"Yes, this is Jimmy Colton. I'd like to resubmit our letter and application, please."

"I'll be glad to help you, Mr. Colton," the woman said.

CHAPTER 6

✦ ✦ ✦

Melissa had learned from an early age not to ask for help. A responsible person does things herself, figures things out on her own. If you rely on others, you'll become dependent, and people will always let you down. You must pull yourself up by your own bootstraps.

This mindset was partly due to how she was raised. After her parents divorced, her father had married another woman with her own kids, and Melissa watched him spend more time with them than her. His new wife never got along with Melissa, and soon it became obvious that the best thing to do was to get out of the house.

Melissa's mom wasn't easy either, and the two butted heads regularly. Melissa struggled to believe either parent loved her, and soon she found herself feeling emotionally abandoned by her own family.

However, Melissa's life and outlook began to change in June when she called the adoption agency. She assumed she was close to three months along. As soon as she explained her situation, the woman on the other end paused. It almost sounded like she was crying.

"I can't tell you how encouraging it is to hear your story, Melissa. You did a brave thing, a courageous, life-giving thing for your baby."

"Thank you, ma'am."

"Have you been seen by a doctor?"

Melissa told her the rest of the story and it sounded like the woman was typing on the other end. By the end of the call, Melissa had information about a doctor only a few miles away who would see her without cost to her. There was also a place where she could get financial assistance for food and vitamins, a pregnancy resource center (she'd never heard of such a thing), and an appointment to meet with a counselor at the adoption agency.

She had assumed she would need to do all of that herself and was surprised to find otherwise.

Brian said he wanted to support her decision, but he had emphasized that it was *her* decision, not theirs. He'd suggested she might want to "stay with someone out of town" while she went through with her pregnancy.

"And who did you have in mind?" she said, hands on hips.

He'd dropped the suggestion but his words brought a double wound. The first pain came from the fact that she was losing confidence that he would stick by her through the coming months. The second wound was the loss of her mom's friend, Addie Young.

Addie had been Melissa's godmother. She was a feisty woman with wild gray hair and tinted eyeglasses that made her look like a wrinkled federal agent. She had a way of staring at Melissa through those glasses that made her think the woman saw more than others did. After Melissa's parents divorced, Addie had let Melissa stay with her on weekends, sensing the weight of that loss. They'd had long conversations about baking and life during the Depression and seeing Addie's brothers fight in World War II, one of them returning, the other killed in the Ardennes during a bloody battle.

One day when Melissa was sixteen and Addie's cough had grown worse, the old woman grew quiet. When she spoke, Melissa leaned in, hanging on every word she got out between coughs.

"There's something you need to know about your mother, Melissa. She was pregnant with your oldest brother before she married your father. That's the main reason they got married. I advised against it, but she was headstrong. She said she could settle your father down."

Addie took her glasses off, her pupils the size of pinholes. "I want you to look at me. Your mother did the best she could. But there's going to come a day when some fellow is going to tell you that you hung the moon and be all sweet to you. Choose a husband carefully. Don't pick one you have to change."

Melissa had spent the next year sizing up young men in the school hallways. She dated a few who needed a lot of changes, guys she knew Addie wouldn't approve of, but then she met Brian. She wouldn't have changed a thing about him. Until, that is, this situation with the baby.

She'd taken Addie's wisdom to heart but had never introduced her godmother to Brian. Addie's health had declined again soon after their talk. She'd been in and out of the hospital and then a nursing home. Melissa hadn't visited or even called her. Then came the call that Addie had died, all alone. Now, as Melissa tried to make the biggest decision of her life, she wished she could talk with her one more time.

When she hung up with the adoption agency, she felt hopeful that things were going to work out. But she worried that as the baby grew, the complications with Brian would increase. That afternoon when he came home from looking for a job, she confronted him.

"I need to know if you're going to be ashamed of me when my belly gets big."

"Of course not. Why would I be ashamed?"

"You suggested I go live somewhere else."

"I was thinking of you, Melissa. If you stay here, people are going to talk. And everyone will find out."

"Are you scared of that?"

"I'm fine if you are. I just don't want you to have to go through anything harder."

"You can't control hard, Brian. Hard's part of life."

Brian pulled into the apartment parking lot, his gas gauge on empty. He'd now applied for a job at six places in the last few weeks and as much as he needed the money, he hoped none of them would hire him. All were minimum-wage entry positions, but so far he hadn't received a call.

He stared at the radio that he could only hear through the right speakers, and all he could think about was the $220 that had been flushed down the drain. How many tanks of gas could he have bought with that?

At least Melissa was getting some financial assistance from the pregnancy resource center, but it wasn't enough for them to live on, and the kind people there could only share provisions for a limited time.

Brian had slowly come to the realization that Melissa wasn't going to change her mind about having the baby. He'd hoped she would come to her senses and he could drive her back to the clinic. He told her he'd talk with the people and explain. They would understand. But she said no, and the way she said it made Brian believe her.

Why would she want to go through nine months of nausea and pain? Why not make a fresh start? He chalked it up to her emotions and a little motherly instinct. But something troubled him that he couldn't tell Melissa. Maybe the truth would help her see things differently.

When he walked inside, she was sitting on the floor by the couch with letters and envelopes spread around her. "What's all this?"

"Jennifer dropped them off," Melissa said.

"Who's Jennifer?" Brian said.

She gave him an exasperated look. "From the adoption agency. She's helping me."

He picked up one of the letters and saw it was from a prospective adoptive parent. Most were handwritten pleas and this one seemed a little desperate to him. He wondered if they were all like that. Melissa had also taped a few letters on the wall behind the couch. He assumed those had made the first cut.

"It's like the baby lottery, isn't it?"

"I don't look at it that way," Melissa said. "These are just couples wanting us to know more about them."

"Well, it's your choice. You're the one doing all the work."

"You could help," she said, holding out a handful of letters.

He took the pages she handed him, kicked off his shoes, and sat on the couch. Each letter had a picture of the couple paper-clipped to the edge. He looked at the photo before him and wondered how you could say no to people that desperate. How could you choose only one?

"Maybe we flip a coin?" he said. "Or tape all of them up on the wall and throw darts. Might be easier."

She looked up at him as if trying to see if he was kidding or not. Brian lifted his hands and smirked, and she went back to the page she held.

"Look, before you go through with this, there's something I need to tell you."

She put the letter down and turned to him.

He rubbed his hands on his jeans and swallowed hard. "I don't want this baby to hate us. That happened to somebody I know. She could never forgive . . ."

"Who?" Melissa said.

"My mother was adopted. Her mom was young, like us. She decided to give the baby away. And when my mom found out, she never forgave her biological mother. It tore both of them up."

"Yeah," Melissa said quietly, studying a picture on one of the letters.

"I don't want somebody feeling that way about you or me down the road."

"I don't either," Melissa said. She put a hand on his leg and looked up at him. "But think about it this way. If your mom's mother hadn't made that choice of having her baby, you wouldn't be here."

Brian looked out the window. He couldn't argue with that, but he also couldn't shake the feeling inside.

"We can't change what's happened. We just have to make the best decision we can right now. And I really believe this is it."

Brian glanced at her, then picked up one of the letters beside him. Melissa did the same, then held up the picture so he could see it.

"What about these people?" she said.

Brian glanced at the photo and quickly said, "No. He looks weird." It was something about his eyes.

"No, he doesn't," Melissa said. She held the picture closer. "Yeah, he does." She put the letter on the couch in a stack of rejects.

Brian dropped the letter he held onto the floor behind Melissa. "What are we even looking for?"

"People like us. I mean, not just like us, but . . ." She thought a moment as if she were picturing the perfect couple to raise their baby. "People that we might like. At least, people that like what we like. Better people than us, but people that would like us if they knew us. I don't know." She looked down at the page.

Brian stared at her blankly. "You're weird."

"No, I'm not."

"Yes, you are."

"Well, you're living with me, so what does that make you?"

She smiled and laughed a little and Brian thought that was best sound he'd heard in a long time. He unfolded another "Dear Mother" letter and saw the careful handwriting on the pink stationery.

"Okay, all right, here we go. 'Dear Mother, as honored as I was to win the prestigious title Miss Southern Alabama TWICE, now all I want is the title Mommy. And that's where you come in!'" He crumpled the page and tossed it away. "This is, ugh."

Melissa had her head down and when she spoke, there was something hopeful in her voice. "Listen to this. 'We like to go camping and fishing, and we love outdoor activities. We've lost two boys to Aicardi syndrome at a very early age. We don't care if it's a boy or a girl—we just want to be parents.'"

As Melissa stared at the paper, Brian said, "I honestly had no idea that this many people were wanting to adopt."

"Me either."

"Do you want to put them on the wall?"

"Yes, but I kind of want to ask them a question."

"What do you want to ask?"

"I wonder if I can call?"

"How? You don't have any information other than this."

"I can go through the agency."

"You really want to do that?"

Melissa smiled at him. They had come a long way from the parking lot of the abortion clinic. How did they get from there to looking at all these letters and choosing who would be the parents of the child Melissa carried?

Melissa picked up the phone.

He wanted to walk out of the room. He didn't want to hear what might happen in the conversation. But he stayed on the couch.

CHAPTER 7

✦ ✦ ✦

Laundry was one of Susan's least favorite household chores, but she always felt a sense of accomplishment when it was done. Plus, it was something that occupied her mind. When she was busy, she could keep the swirling thoughts away—the grief, the questions, the inner struggle.

When Jimmy had asked her to wait on donating the crib to the Millers, she wasn't sure what his motivation was, but his reticence encouraged her somehow. Jimmy was a deep pool—he kept a lot inside and didn't divulge his true feelings until prodded. Even now, she could only guess at his thoughts. But his reaction to the crib stuck with her. Instead of talking about it, she let the deep pool settle. He always shared his heart with her eventually, even if it took some time.

The more she thought about the crib, the more she realized she simply wanted the pain to go away. The crib represented all the losses, all the dashed hopes and dreams of her life. As she finished with the sheets and the comforter and moved to the couch to re-cover a decorative throw pillow, the phone rang.

Jimmy answered and she focused on the pillow. There was a way to make the pillows look fresh and new, but she had never figured out how not to make them come out lumpy.

"Sure, just a moment," Jimmy said.

There was something in his voice that wasn't quite right.

"Susan?"

She turned to him. He stood with his hand over the receiver, like a little boy who had been caught sneaking a cookie before dinner.

"It's the adoption agency."

She couldn't breathe. Why would they be calling? Before she could formulate a question, Jimmy said, "There's a birth mother on the line with a question for you."

"For me?" she said, barely able to get the words out.

She put the pillow down and hurried to the kitchen,

unable to think of why a birth mother would call their house. They had stopped the adoption process long ago.

"I resubmitted our application."

Susan's heart pounded. She tried to process what he had just said but she couldn't. "You did?"

Jimmy held out the phone.

"She's on the line right now?" Susan said.

He nodded and she took the phone. When she spoke, her voice sounded like a teenager's, trembling at being asked to prom.

"Hello?"

"Hi, is this Susan?" someone said on the other end. She sounded young. A little nervous. That made two of them.

"Yes?"

"Hi, um, I was just reading your letter and I just wanted to ask you a question, if that's okay."

Susan stared at Jimmy. "Okay."

"You said in your letter that you like to go fishing. And I just wanted to know how you bait your hook."

Susan did a double take. The question seemed beyond weird, but she shook off the thought. For some reason this expectant mother had that question in her mind.

The silence on the line made Melissa feel she had overstepped some boundary. But in her heart, she knew the answer would tip her off to the type of woman who would raise her child.

Susan's voice relaxed. She sounded almost comfortable answering the question. "Uh, when we go fishing, we use the Cocahoe minnow, and you have to put the hook through the eye of the minnow. That's the way we've always baited our hook."

Melissa glanced at Brian, who had leaned forward to hear the answer. He looked her in the eyes and something passed between them.

Melissa swallowed hard and tried to compose herself. Her voice trembling, she gave a quick laugh and pulled the handset to her mouth.

"That's really good." She paused, gathering her thoughts. Should she say what she was thinking? Should she wait? What came out of her mouth came from somewhere deep inside. "Then I want you to be the mother."

The words hung there, then Melissa hung up the phone.

Brian leaned forward. "Wait. Did you just say what I think you said?"

"Yeah."

"Because of how she baits a minnow? Melissa?"

She shook her head. "No, it's not that. I could tell. She's the one, Brian. She's going to take care of our baby. She didn't just put the thing about fishing in the letter because it would look good. It's who she is. Susan is the mother of this baby."

"I don't understand how you can make that decision with one little piece of information like that. I mean, look at all these other letters, these other people."

She stood and walked toward the kitchen and put the phone on the counter. "When the doctor started the procedure, he had his gloves on and moved toward me. I knew right then I had to get up and get out of there. It was the right thing to do. This is the same. Susan is the mother of this baby."

Brian lifted both hands, gathered the "Dear Mother" letters, and stacked them on the counter.

Jimmy studied Susan's face as she stood motionless, still holding the phone, as if trying to process what she had just heard.

"What?" he said, moving closer, taking the phone from her and hanging it up. "What did she say?"

Susan could barely speak. Her face showed the emotion roiling inside. Finally she said, "She wants me to be the mom."

"What?" He couldn't contain his smile. "Honey, that's wonderful!"

Instead of hugging him, she turned away and with her

voice breaking said, "I didn't know you were going to do that. I didn't know you were going to do that!"

Sobbing now, Susan broke and Jimmy wrapped his arms around her and pulled her into a hug. Her body shook with emotion, and he moved in front of her and looked her in the eyes. "I'm sorry. I'm just not ready to let go."

Susan searched his eyes. Then through her tears she said, "But I can't go through another loss, Jimmy. What if she calls and changes her mind?"

Jimmy guided her to the chair by the desk. His wife was panicking. He could see it. "But we don't know that. She just called and said she chose you."

A little light broke through and Susan nodded and pulled her hair away from her face and there was a smile. "Yeah."

"We want to trust God, right?" Jimmy said. "No matter what happens."

Susan nodded again.

"And we love the baby, we want what's best for the child and what's best for the birth mother. And even if she decides to keep the baby, can we just take this step together and trust God with it?"

Susan's face tightened and she shook her head. "I just don't know . . ."

"Just one step," Jimmy said, holding up a finger. "Okay? Just one step at a time."

Susan finally nodded and leaned forward and the two embraced. And it felt like they had just begun a long journey together.

CHAPTER 8

✦ ✦ ✦

The plan was simple. Keep the pregnancy a secret. Nobody needed to know but them. No family. No friends.

Melissa wanted to get to graduation without any of her classmates knowing that she was expecting, so she visited a thrift store and picked up some baggy clothes. It only helped that loose clothing was in style, so her sweatshirts and oversize sweaters kept her peers clueless.

She also noticed in the first several months that her belly did not bulge out as far as she expected, and she read that sometimes a mother can "carry the baby in her back," meaning the position of the growing child was less obvious when others saw her.

Melissa wasn't close to many of her peers anyway, so slipping away after school each day gave others fewer opportunities to notice anything different about her. Except her friend Kelly White.

Kelly had called and asked why she hadn't seen Melissa after school. She seemed genuinely concerned and told Melissa she missed seeing her on weekends and at the lake.

"Yeah, I'm trying to get a part-time waitress job."

"Are you okay?"

"Sure. I just need income right now. I'm good."

Kelly had asked a few more questions that Melissa dodged. Then Kelly suggested they get together and go fishing again. Melissa said that would be fun and hung up the phone as quickly as she could.

When graduation came, Melissa arrived already in her robe, which she requested one size larger. She kept to herself until time to walk across the stage and receive her diploma. She was amazed that no one seemed to notice anything different. Even Brian acted like they had dodged a bullet.

All the changes in her body surprised Melissa. The nausea had lessened by the end of summer, which she was grateful for, but then came the increase in appetite. She felt ravenous most of the day, and Brian commented on the change.

"I guess you're eating for two?" he said.

She rolled her eyes.

Fatigue was the other factor. She felt exhausted most of the day. She tried not to watch too much TV, remembering her father's coarse words about her mind turning to mush from all the worthless programs. The daytime talk shows interested her, and since she didn't have much interaction with anyone outside of the doctor's office and the adoption agency, she found the shows comforting. At least she got a little human interaction, even if it was from a TV screen.

Through a friend, Brian had found a job at a golf course mowing and retrieving balls at the driving range and maintaining the golf carts. It wasn't what he wanted to do the rest of his life, but it was a paycheck every two weeks. Brian talked about the rich people in their expensive cars who spent lots of money on greens fees and overpriced drinks and candy bars between holes.

"One day you're going to be able join a golf club like that," Melissa said. "You just wait."

"If I ever make that much money, I'm not going to spend it on golf—I'll tell you that right now."

As fall approached, the course let him go. By then the strange flutter Melissa felt inside had intensified and made her call the nurse in the doctor's office.

"I think something's wrong. I feel weird."

"What do you mean, weird?" the nurse said.

Melissa described the flutter and the nurse chuckled on the other end of the line. "Honey, that's the baby moving. You do remember you're having a baby, right?"

Melissa's mouth dropped. How did she not know that? But then, she'd never been pregnant before.

"You're fine. And the bigger your baby gets, the more you're going to feel. My last one was a boy, and it felt like he wanted to be a linebacker for the Colts!"

Melissa laughed and put a hand on her belly. Tears came. Since she'd made the decision on the doctor's exam table at the clinic, she'd known she'd done the right thing. The movement inside gave her a little more courage to continue.

Brian had always been interested in computers. As a kid he took apart old video game consoles and figured out how to put them back together. In the process, he learned how to fix ones that didn't work.

At a family reunion he attended—without Melissa— an uncle came up to him at the bonfire toward the end of the night. As children roasted marshmallows and caught fireflies, his uncle asked his plans for the future.

"Have you thought of going to college?" the man said.

"Sure. I've thought of going to the Indianapolis 500, too, but I don't have the money."

His uncle smiled. "If you went, what would you want to study?"

"Honestly, I'd probably go to a technical college. I like working with computers. I've thought about becoming a programmer."

His uncle nodded. "The community college has a computer course. It's a lot more affordable than going to a university. Do you know Clive Lawson?"

"The TV repair guy?"

"That's him. He's looking for an assistant at his shop. He works on televisions, computers, and small appliances. Not easy work, but you could save up some money and maybe go to that computer course."

The next day Brian drove to the repair shop and Clive gave him a box of tools and told him to pull the fan out of an old IBM computer. He came back with it in less than ten minutes and was hired on the spot.

Brian and Melissa celebrated that night with pizza. She let him put his hand on her belly when she felt the baby moving, and though he couldn't feel anything, he pretended he did. They talked about the future and how long it would take for Brian to make it through school and start work. Melissa said she would start working after the first of the year and they could dream about owning a house.

Two weeks later, Brian was on his lunch break at the shop when a wrecker pulled into the salvage yard next door with a badly damaged VW. He heard the driver say that there had been a fatality in the accident.

About the only thing salvageable was at the back of the car. When Brian saw a familiar bumper sticker and school logo on the trunk, his mouth dropped. He walked over as they removed a few remaining items from the back seat.

Later, he trudged up the steps to their apartment and inside. Melissa smiled and stood, turning off the TV.

"You need to sit back down," Brian said.

"What's wrong?"

He handed her a damaged school notebook with a name on the front.

"This is Kelly's. Why are you showing it to me?"

"They brought a car to the salvage lot next door today. It was in really bad shape. And this was in it."

Melissa stared at the notebook in her hand.

"I'm sorry, Melissa. I made a couple of calls. Kelly was driving it. Somebody swerved in front of her. Or she swerved. I'm not sure which. She didn't make it."

"That can't be right. I just talked with her . . ."

Brian tried to show compassion. He wasn't sure he did, but he tried. "She's gone, Melissa. Her funeral is Saturday."

She stared up at him. "No. We were going fishing.

I told her we would go fishing again out at the lake.
She wanted to know what was going on with me and I
wouldn't . . ."

"I'm sorry," Brian said, and he hugged her until she
stopped crying.

Brian parked at the edge of the cemetery and they watched
the procession from his car. Vehicles lined the side of the
road that led to a fresh grave. Men in suits carried Kelly's
casket. Though they were a distance from the site, he could
see the family was bent in sorrow. Out of the corner of
his eye he saw Melissa in the seat next to him with a hand
on her stomach. The baby was growing and Brian didn't
have any trouble feeling the movement now. A foot would
press against the inside of Melissa's womb and he'd see the
imprint of that foot and those toes. They'd almost taken
that life before it ever had a chance, and he closed his eyes
at the thought.

The family and friends gathered around the grave and
Melissa wept. Brian thought it was mostly due to the loss
of her friend but there was also the isolation. Grieving was
hard enough with others who could carry it with you, but
doing it alone meant you carried a double load.

"I can't help thinking what would have happened if I'd
gone fishing or had her come see me. Maybe if we'd done
some things together this wouldn't have happened."

"You can't let yourself think like that. This is not your fault. You can't control the bad that happens."

She looked down at her growing child. "They did an ultrasound the other day. You know, where they take pictures and tell you if the baby is growing at the right rate."

"Is everything okay?"

She nodded and found a tissue and wiped her nose. "The nurse or technician or whoever it was looked at the screen and asked me if I wanted to know if the baby was a boy or a girl."

"You said you didn't want to know. That would make it harder."

She nodded. "I know. But right then, I forgot. I mean, I felt like I wanted to know." She looked up with tears in her eyes. "It's a boy. We're going to have a boy."

Brian didn't know how to respond. The baby was just something they needed to move past, like some empty grave, but the more it grew and now knowing it was a boy, the more real it became.

When Melissa spoke again, her voice was airy and light, like she was whispering in her sleep. "What would it be like if we kept him? You and me and a baby. Wouldn't that be something?"

Brian stiffened. "Melissa, we've talked about this. We can't raise a child right now. It wouldn't be fair to the baby to bring it into—"

"Him, not it," she said.

"Him. Whatever."

"He's not a whatever."

"Listen, you're doing a good thing for these people. They'll give him a lot better chance than we can."

Her voice was soft when she said, "I know, but at least let me dream a little."

When people began to spread dirt on the casket, she asked him to drive her home. She spent the rest of the night in bed, curled up and crying. Brian wanted to help but couldn't think of anything to say or do. How could you change things that were real?

A week later, he'd come up with something, and when he got his paycheck, he drove to Pawn-a-Palooza on his way home. Then he stopped at a drive-thru and bought some fried chicken and told Melissa he wanted to take her somewhere special. They drove the dirt road to the secluded lake where she and Kelly had fished months earlier. The trees had turned brilliant colors and the lake shimmered with the reflection of the setting sun.

"Where's our gear?" Melissa said when he spread the blanket out for them and put the food down.

"We're not here to fish."

She looked at him like he was a space alien. She stood at the edge of the blanket, her hands on her hips, her back swayed to balance the extra weight she carried. The sun

peeked through her hair and the orange light sparkled
and he wanted to capture that sight somehow. She looked
beautiful and he was the only one who could see it.

"Brian, if we're not fishing, what in the world are we
doing here?"

He looked at her and let her think for an uncomfortable minute. Then he reached in his pocket and pulled
out a small jewelry box and bent one knee onto the
blanket.

Melissa's mouth dropped open. "Are you serious?"

He opened the box and pulled out the ring with a
small stone in it and spoke to the ring. "I don't know how
to do this. I'm not good at speeches. I've seen it in movies,
I guess." He looked up at her and held the ring out. "I'm
going to do everything I can to make you happy and provide for you. I'm asking you to marry me."

She put both hands over her mouth.

"Are you going to take it?" he said.

In tears now, she reached out and took the ring and
held it in front of her face. Then she looked at him and
smiled. "I say yes. I'll marry you."

They sat together on the blanket with Melissa staring
at the ring on her finger and Brian opening the box of
chicken. He was so hungry and figured she would be, but
all she could do was look at the ring and then look him
and repeat.

Finally she took some chicken and coleslaw and a biscuit and they talked about when they'd have the ceremony and who they'd invite and who they wouldn't. Brian asked how much it would cost.

"People spend thousands," Melissa said. "The bride's parents pay most of it, but that's not going to happen with us."

"Maybe we just go alone?"

"You mean to a justice of the peace?"

Brian nodded. "We could have anybody you want go with us."

She held the ring up, the light fading on the horizon. "When do you think we should do it?"

"After the baby," he said. "It'll give you time to recover."

"What about a honeymoon?" she said, smiling. "There will be snow on the ground if we get married in January."

"We could come here and ice-skate."

She laughed and they agreed they would get through her pregnancy and then decide on when and where and how and all the other questions about the wedding.

When Brian came to bed, Melissa was asleep. Before he turned out the light, he saw her with her left hand on her stomach, the engagement ring on her finger. It was a rough start to their lives together, no question. But he was sure things would work out now. The love they both felt would keep them together.

CHAPTER 9

✦ ✦ ✦

Melissa had experienced several false alarms and trips to the
doctor's office. Each time she was sent home, feeling as if
she'd somehow failed. She'd bothered the staff needlessly.
The nurses told her not to worry, that this was normal for
a first pregnancy, but she couldn't shake the idea that she
should have known it wasn't time.

As the baby grew and her body changed, she saw what
was happening as a miracle. Another life was growing,
fed and nourished by her own body, a separate person
yet vulnerable and connected to her, fully dependent
and affected by her choices. She'd seen pregnant women

before, seen the glow they seemed to have as new life grew, but she'd never known why. Now with each heartbeat, she seemed to draw closer to her child, yearning to see him and hold him and feed him. She couldn't get over the excitement of meeting this intimate stranger.

With that growing connection came another thought: the struggle that was ahead to let go of this little person she had nurtured. How could she let go of someone she was growing to love? She felt the dual tug of wanting to give all of herself for her son and yet knowing she would have to place him in another's arms. Her instinct told her to distance herself from the pain of letting go. But how could she become distant to someone so close to her heart?

She felt the struggle every time the baby kicked and moved. She felt it when she was awakened at night by Brian's snoring and by the pressure below that made her desperate for the bathroom. In those waking moments she felt so tired, so exhausted she couldn't move, and she imagined what might be ahead for her son. Sometimes she spoke to him in the night, whispering gently, "It's okay. Everything's going to be okay." But she knew she was speaking those words to herself.

One night in her thirty-eighth week, she threw off the covers and wandered into the living room. Winter had gripped the Midwest but Melissa felt so hot she opened a window and turned on the TV. Brian had rigged rabbit ears and they could only pull in a few stations, but she found the one that came in the strongest and tried to get comfortable on the couch, a pillow between her knees.

She thought it was a talk show at first, then realized it was a religious program. A man and woman with perfect hair spoke to each other. She got up to switch the channel but stood in front of the TV as their conversation turned to the Christmas story and focused on Mary, the mother of Jesus.

"Here was a teenage girl, not married, who was carrying the promise of God, the hope of the world, and that was a baby," the woman said. "Imagine all of the emotions she must have been going through as that child grew within her."

Melissa backed up to the couch and sat, eyes glued to the screen, listening intently. She knew the Christmas story, that Jesus was born in Bethlehem and there was no room in the inn and he slept in a manger, a cattle trough. She pictured it like the quaint Christmas cards with the star shining in the sky and the cattle and sheep and wise men gathered. But as she listened to the two on TV, she realized she'd never considered it a story that made an impact on her until now. She put a hand on her stomach.

"This is the mystery of the ages," the man said. "That God would care so much about us that He would send

His only Son, God in the flesh, Immanuel—which means 'God with us.' And Mary couldn't understand everything that was going on. Like you say, she was a teenager and she had to live with all of the hormonal changes that happen inside a woman's body during pregnancy. I'm sure she had questions and she wondered about the future. But above all, she trusted that God was at work and that He had prepared her in those nine months to give birth to the Savior."

"I love the verse a little later in the Gospel of Luke where he writes, 'Mary kept all these things in her heart and thought about them often.' Other translations say she 'treasured' them. That says so much about what was happening in her mind before and after she gave birth."

As Melissa watched, it felt like the man and woman were talking directly to her. And something came over her, a peace that spread through her and calmed her. She wasn't sure what it was or why it happened, but it was there all the same.

When the program ended, she stretched out and fell asleep.

Three days before Christmas, a pain awakened Melissa and she opened her eyes and took a deep breath. Brian's side of the bed was empty and she remembered he had to get to work early. He had been given more responsibility and was opening up the shop that day. Nobody at Brian's work knew about the baby and the thought comforted her.

She shifted left and right, trying to gain the momentum to roll out of bed, and when her feet hit the floor, she felt something had changed. She stood and walked toward the bathroom, one hand on her stomach, but had to stop in the hall and put the other hand on the wall to steady herself. The tightness had increased. Her stomach felt like a fully inflated basketball. The nurses said contractions were normal, but this didn't feel normal. And just as she took another step, a surge of water gushed from her and stained her sweatpants.

She froze, staring at the wet carpet. The nurses had said something about her water breaking, but she didn't know what that meant. She hobbled into the bathroom and looked in the mirror. Was this really happening?

She turned on the shower. Maybe the water coursing over her would settle her. But another wave of pain hit and she knew she had to get to the hospital.

She called a cab, then with great effort pulled on her maternity jeans, pausing during another contraction. When the cab honked in front of the apartment, she looked at her red high-tops. Brian always helped her because she couldn't get that low to put them on herself. Another honk. She grabbed the gym bag she had packed a month earlier with what she'd need, shoved her bare feet as far into the shoes as she could, and shuffled into the cold morning, her shoelaces flopping.

The cabdriver got out and opened the trunk, but when he glanced at her, his eyes widened.

"I need to get to the hospital. Fast."

He slammed the trunk and opened the back door and helped her in.

She handed the man a ten-dollar bill as they approached the hospital and when he stopped, she didn't wait for change.

A nurse met her just outside the front door and got her to a wheelchair inside. Melissa was never so glad to see a nurse in her life.

The next couple of hours went by in a blur. A female doctor with red hair examined Melissa, and as she put her feet in the stirrups, she remembered that spring day at the clinic. She'd come so close. And yet here she was. Her baby on his way.

On his way.

Her son was coming. Somehow in all the months leading up to this, it had seemed like a dream, like it was so far away. Was it really going to happen today? Would she hold her baby in her arms in a few minutes, a few hours, or be sent home again?

Another wave of pain. Another nurse guided her

through the contraction and she thought of Brian. She wanted him to be with her, but she didn't at the same time. Best to just get through this alone.

And then a contraction came and she squeezed the arm of the nurse so tight she left fingernail prints.

"I'm so sorry," Melissa said, catching her breath.

"You're fine. Just breathe. Do you want me to call somebody to be with you?"

She shook her head. "Here comes another one."

The pain. She'd never felt anything like it. She'd seen births in movies and TV shows, she'd read articles about what to expect, but nothing prepared her for the disorienting, overwhelming pain. Between contractions there were nurses, and a machine kept track of the baby's heart rate. At one point she asked for medicine to relieve the pain and the doctor shook her head.

"It's too close, Melissa."

Melissa screamed at the woman and then quickly apologized.

Finally the doctor sat on a stool in front of Melissa. "You're ready to push."

"Okay," Melissa whispered.

The doctor gave instructions on where to put her hands and how to bear down and focus her strength, but Melissa couldn't hear any of it because of the excruciating pain.

She wanted out of the room. She wanted the baby out. She wanted the pain to stop, but it wouldn't. It rolled on and on like waves against the seashore, but not just waves—a tsunami.

A few minutes later, her face drenched with sweat and holding her breath, she pushed and felt something give way inside. She lay back, her eyes closed, waiting for another contraction, and then she heard the sound that changed everything.

Her son gave a gurgling cry. A nurse suctioned out his mouth and nose and then the doctor cut the umbilical cord and in one motion placed the baby on her chest.

Melissa's eyes blurred. She didn't know what to say. She looked at the doctor, who smiled behind her mask.

"That's a healthy little boy you have there," the doctor said.

"Hey, little guy," Melissa whispered.

The child squirmed and then a nurse took him and wrapped him and weighed him. Melissa couldn't take her eyes off of him. The doctor was tending to the afterbirth, something else Melissa hadn't known about, and there were stitches and monitors beeping, but she focused on the little boy across the room. Her son. What would his new parents call him? She had wanted to name him, but she knew she couldn't. It would be too hard to let go if she did.

Melissa put a hand on her stomach. What had been an inflated basketball was now soft and empty. And the sight of the child being cleaned and weighed on the other side of the room brought an ache inside.

"Seven pounds, thirteen ounces," the nurse said. She put him in a plastic bassinet on a cart and wheeled him out of the room.

Melissa pushed herself up on her elbows to get one more glimpse. Was this the last time she would see him? "Wait, where are you taking him?"

"It's okay," the doctor said. "Lie back down."

Melissa looked at the woman. All she could see was her eyes, but that was enough because there was something in them, a kindness that came through.

"You're doing a good thing, Melissa."

Melissa lay back and tried to relax. Was the doctor telling her the truth or just trying to calm her?

"Once we're finished here," the doctor said, "you'll be taken to your room, where you can rest and recover. You can call anyone you'd like and tell them you've had a healthy baby boy."

"I need to call . . . his father."

The doctor nodded. "We notified the adoption agency while you were in labor. Someone should be here soon."

Melissa looked at the door. "Can I hold him again?"

The doctor stood and pushed the stool into the corner.

She took off her gloves and tossed them in the trash and came around the bed and took off her mask. She placed a hand on Melissa's arm. "You did so well, Melissa."

"Even when I yelled at you?"

The doctor smiled. "Believe me, I've heard a lot worse. At this point, I usually tell my patients that the hard part is over. But that's not true for you. You know that, right?"

Tears came to Melissa's eyes and she nodded.

"A lot is swirling inside you now. Your motherly instinct is kicking in. You want to protect and provide for your son."

Melissa closed her eyes.

"You're doing that. The decision you made, however long ago you made it, was a good one. So when the person comes from the adoption agency, they'll ask you to sign the papers."

"I don't think I can. I don't want to. I just want to hold him."

A nurse rushed into the room. "Doctor, the patient in 212. She's close."

The woman smiled at Melissa and patted her arm, then hurried out the door. The nurse wheeled Melissa's bed down the hall, past the nursery, and Melissa lifted her head trying to catch a glimpse of her son.

Passing the open doors, she saw mothers breastfeeding and families gathering to see the newborn children.

Maybe she could wait to sign the papers. Maybe just a day with her son would be enough to help ease some of the doubt.

When she got to the room, she picked up the phone to call Brian, but the answering machine at work picked up. She didn't want to leave a message. A few minutes later she tried again and finally asked Brian to call her back. As she hung up, the door opened with a soft knock. Her counselor from the adoption agency, Jennifer, stuck her head inside. Her smile eased some of the stress in the room. She had long brown hair that curled and dark-brown skin. She hugged Melissa and couldn't stop smiling.

"Congratulations," Jennifer said. "You did it!"

Melissa nodded, unable to smile back. She stared at the manila folder under the woman's arm.

Jennifer noticed Melissa's gaze and took off her coat and put it on the back of a chair. Then she pulled the chair to the bed and sat. She placed the folder on the floor. "How are you feeling?"

"Physically or mentally?"

"Both."

Melissa put her hands on her stomach. "I've never lost that much weight so fast. And I've never felt that kind of pain."

"Was Brian with you?"

"No, he was at work. I called a cab."

Jennifer gave her a look. "Why didn't you call me?"

"I kind of panicked."

"It's okay. Does Brian know you've had the baby?"

"I called and left a message."

"You'll get through," Jennifer said. "You look good. You've got that glow."

Melissa stared at her hands. "I don't feel like I'm glowing."

"What do you feel?"

"I don't know if I can do it. Something happened inside when they put him in my arms. One look at his face and . . ."

"I understand."

"I don't want to hurt anybody or let people down."

"Melissa, you're going to make a good decision here. When you walked out of that abortion clinic, you put the baby's interests above your own."

"You'll hate me if I don't sign. And so will the adoptive parents."

Jennifer leaned close. "Nobody will hate you, okay? What you're feeling right now is the mom inside of you coming out. You want to love this baby and protect him. You gave him life."

Melissa brushed at a tear streaking her cheek.

"Let me ask you something. You chose Susan and Jimmy from all those letters and pictures. Why?"

"I don't know. They seem like really nice people. And the way she answered my question about baiting a hook, I knew she should be the one to . . ."

"Go on. The one to what?"

Melissa pulled her arms tight around herself. "I hate this feeling."

"What feeling?"

"That I can't give him what he needs, but I can't let him go, either."

Jennifer lowered her head and clasped her hands. It almost seemed to Melissa that she was praying.

CHAPTER 10

✦ ✦ ✦

The grocery store was an unlikely place for Susan to retreat, especially this early, but she felt she had to get out of the house. Her mother and father were over for breakfast and they planned to help Jimmy decorate, something she had put off. She felt the expectation as heavy in the air as the pine-tree scent of the candles her mother had brought as a gift. She loved her mom and dad, but she needed to be alone and where better but the crowd of humanity out early morning grocery shopping this close to Christmas.

The store was decked with wreaths and there was a

strong aroma of cinnamon and pumpkin spice as she walked inside. Cashiers wore Santa hats and everything was "ho ho ho" and "holly jolly" and "the most wonderful time of the year." There weren't as many shoppers as she expected, but the ones there scrambled for holiday turkeys and hams on sale.

She found a bouquet of white peonies at the front and thought they would look nice on the table. She pushed the small cart through the aisles, picking up items and putting them back, walking in a fog of expectation. There was really nothing here she needed other than the space to process her feelings.

It had been a week since Susan had heard from the adoption agency. The last word from the birth mother had been that she was close to delivering. There was even talk of inducing her if things went much further, and that made Susan wonder if the young woman had changed her mind. How could she not have second thoughts after carrying a child for nine months? Susan had done that twice. She knew how close to Michael and John she'd felt when they were born. They were part of her, like delivering half of her own heart. How would this young mom find the courage to let go?

It was in these moments of doubt that Susan tried to hang on to hope. Jimmy had it. But the feeling of loss and pain and what she might do if it came again overwhelmed her. The rug beneath her hopes had been pulled time after time. Why would this be any different?

She looked up and realized she was in the baby food aisle. The young woman's voice echoed somewhere in her heart.

"I want you to be the mother."

Was that a promise? Was it just something spoken wishfully?

Susan closed her eyes. *Father, I can't do this on my own. I don't have the strength to go through another loss like this. But I choose to trust You. I can live in fear of what might happen or believe that You're working all things together for my good.*

She said a prayer for the young woman. She prayed for the baby boy. She and Jimmy had thought of a name, but they hadn't told anyone. She walked to the end of the aisle and saw a display of pacifiers, and the sight took her breath away. Each had a child's name on the ring, and a third of the way down the display she saw one with *David* on it.

She reached for it and then held back, not daring to presume that God would do what she asked, but at the same time believing He had heard their cries. Slipping the pacifier from the metal holder and placing it atop the flowers in her cart felt like an act of faith akin to walking on dry ground through the Red Sea.

As she walked toward the checkout, she saw movement

outside the exit door. Two girls stood by a table filled with boxes of cookies. Susan smiled.

✦ ✦ ✦

Jimmy sat at the kitchen table with his father-in-law, Roy, a five-hundred-piece puzzle spread out in front of them. They were hunting straight-edged pieces to give the border of the puzzle. It was methodical to do it that way and it helped him focus on the task, rather than think of all the things that were out of his control.

Gail, his mother-in-law, was in cleaning mode. She had stored the boxes of decorations and had moved to the kitchen. She was at the sink when the phone rang and Jimmy answered it.

"Mr. Colton?"

A woman's voice. She sounded familiar.

"Yes?"

"It's Jennifer. I'm at the hospital with Melissa. Congratulations—your son is here."

He couldn't breathe. He couldn't think. "I have a son?"

He could tell from her voice the woman was smiling. "Yes. You have a son. Now, I know how long of a drive you have, but if you and your wife could come up as soon as possible . . ."

Jimmy turned and looked at Susan's parents. Their faces lasered on his own. "I have a son."

The two gathered close to him. He wanted to ask Jennifer the most important question, the question he knew Susan would ask. Before he could, Jennifer told him the news.

"She's signed the papers, Mr. Colton. Do you think you can drive up this afternoon?"

"Sure, yes. We can leave right away."

"Your son will be waiting," Jennifer said.

"Okay, thank you."

Jimmy put the phone down and turned.

"Congratulations," Gail said.

"We have to leave right now," Jimmy said. "The suitcases. I'm going to get the suitcases." He ran toward the bedroom.

"I'll take care of the kitchen," Gail said.

Jimmy stopped in the hall and turned, a hand to his head. "I forgot to install the car seat." He reversed course toward the living room. "I've got to get the car seat!"

"The car's not there," Roy said. "Susan has it."

Jimmy stopped. "Susan! I forgot to call Susan." He headed toward the kitchen and picked up the phone, his hands shaking.

"Where do you keep the dishcloths?" Gail said.

"Uh, they're in the drawer." What was Susan's number? He couldn't remember. Then he saw Gail open Susan's coupon drawer and corrected her. That little aside helped him remember the phone number.

"I've got the car seat," Roy said. "And your suitcases."

"Okay, thanks. Put them by the front door."

"Well, what are these cookies doing in the coupon drawer?" Gail said.

Jimmy turned and stared at the box she held. "Wait, what? Where did you find those?"

"Hey, she's here!" Roy said. "She's pulling in."

Jimmy hung up the phone and lowered his voice. "Stay calm. Stay calm, everyone!" He moved toward the front door. "I'll tell her."

"This is so exciting!" Gail said.

Jimmy took his place in the hall, took a deep breath, and tried to calm his heart as Susan walked in, oblivious to the excitement.

"Okay, I did not find our favorite ice cream but I did find our favorite cookies," she said.

Jimmy took the bag from her and put it on an end table. He took the box of cookies from her and placed it by the bag, then took her hands in his. "We got the call."

Susan's face went blank.

"We have a son," Jimmy said.

Susan spoke in a little girl's voice. "We have a son?" Then a look of concern. "Are you sure?"

"I'm sure."

Susan turned her head slightly as if bracing herself. "Jimmy, are you sure?"

"The birth mother already signed the papers."

At those words, the dam broke, and joy spread across Susan's face mixed with tears. "A son," she said, barely able to get the words out.

"Let's go get him!" Jimmy said, moving toward the garage.

"We'll look after the house," Gail said. "You just go!"

Jimmy hurried to the garage with Susan following him. When he saw the luggage and car seat, he hit the garage door opener, then remembered something. He spun around and quickly retreated to the end table and grabbed the box of cookies, then hurried back to the garage and put the car seat and luggage in the back.

He put the box in the driver's-side door. When Susan gave him a look, he said, "We're going to be driving all day. My cookies will help me stay awake."

Susan shook her head and smiled.

✦ ✦ ✦

Melissa stared out the window at clouds that hung low and gray, like something ominous was ahead. The phone rang, startling her.

"Clive told me you left a message," Brian said. He lowered his voice. "Where are you?"

"At the hospital."

"What?"

"Brian, he's here."

"Who's here?"

She closed her eyes and didn't say anything, waiting for him to work it out. When he finally did, he sighed heavily.

"How did you get there?"

She shook her head. "Don't you want to know how I am? How our son is?"

"Of course. How are you?"

She pushed the emotion away. "If you want to see him, you've got to come now."

"Did you sign the papers?"

"Brian, when I looked in his eyes, I had this feeling that we could do it, you know? We could raise him. He's our son. And he's perfect. You should see his little fingers and toes and—"

"Melissa, you signed the papers, right?"

There was something in his voice, an edge that touched a nerve inside. She decided to probe.

"What if I didn't? What would you do?"

"I can't believe it. I knew you would do something stupid like this!"

"Is that what you think of me? I'm stupid?"

"Melissa, you're not thinking straight. We talked about

this. We went over it so many times. You promised those people in Alabama that you'd go through with this."

"Louisiana."

"Wherever. This is the same thing that happened that day at the clinic."

She felt the tears and brushed them away. "At least I know how you really feel."

"This is not about you, Melissa. This is about us. The future. Don't you see that?"

"If it was about our future, you'd want to take care of your son."

A long exhale on the other end of the phone. Hearing the anger in Brian's voice made her feel hollow, as if she were losing everything good and would never get it back.

Finally, in a whisper, she said, "I signed the papers."

"What did you say?"

"I signed the papers. The people are on their way. If you want to see your son, you'd better get here."

"Oh, okay. But I thought . . ."

"Do you want to see him before he goes?"

"Sure. It's just that Clive and I are the only ones here right now and . . . Let me see if I can get away."

Melissa kept quiet, hearing voices and banging in the background of the shop. She imagined him with wires and computer keyboards all around him.

"I'm glad you went through with it," he said. "You did a good thing."

"Did I?"

The nurse came in holding her son and she hung up the phone without saying goodbye. She didn't want to miss a second with him. Melissa pushed herself up on the bed as the nurse approached.

"You ready to hold your little one?" The woman smiled and there was a look in her eyes that made Melissa think she knew more than she let on.

Melissa nodded and held out her arms. It felt like an eternity since she'd first held him, and now he was wrapped tightly in a small blanket. She cradled him close and studied his face as the nurse stepped out of the room.

He looked straight at her and she thought her heart would melt. She kissed his forehead and closed her eyes and smelled his hair and newborn skin.

"Hi," she whispered, touching his nose. "I've been waiting a long time to see you."

His mouth puckered and she laughed, tears coming. He was absolutely perfect. A miracle. As she studied his little chin, she thought of a Bible verse Jennifer had shared with her. It said, "You knit me together in my mother's womb." And that was exactly what had happened.

"What's your name going to be, little guy?" she

whispered. "I wish I could pick it out, but I don't think that would be fair. Your new mom and dad will do that."

Melissa closed her eyes and tried to catalog this feeling. What was it? The baby seemed so content. Maybe that was it—she was just as content here holding him as he was being held. She looked at the ceiling and wondered if somehow she was being held, being given the strength of an embrace just like her baby.

"Do you want to see out the window?" she whispered.

She got out of bed and stepped to the window. The soft December sunlight peeked through the closed blinds and she stroked the baby's head as he closed his eyes and slept peacefully.

How in the world was she going to do this? How could she just hand over something this precious, this piece of her heart, to someone she had never met? She looked in the corner at her gym bag and the thought crossed her mind to get dressed, slip down the back stairs, and walk out the door. Everything in her wanted to take this little one home.

They had been driving at least eight hours when Susan saw the sign that made her heart flutter.

Welcome to Indiana. Crossroads of America. Lincoln's Boyhood Home.

"How about that for a name?" Jimmy said. "Lincoln Colton?"

She rolled it around in her mind, not knowing if Jimmy was serious. "I don't know. It sounds like a lot of pressure when he's in the third grade," she said. "'Can you live up to the name, Lincoln?'"

"Yeah, that would be tough. What about Buck?"

"Jimmy, come on."

"No, think of it. First Christmas he'd get cowboy boots and the next a Stetson and then six-shooters with holsters."

"We're not naming our son Buck."

"Maybe that's his middle name?"

"Stop it."

Jimmy smiled. "If he becomes a country music star in twenty years, you remember this idea."

Twenty years. What would their lives be like in twenty years? What would they be like in twenty *hours*? She couldn't imagine. All she could imagine was holding their son for the first time.

They stopped for gas and Jimmy suggested they get something to eat but Susan shook her head. "I just want to get there."

"Don't worry," Jimmy said. "She signed the papers."

"I know, but . . ." Susan glanced at the restaurant a couple hundred yards from the gas station. "If you're hungry, go ahead. I'm not the one driving."

"Coffee's all I need," Jimmy said. "And another cookie."

When he pulled onto Interstate 65 and headed north, she opened the baby name book she had bought. In the back was a blank section where she had written all the possible names her parents had suggested as well as friends at church. On the last page she had written the names of her other sons.

Michael John Colton.

John David Colton.

"Are you sure we should stay with the pattern?"

"Why wouldn't we?" Jimmy said.

She didn't want to say. She didn't believe in luck, good or bad. Things happened in life that couldn't be explained. And deep inside she felt that even the bad things were not just happenstance or retribution but somehow were for a purpose.

She took her pen and wrote *David Colton*. It looked good. It felt right. "His name will be David. You okay with that?"

"Sure. David Buck Colton."

"No."

"Okay, what's your idea? John?"

She thought a moment, studying the page. Without looking up she said, "I was thinking *James*. After his father."

When she turned to her husband, there was water in

his eyes and he was smiling even wider than normal, that silly grin of his with his dimples showing.

"It's not as good as Buck, but I like it."

✦ ✦ ✦

Melissa held her son and couldn't let go, couldn't put him on the bed or in his bassinet or do anything but hold him close. He slept peacefully in her arms no matter whether she stood or sat. What she loved most in the little time she had was lying back on the bed and letting him sleep on her chest, his stomach rising and falling with the soft sounds of his breathing. Once, he yawned and stretched, pulling his head back, his mouth in an O.

At that moment a flood of guilt washed over her as she thought of what might have been. If she hadn't gotten up from that exam table, if the doctor hadn't taken off the gloves and walked out of the room, she wouldn't have experienced this. She held the child tighter to her chest and willed the thoughts away.

Melissa was on the bed with the baby sleeping on her chest when the door opened. Jennifer entered and crept near the bed and beamed when she saw the child's face.

"It's okay, you can talk," Melissa said. "He kind of likes the sound of voices, I think. Probably reminds him of his old room."

Jennifer smiled and studied his face, leaning close and

gently caressing his thin hair. "I make phone calls. I talk with people. I get paperwork in the mail. And every day I remind myself that this is what it's all about."

"Funny," Melissa said. "The best part of your job is the worst part for me."

Jennifer looked at Melissa with kind eyes. "How are you feeling?"

She shook her head. "Nothing can prepare you for that. I don't care how many classes or videos or books. I thought I was going to die."

"And look at you now. The pain was worth it, wasn't it?"

"Oh yeah. It's just that . . ."

Jennifer sat on the edge of the bed and Melissa shifted a little as if she needed a better position to say what was inside.

"I don't know how something that's supposed to be so good can feel so bad. It's like I'm losing a part of me. It's not supposed to feel this way, is it?"

"Yes, it is. This is a real loss. And it's because you care about him that it's going to be hard. He's your son. He's part of you. So you're going to feel this for a long time."

"Nobody told me that."

"I know it seems like it ought to be easier. If you do something good, that feeling should overwhelm every-thing else. Problem is, you can't just turn off the other feelings."

Melissa looked up at Jennifer. "That's exactly what I told Brian when I said I was going to have the baby."

Jennifer smiled. "And that feeling deep inside is going to pull you through. Because someday he's going to thank you."

Melissa closed her eyes and shook her head, and she felt her chin shaking. "No. He won't thank me. He's going to hate me for not keeping him."

"Why do you say that?"

"Because it's true. He's going to wonder why I didn't love him enough. Why I didn't fight harder to keep him. And I won't have a good answer."

Jennifer stayed quiet as if in thought about what to say or how to remove the guilt. But her cell phone buzzed and she looked at it. "I need to take this." And when Jennifer stepped out of the room, Melissa knew this was the end.

She wanted to hold her son forever. But Jennifer was right. She knew she was doing something good that went against her instincts, and she had to trust that what she was doing for her son would be the best for him, even if it tore her heart in two.

She moved to the window, the sunlight peeking through the shades, and whispered, "I wish I could name you. I wish I could just do that so that you'd always have something I gave you."

And then, as if the glow of the sunlight from the Indiana sky was shining like a Bethlehem star, she remembered something from the TV show she'd watched. The teenager Mary hadn't chosen her Son's name. It was given by the angel who was sent to her. In a strange way, that comforted her and as she stood next to the window, she whispered a prayer.

"God, if You're there, watch over him and protect him."

As soon as she said the words, the door opened and a nurse entered the room. Melissa took a final look at her son, then turned and took six steps toward the woman in nursing scrubs. Those steps felt like a marathon, her legs heavy, like she was climbing the last steps up Mount Everest. When she reached the nurse, she gently put the baby in her arms and whispered, "Here you go."

The nurse took him, held him tightly, but lingered for a moment as if she knew what was happening and how hard that final walk was. Melissa stepped back, her eyes locked on the child. And as she felt her emotions giving way, she looked at the woman and nodded.

As if given permission, the nurse turned and walked out the door.

Arms empty now, Melissa stared at the hall, struggling to breathe. She closed her eyes and turned away, putting a hand to her face. And through the tears and the sobs that came, she whispered another prayer.

"Please don't let him hate me. And please let me see him again someday."

She closed the door and sank to the floor and hoped no one would hear her crying.

✦ ✦ ✦

Susan retrieved the diaper bag as soon as they parked at the hospital. Jimmy grabbed the baby blanket and they walked hand in hand as evening shadows fell. It almost felt like she was walking on air as she entered the hospital.

Jennifer, from the adoption agency, met them and hugged Susan. She passed them off to a hospital representative, Scott Davidson, who escorted them to the meeting room.

"Do you do this kind of thing a lot?" Jimmy said as they rode up the elevator.

"Not as much as I'd like," he said. "Sure beats budget meetings, I'll tell you that."

"With your experience," Susan said, "how often does it happen that . . . ?" She couldn't finish the sentence.

"How often do adoptive parents walk out and have the birth parents cause trouble?" The elevator door opened and he let them get off first and showed them to a room down the hall. When they were inside, he closed the door. "Mrs. Colton, I can't give you a 100 percent guarantee. But working with the agency the past few years and seeing how thorough they are, I would be very surprised—" he paused—"no, I would be shocked if anything happened with your son."

The way he said it, how sure he was, comforted her. And when he said "your son," her heart skipped a beat. Susan glanced at Jimmy, who raised his eyebrows and smiled, his dimples showing again.

The door opened and a nurse walked in cradling an infant. He was bundled in a blanket and wore a striped knit cap that fit perfectly over his head. The nurse handed him to Susan and all she could do was look in his face.

"He feels perfect," she said, her voice trembling. She stroked his head and when she choked the same words out again, the nurse put a hand on her shoulder.

"Do you want to hold him?" she said to Jimmy after a few minutes.

"I like watching you hold him," Jimmy said.

Jennifer came into the room and Susan looked up. "Is there something wrong?"

"The only thing wrong is that it's getting late and you two have a long drive ahead," Jennifer said.

"Is there anything else we need to do?" Jimmy said. "Sign any more papers?"

Jennifer looked at Scott and they both shrugged.

"You're good to go," Scott said.

"Wait, what's his name?" Jennifer said. "The birth mom wanted to know."

"His name is David James," Susan said. "And tell her we can't thank her enough for this gift."

Susan held David out as Jimmy wrapped him in the yellow blanket they had brought and they walked downstairs. When they made it into the cool December night, Susan looked up. The sky had opened a shower of perfect snowflakes, as if welcoming their son into the world.

Susan lifted a hand to feel the flakes as they fell and it felt like a moment of pure praise for God's answer to her prayers. Jimmy kept David's head shielded from the snowflakes with a hand. Then they walked to the car with their son.

✦ ✦ ✦

Melissa stood at the window, the blinds open, and watched the snow fall on the parking lot. The way it fluttered to the ground past the lights below looked pretty, but she felt separated from the world now, like her reason for living had been stolen.

She watched people scurrying along the sidewalk in the snow and wondered if the parents were there. Would they drive back to Louisiana tonight or get a hotel? She didn't know and never would.

Jennifer walked into the room and put her arm around Melissa. "I'm proud of you."

"Thanks."

"You should have seen them, Melissa. They were over the moon. They're going to be such good parents to David."

Melissa looked at the window again. "David. I like that. He looked like a David to me."

Jennifer retreated to the bed and sat. "So when are they letting you out of here?"

"The doctor said sometime tomorrow."

"Want me to pick you up?"

She looked at the door and saw Brian.

Jennifer glanced back, saw him, and stood. "I'd better get going. Call me if you need anything." She stopped and made sure Melissa heard her. "Anything, okay?"

Melissa nodded and Brian walked into the room. "Hey."

"Where were you?"

"You know where I was. At work."

She walked up to him and he backed away. He had a handful of breath mints in his mouth and she guessed why.

"How you feeling?" Brian said.

She wanted him to hug her and tell her everything was going to be all right, but he stood on the other side of the room. She sat on the bed and shrugged.

"Hey, I saw two people carrying a baby out in a yellow blanket. Do you think those were the people who adopted your baby?"

"Our baby," Melissa said. "Did you see their car? Did it have Louisiana plates?"

"I just passed them in the parking lot. I didn't stalk them."

She wanted to cry. She wanted to run down the stairs and into the falling snow barefoot. She wanted to get out of the hospital and away from the empty feeling. Anything to lessen the pain inside.

"You want me to get you something to eat?" Brian said.

"Not hungry." And she doubted she ever would be. She had watched what she ate because she knew it would affect the baby. Now nothing she ate would affect him and that thought sent her reeling. She had watched the doctor snip the umbilical cord, and even though she had held David and kissed his face and felt closer to him than anything in her life, he was gone.

"You want me to go, then?" Brian said.

"Why didn't you come see him? You could have at least done that for me."

Brian shifted his weight from one foot to the other, a habit when he was nervous.

"Don't lie and say you were at work all day."

Shoulders slumped. "I'm here now, aren't I? Everybody

handles things different, Melissa. I'm not good with stuff like this. Hospitals give me the willies."

She stared out the window at the snow that came harder now. "It's like it never happened."

"What do you mean?"

"For you, it never happened. You can go on with your life. You never even looked him in the eyes."

"I thought that was the point. You said you couldn't turn things off. You couldn't just get rid of it. I've been here. And I'm going to be here in the future. But you can't make me be something I'm not."

"I'm not asking you to be anything other than human and care for somebody other than yourself."

Brian's jaw dropped. He scowled and shook his head. "I'm not taking that. I'm out of here."

He stalked out of the room and she heard his work boots clomping on the hallway tile. She had never felt so alone in her life.

PART 2

PART 2

CHAPTER 11

✦ ✦ ✦

The wedding was held in April at Brian and Melissa's apartment and officiated by a justice of the peace.

Melissa had debated whether to invite her mother. On the one hand, she didn't want any drama that could ruin the day for her and Brian. But on the other hand, she wanted her mother to see that she was an adult now and moving on with her life in spite of the family friction she left behind.

Surprisingly, her mother said she was coming, though there was tension on the phone when she learned that the wedding would be in a small apartment with little to no decorations. Melissa shoved aside any feelings of shame at the humble location. She was about to become somebody's wife, and her mother would just have to accept it.

Brian's mother agreed to come too, which shocked them both. Yet the guests that Melissa was the most honored to have in the room were members of Kelly's family. It would be bittersweet, but they knew that Kelly wouldn't have wanted to miss this day for the world.

Planning the wedding on a shoestring budget, Melissa had decided to buy a nice dress she could wear again. But a phone call changed that idea. It was Kelly's mother, who said she had a gown she'd been saving for Kelly's wedding. Melissa had said she couldn't take the gift, but Kelly's mom insisted.

"She would have been your maid of honor if she were here, wouldn't she?"

"Yes," Melissa said. "She wanted me to be the same for her."

"Then let her do this for you. She would want that. I was saving this for her. But since she can't be here, it'll feel like a little of her is. I can't wait to see you in this dress."

That thought had convinced Melissa and when she tried it on, she couldn't believe how it fit. She thought of how much the dress would have been shortened if Kelly wore it. That made her smile.

As they stood in the small living room, she looked at those gathered, knowing only one person there knew the truth about David. They had kept the secret well.

Brian stood next to the justice of the peace. He had his hands clasped in front of him, with a nervous smile. He looked like there were about a thousand places he would rather be, not because he didn't want to marry her, but because he wasn't comfortable being the center of attention. He would much rather be fishing or repairing a computer or watching a wrestling show.

They made it through their vows and everyone clapped when they kissed. Then the whole group went to Red Lobster for the celebration dinner. Melissa knew she would have laughed had she heard of someone else doing that on their wedding day. But this was her day, and for some reason she decided not to let it bother her.

There was no honeymoon because they couldn't afford it. Brian said they could save up for a trip on their first anniversary but she wondered if that was a promise or simply an idea to consider.

Back in the apartment, Melissa smoothed out the dress and hung it in the closet. She couldn't help thinking of Kelly and the fun they would have had. Kelly's mother said the dress was Melissa's now and that she should save it for her own daughter to wear.

Was that simply a wish too? Would she have more children? Would she ever have a daughter?

Sitting on the edge of the bed, staring at the dress illumined by the naked bulb in the closet with Brian already snoring behind her, she whispered the name.

"David."

He was four months old now. She had read in a book what happens at each stage of development, and she imagined David grabbing his feet and putting his toes in his mouth. But that was all she could do—imagine. There were no pictures, nothing to go on but her own thoughts of what his life might be like.

It was funny how life went on. After Kelly died, she'd thought of her and even picked up the phone once or twice wanting to call her before she remembered what had happened. And life went on without her son, too.

She had gotten a full-time job in an office in town, and she and Brian were talking about buying a small house. She filled her days with obligations, the inevitable to-do list of life. But at night, when her head hit the pillow, she felt an ache inside. And when she closed her eyes, she saw him in her arms, his perfect little face, how alert he was, his eyes open, even less than a day old. In those moments she could only see what she didn't have, her empty arms.

She went to sleep with the ache and woke up each morning with the same. And in a strange way, the ache became a friend, a constant companion she could always count on being there.

The first letter from Susan came a few days later. The adoption agency had put together a schedule for the adoptive parents and birth mother to correspond for the first year. Susan gave an update on David's growth, and Melissa got her first look at her son in another mother's arms.

As the months went on, Melissa looked forward to getting the letters, but at the same time they set her back. Every time she saw his little face and how it had changed, she thought of what she had missed. She didn't put any of those feelings in the letters she wrote Susan and Jimmy, of course, knowing that at some point David might see them.

When David was nine months old, Susan wrote:

Melissa and Brian,

David is growing up so fast, we can hardly believe it. He's such a happy child, always smiling. I catalog these things with our camera and video recorder, but Jimmy is even worse than I am. He has to catch every significant moment, such as first time in his high chair, first time to eat real food, and more.

As I said in my letter before he was born, we've lost two sons and we want David to know about Michael and John. And when the time is right, we want him to know about his adoption.

We're headed to a lake to go camping. I'm hoping to send a photo of David's first fishing expedition. I'm sure Jimmy will take about a thousand pictures.

My favorite thing to do each day is sit with David and read. He fits so perfectly right beside me and he snuggles in. He's such a smart little thing. He points at pictures on the pages and laughs so hard.

He does a funny thing with his fingers, too. When he goes to sleep, he puts his middle and fourth finger in his mouth and then he wraps his blanket around his other hand and touches his nose until he falls asleep. I could go on and on describing him, but I'll stop.

We hope you are well and this letter will encourage you about this little life that has grown our little family.

With gratitude,
Susan Colton

When Christmas neared, the ache inside Melissa began to feel more like a sharp pain. At first she didn't understand what was happening—the anxiety, the troubled feeling that something wasn't right. She snapped at Brian for little things, and the tension leaked out at her work.

She had secured a new job at a local bank. Kelly's

mother had suggested she apply. The woman had put in a good word for her. But when the boss said he was ordering pizza for the office Christmas party, Melissa made a snarky comment that led to a full-on argument. She told him it was a stupid choice and that anyone with half a brain wouldn't do such a thing.

"Who orders pizza at a Christmas party? Deep dish and candy canes don't go together. Makes me sick thinking about it."

She regretted saying that almost as soon as it left her mouth and she could tell by the looks on her coworkers' faces that she had crossed a line. Her boss had ended the argument by leaving the room but called her into his office and told her she could leave early that day.

"I don't need to leave early."

"Yes, you do. I want you to go home and think about whether you want to work here," he said with a stern face. "We operate as a team and you need to decide if you're on it."

She picked up her purse from the desk and saw the calendar underneath. When she glanced at it, she realized she was only two weeks away from David's birthday, and a flood of emotion hit her. Her eyes blurred and her boss asked her what was going on. No wonder she was on edge. But there was no way she could tell her boss or anyone else. She had to keep the secret.

On the drive home all she could think about was how different things would have been if she had kept David. And she would have kept him if it weren't for Brian. A gloom came over her that only increased as she saw all the lights and tinsel and happy families with smiling children and the TV shows where every problem was solved in half an hour. Why didn't any of her problems get solved that way?

She stopped at a big-box store near her house for paper plates and a rotisserie chicken for dinner but she got sidetracked by the toy aisle, imagining what she would give her son on his first birthday and how she would separate his birthday from Christmas morning. All the brightly colored toys brought back the truth of what she didn't have.

When she arrived at the apartment and checked their mailbox, she saw a small brown envelope and knew what was inside. With David's birthday approaching, this would be the last letter from the Coltons.

She hurried to the living room, opened the note, and found a picture of Susan and David at a Louisiana lake. David had grown so much. Susan was holding him with one arm and with the other she held up a huge catfish. That made Melissa smile.

Melissa focused on her son and put her finger on the picture as if he might be able to feel her touch. She opened the note and read.

Dear Melissa and Brian,

We can't believe this is our last letter. It seems even harder to write than the first. We don't feel like we have said thank you enough.

This year has been the greatest of our life. Not necessarily the easiest. There've been lots of adjustments and it has gone by much too quickly.

We will always be open with David about his adoption. We look forward to your last letter and to sharing it with him.

Sincerely,
Susan and Jimmy Colton

Somehow the words rang hollow. They were fine on the page and pushed all the buttons, but this letter was shorter than the others and didn't share many details. It felt like Susan and Jimmy were glad to be moving on and the letter was the final cutting of the umbilical cord.

And what did Susan mean by "not necessarily the easiest"? Were there physical problems with David? Had their family been through something they hadn't told her about?

Melissa studied the picture again. David's nose and mouth looked a lot like Brian's. His eyes were hers. And in every picture he seemed to have a beaming smile, the proverbial happy baby.

She had so many questions but decided to push them aside. As she balanced her notebook on the arm of her chair, she wrote a response in red ink. From early on her teachers had commented on how neat her papers were, the way she printed her letters. She let the words flow but decided to keep the letter brief.

Jimmy and Susan,

I can't believe it's been almost a year. I know it will be the last update. It just doesn't seem possible. But I understand that we will have to get on with our lives. I cannot make out like I don't miss David because there's still a part of me that feels empty. I'm just glad that we chose you two.

I'll be praying for David as he grows up. We know he'll have everything he needs. We think of you guys every day. Thank you for sending the pictures.

Love,
Melissa

She didn't sign Brian's name because the letter wasn't from him. In fact, he didn't seem to want anything to do with them. She'd shown him pictures of his son but he had looked at them quickly and handed them back without much reaction. He had actually told her that he'd be glad when the letters and pictures stopped.

"Why is that?" she said.

"So we can get this behind us. We need to move on."

But she couldn't "move on," whatever that meant. She couldn't close the door on the past, especially something as life-changing as having a baby. She didn't think she could ever "move on" from that event.

She tore the page from the spiral-bound notebook and folded it. As she was addressing the plain white envelope, she compared Susan's note with hers. Susan's was on nice stationery with a border design. Her note had three holes along the side and perforations where she had torn it. It was another indicator of how different their lives were. She pursed her lips as she licked the back of the envelope.

They can give you so much more than we could. But I still love you, little guy. I don't know why that wasn't enough to make me keep you.

She pulled the page out of the envelope and cut along the red line on the left side to make it look neater. It was the best she could do. She stuffed the page back into the envelope and put it in the mail.

CHAPTER 12

✦ ✦ ✦

Jimmy was thrilled for Susan and watched in amazement as she blossomed as a mother. There was such tenderness in the way she treated David. She insisted that she be the one for late-night feedings, but Jimmy sometimes beat her to the crib instead of turning over and going back to sleep.

There were few arguments about child raising. Jimmy let Susan take the lead and make decisions, but she always consulted him. His usual reply to any idea was simply "I'm good with that."

As he watched David grow into his personality in the first few years, Jimmy's prayer was that David would always maintain his patented wide smile. He wanted his son to feel secure, provided for, loved and treasured, and to believe that he could accomplish whatever he set his mind to. More than anything, Jimmy wanted David to see him not simply as the man who had stood in place as his father, but as his real father. He wasn't sure how to accomplish that or if it could be accomplished once David was old enough to know the truth. But Jimmy hoped that would come to his son and that the bond they formed would be lasting.

Their first camping trip once David could walk was a disaster. Jimmy and Susan had camped dozens of times, but they'd never done so with a toddler. Though they used repellant, the mosquito bites made red splotches that swelled on David's arms and legs. Instead of fishing from their canoe, they spent the ride trying to corral him and not capsize. And since they didn't bring a crib, David used his freedom to bound over their sleeping bags most of the night.

"I've never been so thankful for a zippered tent," Susan said the next morning when they found David curled up between them. They called it quits after two nights, hoping things would be better next time.

After losing two sons, Jimmy was concerned that Susan might be overly protective of David and not allow him to simply be a boy and explore and, at times, fall.

But from the outset, she was able to do the hard work of letting go a little bit each day. They talked about that one night after David turned three and had bumped his head on the coffee table after jumping off the couch with his Superman cape flying behind him.

"I have fears of him getting hurt or that I'll be driving and get into an accident," she said, "but from the first moment I held him, I told God I would trust Him. I don't want him to grow up afraid to live. And that kind of attitude is caught more than it's taught."

"Can I still insist he wear a helmet when he gets his first bike?" Jimmy said with a smile.

Three years into their marriage, Melissa felt her relationship with Brian slipping. They had tried to save for a house but car repairs and monthly bills got in the way. And so did a bass boat Brian came home with one day. He'd bought it from a friend of a friend who gave him a great deal, he had said. Melissa couldn't contain her anger and he shut down after the argument. Her first problem was the fact that he hadn't even talked with her about the purchase. And they had never taken the promised honeymoon, so she felt it a double wound. Then came the fishing trips on weekends with his buddies. That angered her even more. She could fish better than the whole load of guys Brian hung out with, but that was the problem. They did less fishing and more drinking.

She thought a baby might be the very thing to bring her and Brian together. But each month when her period came, she felt like God might be punishing her. Maybe she wasn't fit to be a mother after what she had considered with David. The months turned into years.

Then, just as she was thinking seriously about leaving Brian, she began getting sick in the morning. The feeling brought back memories of the morning sickness she'd had with David.

After her positive pregnancy test, she handed the results to Brian.

"Is this what I think it is?"

"Depends on what you think it is," she said.

He ran a hand over his face. "Seriously, Melissa? Just when we're getting our feet under us?"

"You knew I was trying to have another baby."

"Yeah, but I thought it wasn't going to work. This changes things."

Brian was right. It did change things. Instead of drawing them together, the pregnancy pushed them further apart. But when she went into labor, he actually drove her to the hospital and stayed until their daughter, Courtney, was born. Melissa gave her the middle name of Kelly and gave Kelly's mother a picture.

For the first few months Brian seemed like a new man. He held Courtney and was at least trying to pitch in. He'd bring her from her crib to the bed to be bottle-fed and then fall back asleep.

He still went on weekend trips but always found a way to get back for the Colts game on Sunday. And his anger issues seemed to surface more often. Early in their relationship he would get upset with Melissa and yell and say demeaning things. Melissa could play that game too, and did quite often, giving him the same and more.

The moment that changed everything came when Courtney was almost two. She was sitting in her high chair eating breakfast when Brian came down the hall, late for work. He'd overslept because he'd been out with his friends the night before.

"Why didn't you wake me up?" he screamed.

Instead of yelling back, Melissa said something calmly to defuse the situation. But it was the look on Courtney's face that got her. She would jump when Brian raised his voice in anger. That day Melissa made the decision. She knew if she went to somebody in the family, Brian would be there trying to talk her out of it, so she called Kelly's mother.

"I've got two spare rooms in the back of the house," the woman said. "Bring whatever you need and I'll find the rest."

Brian didn't want a divorce and he made that clear. When he learned that Melissa had hired an attorney, he was livid. His mother called Melissa and talked with her. She had always been able to calm her son, and she knew he was dealing with a lot of anger inside.

"I had my doubts if Brian was ready for marriage to begin with," she said. "I don't think either of you knew what you were getting into."

"I thought he was the one," Melissa said.

"Well, I hate to see you two split, but I want you to know Courtney will always be my grandbaby. And you're welcome over here anytime you want to come."

Things escalated when Brian discovered the cost of child support. It was the longest season of Melissa's life, with the lawyers going back and forth. When the judge granted the divorce with joint custody, she felt a part of her life close like a door. She and Courtney would set out on their own. And like always, Brian would just move on as if what had happened in the past was gone and didn't make any difference.

The two tried to be cordial, especially around Courtney. Melissa had to give Brian credit for that. On the weekends when Courtney would spend the night with her father, and eventually her new stepmother, Azure, Melissa was alone. That was the time when she would pull out the box she kept hidden in her closet, the one with the letters and the pictures of David.

What would have happened if she had kept him? What was he doing now? Did he look more like her as he grew? When and how would she tell Courtney about her brother? That thought sent her reeling.

And did David ever wonder about her or think of her? Was he old enough to even entertain those thoughts?

She'd seen a TV show about a mother who searched for her biological daughter for decades and finally, as the woman was dying of some disease, her daughter found her. Melissa was glad she was alone that weekend because the tears flowed and she couldn't stop them. And she began to write her own script of what it might be like in the future to meet her grown son and reunite with him.

There was only one problem with her version of that story. It was the old whisper that told her how bad she was, what a terrible person she had been for considering taking the life of her child. In the movie-of-the-week of her life, she would look her son in the eye and see the man he had become. But instead of a warm embrace, he would speak with venom, telling her he hated her and to stop trying to ruin his life.

He would turn and walk away, and Melissa would be left on the ground in tears.

You can't risk that kind of reaction, the voice inside said. *Don't risk the rejection you'll receive. Keep the secret. Bury the desire to ever reach out to him.*

The voice won. She put the box of letters and pictures away and promised herself never to open them again.

CHAPTER 13

✦ ✦ ✦

Wilson Elementary was a yellow-brick building constructed during the Depression—and it looked like it, sad and faded. Hallways were made of glazed concrete and patrolled by zealous sixth graders handpicked as safety patrols. They blocked water fountains after the recess bell rang and instilled fear in any child caught in one of the innumerable infractions such as running in the hallway.

The classroom floors were hardwood on top of concrete and the sonic effect was that every noise in the building was amplified. A slamming door, a crying child hurt on the playground, a teacher rolling a projector from the library, a thirsty third grader who made it to the fountain five seconds after the bell—all noises reverberated in a cacophonous roar.

It was at the first-grade door on the east side, ground level, that David Colton took his place in line, head down, staring at the shoes of other children in front of him and cataloging what he saw. Some wore shiny shoes and crisp, new jeans. They looked like children from back-to-school ads in the Sunday paper. Others wore sneakers held together with duct tape and prayer. David could see this disparity, even at six. His mother had told him never to judge people by their clothing, that what was inside was the important thing.

He glanced to his left toward the parking lot only once and saw his mother and father. They were standing outside the car. His dad had his arm around his mom and she waved and brushed something from her face. David had attended kindergarten at the church-run school near their house. They'd walked with him each day, but for some reason they had decided to have him attend the local public school for first grade and David didn't object. He trusted them.

They had made a big deal about driving him for his first day but told him he could ride the bus the next day if he wanted. Part of him wanted them to drive him every day. Part of him wanted to take the bus. He looked away, trying to find something to catch his attention. The last thing he wanted to do was cry, and the feeling inside was like a weight pressing on his chest.

His eyes landed on a kid running toward the line with a *Star Wars: Attack of the Clones* lunch box, his backpack bouncing. The kid stuffed something in his mouth as he came to a stop, and his cheeks puffed. He was husky with thick red hair that hadn't been tamed by a comb. A girl who looked a little older trailed him, and when she passed, he said something unintelligible to her because of his full mouth. She rolled her eyes and walked past the line of first graders toward the back door of the main building.

David's teacher came out of the room and walked down the line. Mrs. Hayes was a short, full-figured woman with dark hair and a shiny forehead. He had met her a few days earlier when his mother brought him for orientation. She smiled at him as she walked the line.

"Good morning, David."

"Good morning," he said.

The bell was mounted just below the eave above them and the sound was so deafening when it rang, David had to cover his ears. He filed into the room behind the others, looking for the desk Mrs. Hayes had assigned to him. He found his chair and was putting his backpack on it when the redheaded kid barreled up and put his lunch box down.

"This is my desk," David said.

"Who said? I don't see your name."

David pointed at the teacher. "Mrs. Hayes told me this was—"

"Nathan?" the teacher said. "You're over here, right next to my desk."

The boy frowned and picked up his lunch box. "Thanks a lot," he said.

David picked up the scent of sausage from the boy's breath. And there was something about the way he charged to the other side of the room that made David feel unsettled. He seemed the type of kid who might be a bully. His dad had warned him about them. But there was something else. This Nathan seemed so sure of himself. Confident. And David wanted to be confident instead of the way he was. He wasn't sure what to call that, but it was anything but confident.

At lunch, Mrs. Hayes led her class to the gym that was also the auditorium and the cafeteria. David took a tray from the shelf and carefully walked to the long table where Mrs. Hayes stood. On the stage at the front, a group of sixth graders stood on risers with the music teacher at the piano. They practiced a song they would later sing at an assembly.

The redheaded kid, Nathan, barreled through the doors, grabbing a carton of milk and dropping his metal lunch box loudly next to David. He sat, the table bouncing with the intensity of his descent, and in one motion he opened the lunch box and dumped the contents in front of him.

"I'm on a special diet," he said. "I can't eat the stuff they serve here."

David wasn't sure if he was talking to him or the kids across the table.

When Nathan took a bite of his sandwich, he turned and noticed the sixth graders onstage. "Hey, look, food and entertainment," he said, his mouth full.

David glanced at the kid and though he tried hard not to, he smiled. Then he chuckled and tried to turn it into a cough. He didn't want to be near a bully.

"I'm Nate," the kid said. "Don't call me Nathan. What's your name?"

A hesitation. "David."

"David what?"

"Colton."

Nate put out a pudgy hand. "Nice to meet you, fellow prisoner."

David shook his hand limply, unlike how his dad had taught him.

Nate stared at the end of the table. Then he leaned over and whispered, "Have you noticed how shiny her forehead is?"

David shrugged.

"My dad can't get that much shine when he waxes his car. Seriously, she came over to my desk and I could see myself, like in a mirror."

David went back to his lunch. Nate talked so fast, almost faster than David could think.

"Look, I'm sorry about the desk and all. They put me next to the teacher's desk in kindergarten and I didn't want to go through that again."

"Why do you have to sit close to the teacher?"

Nate opened a package of gluten-free crackers and shoved a handful in his mouth. "I don't know. They think I'm a troublemaker, probably, but I'm not." A slight pause and then Nate said, "Hey, have you seen *Revenge of the Sith*?"

"No."

"Aw, man, it's so good. Special effects are awesome. Reese and I rented it the other night from Blockbuster. I want to buy it so bad. What's your favorite movie?"

David thought a minute and before he could come up with an answer, Nathan had suggested three movies he ought to see and why he should see them.

When Nate paused to take another bite of his sandwich, David said, "Who's Reese?"

"My sister. She's in third grade. She's a pain. You know how sisters can be."

"No, I don't have any."

"You're lucky. She bosses me around and then gets me in trouble. Maybe she's the reason they put me near the teacher."

"Is she the one who passed you in line this morning?"

"Yeah, long brown hair." Nate held out his arm. "Sharp fingernails. Don't get too close. I don't think she bites, but you can't be too careful."

The next day when he got on the bus, David's stomach was in knots. His parents walked with him to the bus stop, then watched from a distance. The door opened and he climbed the steep steps and saw the bus was packed. The kids in the first few rows turned their heads and looked away as he was swallowed into the rows.

"Sit down!" someone yelled.

"Yeah, sit down so we can go," another chimed in.

David turned and saw the bus driver in the mirror watching him. That's when he heard someone yell his name.

"David, back here!"

David moved toward the voice and finally caught sight of Nate's red hair above the sea of faces. He made it to the row and Nate scooted over enough for him to sit and the bus moved forward.

"Thanks."

"You've got a seat back here any day."

They passed his parents and David turned to look out the back window and wave but they didn't see him.

A girl turned and looked at him. She was cracking her gum loudly.

When she turned around again, Nate said, "That's Reese." He lifted a hand like it was a lion's claw and brought it down. "Be careful."

As David got off the bus at the end of the day, his mother was there to meet him. They walked up the street to their house in the plume of exhaust.

"I was talking with your teacher today, Mrs. Hayes."

"You were at school?"

"No, she called. How do you like her?"

"She's nice."

"She told me you've made a new friend. That sounds exciting."

"I guess."

"Nathan, right?"

"He goes by Nate. He wants me to come to his house to watch a movie. Can I, Mom?"

"We'll see. Let me talk with your father. Maybe we could have him come here and have dinner with us one day?"

"Could we?" David could hardly contain his excitement.

"How did you meet him?"

David explained the first day and what had happened on the bus and how funny Nate was, the things he noticed in the lunchroom. He didn't mention the observation about Mrs. Hayes's shiny forehead.

When his father got home from work, David told him about Nate in one long, run-on sentence. David looked up at him expectantly.

"Why don't we call after dinner and see if he can come tomorrow?"

"Yes!" David said.

After dinner, David helped his father clear the table and put the dishes in the dishwasher while his mom called Nate's mom. After a few minutes, she hung up and said Nate had something to do the next night. "His mom said maybe next week."

David's shoulders slumped.

"Hey, how about going over to the pond and putting a line in the water before the sun goes down?" his dad said. "What do you say, sport?"

"You're not going without me!" his mother said.

They walked to the nearby park and sat on the bank. From the start, his mother had insisted that David learn to bait his own hook. She had been the first to show him how and David wondered if all moms were as good at fishing as his.

David sat between them as they watched the September sun sink to the tops of the trees. A goose came walking up the hill on the other side of the pond. Trailing it, walking the edge of the hill, were several goslings. The goose surveyed the water as if making sure everything was safe for her offspring. Then it ventured in and the goslings followed, one by one.

"They're so cute," David's mother said.

"Hey, Dad, it's like the story you tell."

His dad laughed. "Yeah, that could be the family I tell you about."

"What story?" David's mother said.

"Oh, we were out here the other day and I made up a tale about a goose and her husband."

"I've never heard that one," she said.

"Let me tell it, Dad."

His dad glanced at his mom as David started in.

"So there's this goose who lays some eggs and sits on them and tries to get them to hatch, but they don't. One gets taken by a . . ."

"Snake," his father said.

"Yeah, one gets taken by a snake. And then a racoon. And then the others get stepped on by somebody who doesn't see them. It was an accident, but the goose is really sad. She doesn't have any babies."

"That is a sad story," his mother said.

"Wait, I'm not done. It gets better. So there's another goose and she only has one egg. So the goose takes care of it until one day the egg cracks and a little beak comes out." David looked up at his dad, who nodded, encouraging him to continue. "So the little goose gets out of the egg and the mother goose loves her goosling, and she—" David stopped when he noticed his mother giggling. "What?"

"Nothing, go on," she said.

"No, why are you laughing?"

"It's called a gosling," his dad said.

"Oh yeah, right. Gosling. So the mother goose loves him a lot, but she can't take care of him the way she wants. So she meets this other goose who didn't have any goos—goslings of her own. And so the goose becomes a mom. And that's pretty much the end of it."

David looked up at his mother and noticed she was staring at the pond. Then she turned and rubbed at her eyes.

"I'll bet the mama goose takes good care of the little one," she said.

"Yeah," David said, mimicking his father. "She loved him like he was her very own." David reeled his line in and instead of casting again, he looked at his dad. "You know, that's kind of like the story you tell of the fish."

"What story is that?" his mother said.

"There's a mama fish and a papa fish who don't have any baby fish and one day they find a baby fish and they take him in and he swims with them. Isn't that how it goes?"

"Something like that," his father said.

His mother leaned forward so she could see David's dad. "Sounds like a recurring theme."

"What does that mean?" David said.

"It means the same thing happens to the characters in different stories. Like in the Bible, when David goes up against Goliath. There are lots of stories about facing giants and overcoming them."

David cast his line into the water and it sailed high and fell with a plop. "Did you see that, Dad? That's farther than you cast it."

"Perfect timing on the release. That was excellent."

A silence fell between them and there was nothing but the sound of the water gently lapping the shore and the honk of passing geese. Somewhere a lawn mower droned and struggled in tall grass. And there came the call of frogs and crickets welcoming the evening.

David crawled into bed later that night and pulled the covers up. His father entered the room and sat on the edge of the bed.

"Did you have fun at the pond today?"

David nodded, then frowned. "But we didn't catch anything."

"That's actually part of the fun of fishing. You never know what will happen with the fish. But if you pay attention, you'll have fun seeing the geese and listening to the birds and being with those you love. You can't force a fish to come up and take the bait. You have to wait."

"Waiting is hard, isn't it?"

"It is. But think about it. That's what makes Christmas morning so special. You have all the waiting that leads up to it."

David had a stack of books by his bed and he looked at them.

"Which one tonight?" his dad said.

"I don't want you to read one. I want you to tell one. You know, like the goose and the gosling."

"Why do you want to hear that?"

David shrugged and sank a little further under the covers. There was a feeling he had when his dad sat on his bed and took the time to read or talk. Something warm spread through him he couldn't describe.

"All right, let's see," his dad said, looking at the plastic stars on his ceiling that glowed when the lights went off. "I've been thinking about a new story that has people in it."

He stood and pulled the chair from David's small desk

by the window close to the bed and sat. He leaned forward with his elbows on his knees, his face inches from David's.

"Once there was a man and woman who wanted to have a baby. And they waited and waited. They waited such a long time."

"Just like fishing at the pond."

"Exactly. And just when they thought they could wait no longer, the doctor said they were going to have a child. And the woman and the man were over the moon."

"What's that mean?"

"*Over the moon* means they were so happy they couldn't stop smiling. Their hearts rose so high just thinking and planning their life with this child. They painted the baby's room and they bought a crib and they told their family, and everyone was so happy."

David propped himself up on his elbows. "Wait. Something bad is going to happen."

"Why do you say that?"

"Because in your stories, something bad always happens before the good thing. An egg gets stolen or stepped on."

His father ran a hand through his hair and gave David a strange look. "Do you want to hear this?"

David relaxed and nodded.

"You're right. Something sad happened after the baby was born. It was a baby boy and he was sick. The mom and dad prayed so hard. And the doctor did everything he could. But the little boy was so sick that he died."

David stared at his father, then looked away. "I told you."

"The mom and dad were very sad. They loved the little baby boy so much. And it was really hard for them just to keep going because they had such hopes for that little boy. After a while, the doctor said that the mother was going to have another baby. And they were really happy, but they were also really scared. Do you know why?"

"They didn't want the second baby to get sick?"

"Yes. But they decided that no matter what happened, they would trust that God would help them and the baby. And after nine months their second baby boy was born."

"And he was okay, right?" David sat up again. "Dad, don't tell me he got sick too."

David's father nodded.

"That's not fair. I don't like this story."

"I understand. It's a hard story. But it's a good one too. Sometimes the hard stories are the best ones."

There was movement in the hall and David's mom leaned against the door.

"Mom, can you get Dad to tell a different a story? This one is so sad."

She came around the bed and sat on the other side next to David. "I've heard this one. It gets better. A lot better."

David yawned and stretched. "Okay."

David's dad took off the glasses he had begun wearing and put them on the nightstand. The glasses left two marks on the bridge of his nose and David stared at them as he continued.

"The man and the woman were sad. But even though their hearts were broken, they felt like there was room for someone else. So they found some people who worked with women who were having babies but knew they couldn't take care of them."

"Like the goose mom?"

"Right. And one day they got a phone call that a baby had been born and they had been chosen to come get that baby."

"And love it like their very own," David said.

David's dad nodded and turned his head away for a minute. "So the man and woman drove a long way, all day, and finally got to the hospital. And the people there brought out this perfect baby boy and placed him in the woman's arms."

His mother rubbed David's arm and leaned close. "The baby boy was wrapped tightly in a blanket. It was soft and smooth and the baby was snug inside."

She held out David's old blanket, the one he'd carried around as a toddler. The one he didn't want to let go.

"Where did you get that?" David said.

"I put it away," his mother said. "I have a lot of things I've kept for you. And this is the blanket you were wrapped in when we brought you home from the hospital that day. The snow was falling outside. And your dad and I almost floated home because we were so happy."

David looked at her, then at his dad, then back to her. "Wait. This is about me?"

His dad touched his arm. "David, there was a young girl who was going to have a baby and she knew she couldn't take care of him. She heard about how we had lost your brothers, Michael and John. And she chose us to be your mom and dad."

"And we love you like our very own," his mother said, wiping something from her eyes.

"Whoa," David said. He held the baby blanket up and rubbed his nose with it.

"That's what you used to do in your crib," his mother said. "You would hold this in your hand and rub your nose with it. You were such a cute baby."

His mother hugged him and then his father did the same and kissed the top of his head.

"We love you, David."

"Like your very own," David said, turning and pulling the covers to his chin. When his dad turned out the light, he saw stars on the ceiling and fell asleep.

CHAPTER 14

✦ ✦ ✦

On Courtney's second birthday, Melissa took her to a park
and let her run and play on the slides and pushed her on
the swings. Courtney always asked to be pushed higher.
The rusty chain link squeaked with the back-and-forth
of the swing and that sound felt familiar to Melissa. Her
life was filled with rusty squeaks no amount of WD-40
could quiet.

When Courtney got tired, Melissa could always tell by
the way she whined. She put her in the car seat and drove
to her daughter's favorite restaurant, a place that served

breakfast all day and piled stacks of pancakes in front of Courtney and topped them with a whipped cream face, along with chocolate chips. Melissa knew one of the servers and they let her light two candles and three servers sang "Happy Birthday" at their table.

"Make a wish, sweetie," Melissa said.

She took a picture of Courtney with her hands together, a huge smile on her face, as she blew out the candles.

What did she wish? Melissa wondered. *What does she want most in life? Does she even have the ability to want anything?*

Melissa only ordered a cup of coffee. Her stomach swirled as she cut Courtney's pancakes. When the stack was cut into bite-size pieces, her daughter's chin puckered.

"What's wrong, my spider monkey?"

"It's not a face anymore." She said it in a tired whine, then the tears started and she tried to wipe them away.

She was right. The face made with whipped cream had been marred by the cutting.

"At some point you have to eat it," Melissa said. "You can't sit there and look at it all day."

Courtney dropped her fork with a clatter.

In that moment, Melissa saw a flash of childish innocence. She recalled the old saying "You can't have your cake and eat it too." That was what Courtney wanted—to preserve the pancakes and consume them as well. Melissa saw that clearly, but she couldn't force Courtney to see it and she didn't know what to do.

Had David gone through this? What had her son wished for on his birthdays? He was eight now. A melancholy swept over her and as she watched Courtney dissolve into tears, she realized she was looking in a mirror.

Melissa wanted life to be something she could have in front of her with everything neat and clean and tied in a bow. But her life was messy and there was no bow big enough. The decisions she had made and the decisions others had made encircled her life.

"Is something wrong?"

The voice startled her and she looked up at her friend. "Courtney's upset because she can't see the face anymore."

"Oh, sweetie," the server said, kneeling beside the girl. "I think I can help. You wait here. And go ahead and take a few more bites. I'll be right back, okay?"

Miraculously, Courtney obeyed the woman and began to eat what was in front of her, wiping at her eyes and getting syrup and whipped cream around her mouth. Melissa dipped a napkin in water and cleaned her face a little, but it was a losing battle. A few minutes later the server returned with a plate that contained a single pancake with a perfectly drawn whipped cream face, complete with hair that looked just like Courtney's.

As Courtney ate, she kept her eyes on the lone pancake

beside her, and Melissa imagined David sitting beside Courtney. Maybe he would have cut her pancakes for her. She tried to morph his face in her mind—what would he look like compared with the last picture the Coltons sent? How tall was he? When did he begin to walk or run or talk? What did his laugh sound like? All of that was filtered through Courtney and the milestones of her first word, first steps. Melissa had missed those with David by her own doing, and she hated herself for that. She was sure she would never know the answers to her questions because she would never see him again. Why would he want to meet her? She had given him away. Abandoned him to another family.

She had wanted a tattoo to remind her of David every time she looked at it. So she had his birth date etched on the underside of her wrist. And every day when she saw it and every night as she hit the pillow, she remembered her prayer in the hospital for God to take care of him. But instead of bringing her comfort, the date on her wrist added to the guilt and the shame of the secret she and Brian had kept.

The server carefully placed the lone pancake in a Styrofoam box, and Melissa tried to get home without jostling it too much. When they pulled into the driveway of the little house she rented, Brian's car was parked on the street in front.

Melissa unbuckled Courtney and took her inside. Brian came to the door with a package.

"I know I'm getting her on the weekend, but I wanted her to have this today," he said.

Melissa gave him a hard stare, then glanced at Brian's car. His new wife was sitting in the front, window rolled up. There was so much pain and distance between them. "This is not the agreement we had."

"I know, but like I said, I just wanted her to have this today and not wait until Saturday."

"Make it quick," Melissa said.

She followed him into the house. Courtney was at the kitchen table trying to get the Styrofoam box open. She had turned it over and Melissa could only imagine what the whipped cream looked like.

"Spider monkey, look who's here with a present."

Courtney turned and smiled. "Daddy!"

She toddled over to Brian, who hugged her and got down on his knees and handed her the brightly wrapped package. From the looks of it and what she knew about Brian, she figured his wife had wrapped it.

Melissa glanced out the front window. "You want her to come in from the car?"

"No, she's good."

Beneath the wrapping paper was a doll tightly held in a box by twist ties. Courtney tried to open it and Brian took over, unwinding the ties and finally releasing the doll from its cardboard prison. Courtney squealed and ran down the hallway to her room.

"She likes it," Brian said, watching her go.

"Yeah, you can't lose with a doll as far as Courtney goes."

Brian stood and headed for the door. "I'll be here Saturday morning to pick her up."

"I'll have her ready," Melissa said.

Brian opened the door and Melissa couldn't resist saying what was on her mind.

"Does she know?"

Brian turned. "Does who know what?"

Melissa nodded toward the car outside. "Have you told her about our son?"

Brian looked at her with squinted eyes, mouth agape. "What? Why are you bringing that up? That's over, Melissa. It's done."

"Not for me," Melissa said.

"Well, it ought to be. When I move on from something, I move on. As far as I'm concerned, it never happened."

"It did happen. David is real. He's part of the story."

"You need to forget it, Melissa."

"Not a day goes by that I don't think about him and wonder what he's like, what he's interested in, what he looks like."

Brian shook his head. "You can't drive a car looking in the rearview."

"You can't keep secrets all your life. They'll eat you up inside. They'll tear other people apart too." She looked out the window. "At some point you'll need to tell her."

"At some point you'll need to let go of it." He released his hold on the door and stepped toward her, pointing a finger. "Don't you ever tell Azure. You hear me?"

"So she doesn't know?"

"I mean it, Melissa!"

Both hands up, Melissa said, "That's between you and her. But at some point, I'm going to tell Courtney. And when I do—"

"You leave her out of it too," Brian said, his face red. "There's no reason to drag her into our mistakes."

"Is that what you think he was? You think David was a mistake?"

"You know what I mean. We messed up. But you went and did what you thought was right, and because of that he's got a life and people who are taking care of him."

"How would you know? You don't even think about him."

"Don't tell me what I think and don't think."

Melissa heard a noise and turned to see Courtney peeking around the corner, her thumb in her mouth, the other hand cradling her new doll.

"You like your dolly?" Brian said.

Courtney nodded.

Melissa turned back to Brian and glared at him. He avoided eye contact and spoke to Courtney.

"I'll come by Saturday and pick you up, okay?"

Courtney stared at him.

Brian walked out the door, giving Melissa a final look that said as much as his words could ever convey. The slamming door made Courtney jump.

✦ ✦ ✦

Jimmy tried to include David in as much of his life as he could. He took him to work with him once a month and David enjoyed the extra attention. The three of them camped and fished, but there were times when Jimmy and David went alone, just guy time. But Jimmy didn't want every outing to be a planned "fun" time. He knew from his own childhood that doing mundane, ordinary things with his father gave them time together and presented opportunities that couldn't be planned. Conversations about life and friendships and work and God often came at unguarded, unexpected moments.

He was headed to the hardware store for a new toilet flapper to replace one that perpetually leaked and invited David to come along. Jimmy let David walk the aisles and see if he could find the right part.

"This one!" he yelled, a few steps ahead of Jimmy.

"It looks a lot like that," Jimmy said. "Same color. But the size is different."

"Oh yeah, ours is a lot bigger."

"Look up on the top row," Jimmy said.

"That one?" David said, pointing.

"I think you're right."

"Let me get it," David said, crawling up on the shelves.

"Hold on, let me hold you up there."

Jimmy lifted David and he chose the right flapper from the display and beamed as he carried it to the cash register in front.

"Looks like you have a good helper there," the cashier said.

"The best," Jimmy said.

When the cashier told him the total for the flapper, David turned. "That much just to fix the toilet?"

In the car, Jimmy explained the ins and outs of supply and demand and how many people were paid in the process of getting the replacement part to the shelf at the store. "There were people at the factory who worked on this. Then there was the person who drove the truck. The owner of the store has employees. We're not just paying for the flapper, but for all the people involved in getting it to the shelf so we could buy it. Understand?"

David nodded and looked through the plastic bag

at the red flapper inside. Then he said something that floored Jimmy.

"Did you know them?"

"Did I know who?"

"The mom who had me. And the dad."

"Your birth parents?"

David nodded.

Deep breath. Answer the question honestly. But don't give him more than he asks. That's what the counselor at the adoption agency had told him. Susan had read the same thing in a book.

"I didn't know them, David. They lived in another state, a long drive from here."

"How did they find you?"

David explained that they had contacted the adoption agency and out of all the applications sent, the birth mother had chosen them.

David looked out the window for what seemed an eternity. Then he said, "Does dog food taste good to dogs?"

Another suggestion by the counselor was that if David changed the subject, they should go with him and not try to force anything.

"I don't know," Jimmy said. "You want to try some when we get home?"

David turned with a startled look, then smiled.

Two weeks later as they drove home from church, Jimmy suggested they stop at Susan's favorite restaurant. When they were seated, David had to try the straw trick, pulling the paper down and then getting it wet so that it moved like a worm. With his eyes focused on the table, David said, "Do I look like them?"

Jimmy glanced at Susan. Then, calmly, he leaned down to the table. "You mean your birth parents?"

David nodded.

"Well, your dad has the same smile as you. And your mom has green eyes. So I would say the answer is yes."

David closed his eyes. What was he thinking? Jimmy put a hand on Susan's arm and they both held their breath and wondered what was coming next.

"Are you ready to order?" the server said, snapping them out of their reverie.

David sat up straight. "Chicken fingers and fries for me."

Susan and Jimmy ordered and the server took their menus. When she left, David said, "Can I go see her? Would that be okay?"

Susan put her hands on the table and smiled. "Sweetie, if you were to meet her, what would you want to say?"

Without hesitation he said, "I would just say, 'Hi, my name is David.'"

"That sounds like a great thing to say," Susan said.

"And the answer is yes, you can reach out to her when you're older. If she agrees, the two of you can meet."

David relaxed and switched the conversation to a funny story Nate had told him. Their meals came and as they ate, Jimmy asked what David had learned in Sunday school. It was a story about Jesus healing a man who couldn't move on his own.

"So his friends brought him to this house where Jesus was," David said, animated. "And it was so crowded in there, the man's friends climbed up on the roof and made a hole and let the man down. Can you imagine all the noise and the stuff falling down around them?"

"That man sure had some good friends, didn't he?" Jimmy said.

"Yeah, I want to be like that to somebody."

Jimmy glanced at Susan and smiled.

As they got in the car and David buckled in the back seat, Jimmy heard his little voice. "Do you have a picture of them?"

Jimmy glanced at Susan.

"Yes, it's at home," Susan said.

"Can I see it?"

"Sure," Jimmy said.

As soon as they pulled into the driveway, David went to his room and put his Bible and Sunday school papers away. Jimmy followed Susan into their bedroom and she handed him the picture from the envelope she kept in her nightstand.

"You want to show him?" Jimmy said.

"I think it'll be good for you to," she said.

Jimmy studied the Polaroid photo. Brian wore a hooded sweatshirt and had his arm around Melissa. She had long brown hair. They were both smiling.

Jimmy walked into David's room and found him at his desk. He placed the photo in front of him and David leaned closer, careful not to touch it. He stared at the faces, his head moving left to right, then back again.

Finally he looked up at Jimmy. "Can I hold it?"

"Sure."

David sat back in his chair. He was quiet a long time and Jimmy wanted to fill in the silence with information about where they lived and how old they were and other details. Then he thought of the counselor's advice. *Only answer the questions asked.* So he sat on David's bed and watched and waited.

Finally David spoke. "Wow, they look like nice people."

"They sure do, sport."

Then, as if all his questions were answered, he handed the picture back. It was all Jimmy could do to hold back and not ask what he thought, what was going through his mind. He thought David would ask when he could go and see Melissa and how long of a drive it would be and a million other questions.

Instead, David said, "Can we go fishing?"

Jimmy smiled and nodded. "That sounds like a great idea."

CHAPTER 15

✦ ✦ ✦

Melissa had resigned herself to the life of a single mom. It wasn't her dream, but it was her reality. She had met a few men in recent years who seemed interested in her, but when they found out she had a child, their interest waned. A man who worked in a different department at the bank had invited her to dinner, but when she mentioned needing to get a sitter, he told her he'd get back to her. She knew he wouldn't and she was right.

The divorce from Brian had left a scar she wasn't sure would ever heal. She struggled with numbing herself with alcohol, but on the morning when she woke up unable to stop her head from pounding, unable to care for Courtney, she vowed she wouldn't repeat that mistake.

Still, there was something empty inside, as if someone had hollowed out a place in her soul that nothing could fill. Even in her most contented moments, when she was able to pay the bills and watch Courtney go to school and just relax a little, there was an ache that wouldn't go away.

Melissa thought the ache was the load of things in her wagon from the past. There was the memory of David and the choice she had made to let him go. There was her divorce, her inability to find a man who really loved her, and losses that added to the weight. But the further away from those events she traveled, the more she thought there was something deeper going on.

She decided that she wanted to give Courtney the experience of going to church. She took Courtney to the church Addie had attended just to try it out. When the young people were dismissed to "children's church," Courtney bounded out of the sanctuary with the others and Melissa settled in to listen to the message.

That day, it felt as if there were no one else in the room and the pastor was speaking directly to her. There was something about the verses on the screen that touched the hollow inside.

*"Then Jesus said, 'Come to me, all of you who are weary
and carry heavy burdens, and I will give you rest.'"*

Rest was the one thing she'd had a hard time finding.
She was always on the go, always striving to stay two steps
ahead of the bad things life might bring. There was never
rest or a sense of peace inside.

She had always thought that pleasing God was like getting on a spiritual treadmill that went faster and faster. As
long as you didn't fall off and you didn't make too many
mistakes, you'd be okay. Let your good outweigh your
bad. But the pastor framed things differently that day. He
said you could never do enough good things to outweigh
the bad because God was holy and you needed to be
perfect in order to be accepted. At first, that crushed her.
There was no hope for her because she had made so many
mistakes in life.

"That's why it's called the gospel," the pastor said.
"That word means 'good news.' And if you are weary
today and carrying a burden that's too heavy, if you have
a hollow feeling in your soul, God wants you to listen."

Melissa couldn't believe he had used that phrase, *hollow feeling in your soul,* because that was exactly how she
felt.

"God knew you could not live a sinless life," he continued. "So He sent Jesus to live the life you could not
live on your own, and God the Father made Jesus the

Son to be sin, to pay the penalty you deserved, and then raised Him to new life so that you could experience the same.

"You see, God doesn't just let us into heaven by looking the other way at our sin. When you believe in Jesus, He robs your sin and gives you His righteousness. So you enter God's presence not on the basis of anything good you've done, but on the holy life Jesus gives to you. And if you put your trust, your faith, your confidence in Him and what He accomplished for you, God looks at you as if you had always done everything right, just like Jesus did. And you can be forgiven and restored and know you have a place in heaven because Jesus paid the debt you couldn't."

Melissa had heard pastors and teachers before. She'd heard the Christmas message on TV when she was pregnant with David. But nothing had ever reached so deep inside.

She realized others were standing around her, singing a final song. She stood and tried to sing along, but there was such emotion bubbling that she slipped out the back door of the church and stood by the railing.

A woman she would learn later was the pastor's wife came out and stood beside her. "I saw you leave. Is there something wrong? Can I help?"

Melissa turned and wiped her eyes and laughed

nervously. "I'm fine. I just . . ." She stopped and studied the woman's face. "I've been to churches before, but something was different today. Is what he said true? Can God really wipe all your mistakes away like that?"

The next week she came for Sunday school and got Courtney situated in her class and then found a room off the sanctuary for something called the Explorers Class. These were adults who had questions about what the church believed, what the Bible said, and there were a few skeptics. The pastor was there to begin the discussion and study, and there was another man who took over toward the end when the pastor left to get ready for worship.

"I'm Shawn Cates, and I'm glad you're here today. I've been listening to your questions and the discussion and it's encouraging to have you here. We're all on a journey, coming from different backgrounds. In fact, the pastor asked me to be here because, well, about a year ago I was sitting where you are. I was kind of at the end of my rope and there was no knot to hang on to, and I began to learn about how much God loves me in spite of all my mistakes. I found answers here. And something happened on the inside—ask anybody who knew me a year or two ago and they'll tell you, there's been a big change. And I don't take any credit for it."

Shawn was a few years older than her, Melissa guessed,

tall with a big smile and a salt-and-pepper beard. She thought he looked a little like a lumberjack with his broad shoulders. Afterward, when some others had left the room, she went up to him.

"So are you a pastor here?"

Shawn laughed. "No, I just volunteer. It's Melissa, right?"

"How did you know?"

"The pastor's wife told me she spoke with you and invited you. I can't tell you how good it is to have you with us."

They spoke for a few minutes and then Melissa glanced at the clock. "Oh, I have to go . . . There's something I need to do before the worship service."

"Okay, I'll see you in there, then," Shawn said.

Melissa checked on Courtney, then went back to the sanctuary and sat three rows behind Shawn. He sat alone and she watched him as he sang and opened his Bible during the pastor's sermon. There was something swirling inside that made it hard for her to concentrate on the message.

When the service ended, Shawn turned and got her attention. "Hey, the pastor and his family open their house on Sunday afternoons for lunch. You're welcome to come."

"Wait, you invite people to someone else's house?"

"They trust me to invite anyone who looks like they could use lunch."

"That's nice but I can't today," Melissa said.

"Really? You're welcome to come and bring your daughter."

How did he know she had a daughter?

"They have a great swing set in the back. She'd have fun."

Melissa took a step back. "Maybe next week."

"Sounds great. See you then."

She retrieved Courtney from her class and as they pulled out of the parking lot, she saw a few families heading across the road to the parsonage.

"Where are they going, Mom?"

Before she could answer, they passed Shawn on the corner. Melissa rolled down her window.

Shawn leaned down and waved at Courtney, then looked at Melissa. "You sure you don't want to come?"

By the time they left the pastor's house, it was dark and Courtney was exhausted from playing in the backyard with her new friends. After that, the Explorers Class led to a home Bible study at Shawn's place. Melissa learned so much as she read through the Bible. They all brought up questions and made observations.

"I've never really read the Bible before," she said to Shawn after the study ended one night.

"I was the same way. And now I can't go a day without getting my nose in there and seeing what good things God has for me."

On their first date, Shawn insisted Courtney come along. He took them bowling and said he brought Courtney so he could have an excuse to raise the bumpers. But Shawn seemed better at bowling than he let on. Melissa wasn't sure if he let her get close to his score on purpose so he could get three strikes in a row at the end. He beat her by two pins. It was almost like he had planned it.

The next year, as they were getting close to Christmas, Shawn got down on one knee in the middle of the Bible study and proposed. The group cheered when she said yes and Courtney was elated when she heard the news.

A week later, Melissa showed up at Shawn's house in tears and gave the ring back.

"What's this? Melissa, what are you doing?"

"I can't do it. You don't understand. You don't know me."

"That's the point, isn't it? We're going to get to know each other as we spend the rest of our—"

"That's not what I mean. There are things I haven't told you."

LIFEMARK

Welcome to the set of our eighth movie! I hope you enjoy seeing a little bit of what goes on behind the scenes. We filmed *Lifemark* in Columbus, Georgia, in the spring of 2021.

These photos cover only one week of production. It might be news to you that a film is shot completely out of order. That's because most movies are shot by location—it's more productive to film every scene that happens in a certain spot before moving to the next place. We also have to plan shooting days based on the weather, actor availability, or a myriad of other factors. One thing never changes, though: Every day on the set costs money, and we must be good stewards of our resources to avoid those two deadly words—*over budget.*

In some of these shots you'll see folks who keep things running behind the scenes. Obviously cameramen are critical, but we also rely on people who serve the project through wardrobe, makeup, props, lighting and sound, and the wonderful folks who feed us all. It takes a small army, but by the end of production, we've become like family!

—ALEX KENDRICK

DAY 1

David's biological father, Brian (Lowrey Brown), learns that David is interested in meeting.

Alex Kendrick and director Kevin Peeples pray over the cast before shooting a crucial scene.

Stephen Kendrick (right) stands with producer Aaron Burns (left) and assistant director Adam Drake.

Shooting a powerful speech by David (Raphael Ruggero) near the end of the film.

DAY 3
ON THE SET

A stunt truck chases Shawn (Alex Kendrick) on an ATV.

Cameramen Sam Willy and Dave Svenson prep for an action shot.

Melissa (Dawn Long) and Shawn are ready for the chase.

Baby on board! Susan (Rebecca Rogers) holds baby David.

On set for a humorous but emotional scene with Raphael Ruggero.

David prepares to give his speech about being adopted.

Nate (Justin Sterner) talks with David at school about a girl he likes.

Stephen Kendrick talks with actor Kirk Cameron about a scene.

Jimmy (Kirk Cameron) and Susan cheer for David at his wrestling match.

Filming at Calvary Christian Academy in Columbus, Georgia.

He took her by the arm and pulled her into his house. "Melissa, nothing you could tell me would change the way I feel. Do you understand?"

"You don't know."

"All right. Tell me, then. See if it changes anything."

"I can't," she said.

He moved around her to the door, blocking her way. "Come in and sit down and tell me why you're so upset."

She retreated to his couch and they sat, side by side, as she told him about her first pregnancy and about placing David for adoption.. Shawn grabbed a box of tissues and set it beside her, and she couldn't stop the tears.

When she was finished, Shawn said, "So all of this came up because it's David's birthday today, right?"

"I don't know," Melissa said, shaking her head.

"Listen to me," Shawn said. "What you did took a lot of courage. It was a selfless thing. You made such a good decision. That little boy has life because you didn't think of yourself, you thought of him. Melissa, that doesn't make me love you less. It makes me love you more."

"Really?" she said.

He handed the ring back tenderly. "Really."

They were married in a small ceremony with the pastor officiating and Courtney as flower girl. Members of their Bible study and some of the people from the Explorers

Class were present. Melissa decided to invite her family, and she was pleased that everything stayed cordial.

There was a slow, steady drizzle of rain all day, with low-hanging clouds and a chill in the air. It was a dreary, awful day as far as the weather was concerned. But to Melissa, it was the beginning of something good. A few dark clouds couldn't take away her joy.

After the ceremony and small reception, Shawn and Melissa drove to Brian's house and Melissa walked Courtney to the door.

"I want to go with you," Courtney said. "I don't want to stay here."

"I know, sweetie. It's only for a few days."

The curtain fluttered and Melissa saw Azure. Brian opened the door a few seconds later.

"You excited to stay with us for a few days?" he said to Courtney.

"Yeah," Courtney said, pushing past him into the house.

Brian looked at the driveway and lifted his head toward Shawn, who waved. Melissa handed Courtney's suitcase to him and turned to leave.

"Hey," Brian said.

She stopped and turned, raising a hand to block the rain, which was falling harder now. "What?"

"Congratulations."

She studied his face and concluded that he actually meant what he had said. And that shocked her.

She smiled at him. "Thanks."

PART 3

PART 3

CHAPTER 16

✦ ✦ ✦

They called it the cliff, and David did not tell his parents what Nate had asked him to do. Soon, he would be eighteen and making decisions on his own and this seemed like a good test. His mom and dad had been supportive with every sport he had wanted to try, but looking up at the ledge where he would jump took his breath away. When he reached it, looking down at the water terrified him.

Nate controlled the drone a long distance from the ledge and told David how the shot would work as he watched the monitor. He knew the exact overhead angle and the exact place where David needed to enter the water. He had explained all of this in great detail, but David couldn't hear any of it because he kept looking at the ledge.

What if he misjudged things and hit the water flat? What if there was something floating just underneath the surface? There were a thousand things that could go wrong, including hitting the water too close to the bank and breaking a bone. Or worse.

"What's the risk/reward ratio?" David had asked the day before at school.

"The risk is minimal."

"Yeah, to you. I'm talking about me. I'm the one jumping."

"You'll be fine," Nate said, switching to his salesperson voice. "This is going to be the highlight of your life. Trust me. Just meet me us out there tomorrow afternoon."

"Who is *us*?"

"Sam and Justin are coming to help."

David had rolled his eyes. "Help? Yeah, right. They'll be witnesses to my demise."

Barefoot, David now made his way through the trees and leaves and pine cones to the ledge. He took a step closer, then one more, and leaned forward to look at the water below.

"Okay, I'm filming," Nate yelled from his perch down the hill. "All systems go."

David had jumped from the high dive into the pool at the aquatic center in town, but this was in a different league. The wind made ripples in the water below, and he knew he would have to push off a few feet to gain clearance.

"Don't think about it. Just jump," Nate yelled, his voice echoing off the rock wall.

"Don't tell me not to think about it," David said, pointing at Nate.

"Just jump!"

"All right, just give me a second." David took several deep breaths. He heard a noise above the wind through the trees and looked up to the drone hovering above, propellers spinning. "What's this thing going to do?"

"It's going to follow along as you go. Now go!"

David looked down once more. "Okay." He took a few steps back from the ledge, moving sticks and leaves for a clear running path. He measured the steps again, like a field goal kicker backing away from the holder's spot.

The voices of Sam and Justin echoed off the rocks as they rhythmically chanted, "David! David!"

One more deep breath. He took five running steps, launched from the edge of the cliff with his arms above his head, and felt nothing but air beneath him. His arms windmilled, but he managed to keep his feet down. The water rushed up at him and he hit with a splash and plunged below the surface.

✦ ✦ ✦

Nate watched David's descent in the monitor and knew he had something special. Sam and Justin reacted to David's contact with the water, cringing.

"Nice," Nate said. "Guys, check this out. This is sick. Oh, that is buttery smooth right there. Tell me that is not the best shot I've ever gotten."

Sam and Justin leaned in, admiring the camera work.

"I'm about it," Nate said, slapping their hands in victory. "You know what I mean?"

As David swam to the edge and made his way toward them, Nate replayed the jump, catching a subtle way to make the next shot better. When David arrived, he said, "Hey, that was pretty good. But the next one could be better, so let's get up there and do it again. Just do a flip or—"

David put a hand on his shoulder. "I'll start taking your directions when you actually get in the water."

"Dude, I'm the cameraman. I can't get wet!"

"How much was the drone?" Sam said.

"Millie here was eight hundred bucks but I still owe five hundred."

"Millie?" Justin said.

"Millennium Falcon," David said.

"You're kidding," Justin said.

David gave a smirk. "I'm not."

"Dude, you can make five hundred bucks at the speech competition at school."

"I'm a video blogger. I don't do live speeches to impress small crowds."

"You don't do speeches to impress any crowds, actually," Sam said.

"Dude, I'm producing impressive videos for a targeted online audience."

"The ladies?" Justin said.

"I never said that," Nate said. "But yes. All right, look. This next one's got to go viral, okay? So I need somebody to do a belly flop off the cliff and I need it to look painful. David, how about you?"

"No, no thank you."

"Don't be a diva. Just get up and do it."

"Nate, I'm already starting to get a headache. How about you get a shot of all three of us jumping at the same time? How's that sound?"

"All right," Nate said. "That'll work. Let's do it. Get back over there. I'll get Millie all situated."

The three trudged to the ledge while Nate took the drone through the shot one more time. He thought of the drone not as a machine but as a good friend who was going to help him reach his film goals. Nate saw life as if he were constantly looking at it through a lens and had dreamed of shooting at the cliff, cataloging the death-defying jumps of his friends.

"All right, you ready?" he yelled.

The three stood at the edge looking down and Nate maneuvered the drone above them, catching light and shadows and the faces of the three. He gave them a count-down and the three jumped together, hitting the water almost simultaneously.

The leap was perfect but Nate glanced in the corner of the screen and noticed the red light wasn't lit.

"No! I wasn't filming!" As the three surfaced and began to swim toward shore, Nate yelled, "Guys, can we set it up again? Let's do it again. Let's just go back to the top, all right? I gotta bring Millie back and then we can roll it."

He studied the screen and moved the controls but nothing happened. He glanced up, listening for the whir of the drone's blades. "Millie?"

They spent an hour trying to retrieve Millie from the tree she was in. Sam and Justin left and David was the one who climbed the tree and finally rescued the drone. One propeller was damaged but Nate was sure he could repair it.

"What are you going to do when I'm not around to jump in the water or climb trees for you?" David said.

"Hey, I will give you all the credit when I win my first Oscar, okay?" Nate changed his voice and dramatically said, "But I want to dedicate this award to the friend in high school who saved my drone, Millie, from ignominy."

"Ignominy?"

"Yeah, when you give speeches at the Oscars, you have to use big words like that to impress people."

David laughed then stopped along the trail. He put a hand to the back of his head and bent.

"What's wrong, man?"

"It's my headache again."

"Maybe jumping into the water made it worse?"

"Couldn't have helped any. But I was glad to do it. Especially since you're going to give me the Oscar after you win it."

"Hey, I never said I would give it to you. I said I'd mention you in my speech."

Susan had taken each birthday seriously, cataloging David's growth with pictures and videos. On his tenth birthday, the three of them had gone camping in Yosemite and she'd caught David crying on their last day there.

"What's wrong, honey?"

His chin had puckered. "I'm never going to have this much fun again."

She had hugged him and promised he would.

On some birthdays there had been groups of friends at the house, but on this one, his eighteenth, David asked that G and Paw Paw join them for a quiet celebration. She ordered takeout from David's favorite restaurant and they ate crawfish, shrimp, and biscuits, and David had the blackened catfish all to himself.

After the meal, Jimmy set out the plates for dessert and placed eighteen red candles in the cake. He lit them, and David closed his eyes, smiled, and in one breath blew them out.

"Hey, open up your present before we cut the cake," Jimmy said.

"Oh, wait," G said, grabbing the small red party bag. "We want you to guess. What do you think it is?"

David closed his eyes in concentration. "Let's see, it's a new phone."

"No, it's not a trombone," Paw Paw said from the end of the table. "A trombone wouldn't fit in that little bag."

"No, sweetie, that's not what he said," G replied.

"Well, he doesn't even play the trombone," Paw Paw said.

"You're right, dear," G said and they all laughed as David took the party bag.

"You're going to love it," Jimmy said. "We all pitched in."

Susan studied her son's face as he removed the yellow tissue paper and looked into the bag. There had been so many presents that seemed perfect for David through the years, but none that quite matched the meaning behind this one.

David's mouth dropped open and he glanced at Jimmy, then Susan, and pulled out a printed sheet. "Train tickets?" he said, smiling.

There were tears in Susan's eyes as she nodded.

"No way!" David said.

"You've always loved trains," Susan said.

"They're good for a round trip anywhere in the US," Jimmy said.

"Sweet!" David said. "Thank you! This is awesome."

"You're welcome," Jimmy said.

"You've been working so hard, honey. So maybe a trip this summer before college?"

"Just not before our camping trip," G said.

"I wouldn't miss that for the world," David said.

Paw Paw's resonant voice came from the end of the table. "So, David, what are your plans, after you graduate?"

"Well, there's the wrestling competition coming up and if all works out, then—"

"It will," Jimmy said.

"I mean I heard that there are scouts coming, but I'm not sure if I'm good enough for a scholarship."

"Listen, scholarship or no scholarship, we will make sure you can go to college."

"You know if it doesn't work out, I could always join Nate and we could become Internet sensations making viral YouTube videos. "

"Oh," Susan said with a lilt in her voice. "No. That's not going to happen. Where is Nate? I thought he was coming."

"I don't know. He said he was going to be here."

Jimmy broke the silence. "David, God has something very special for you. I'm sure of that."

"I'm pretty sure that's just something parents like to say."

Jimmy smiled and said, "We'll see."

CHAPTER 17

✦ ✦ ✦

On Melissa's next birthday, Shawn threw a surprise party for her. Friends from church and the neighborhood were there, mostly people from the past few years of Melissa's life. Several men brought their grills to add to Shawn's and they cooked steaks and burgers and bratwurst. Melissa was made to sit and watch and do no work for the whole affair, which was nice, but she realized that activity helped her forget the things she didn't want to remember.

That night, as Melissa tucked her into bed, Courtney propped herself up on an elbow and said, "Mom, are you happy?"

"Of course. Why do you ask that?"

"I don't know."

Melissa sat on the bed and stroked her daughter's hair. "What do you think *happy* means?"

Courtney shrugged. "I guess it's a feeling inside that makes you smile, even when you don't know you are."

"I smile when I look at you, spider monkey."

"Yeah, but all night it seemed like you were under a cloud. Like you were at the party but not at the party."

Melissa turned to the wall and stared at the drawings Courtney had taped there. Horses, mostly. One showed a man and woman standing together watching a girl in a field of flowers.

"You know, I was a tomboy when I was your age."

"What's a tomboy?"

"I liked to do things boys do. I've always been more comfortable in jeans and boots than a dress."

"Kind of like me, even though I don't mind pretty dresses."

Melissa paused for a moment. "Yeah, kind of like you. And I would find myself smiling when I was fishing or hunting or working on your grandfather's farm."

Courtney sat up, light in her eyes. "Maybe if we got a horse, you'd smile more."

Melissa kept her lips together, then let her daughter see her grin. "I think a horse would make you smile a lot more than it would me."

"Think about it, Mom. We could keep it in the shed and ride it on the trails."

"Now's not the time to be talking about a horse."

Courtney put her head back on the pillow and stared at the ceiling.

"Sometimes I get to thinking about things and I get kind of moody, you know?" Melissa said.

"What things?"

"Just choices I made and didn't make."

"You mean with Dad?"

"Yeah, he's part of it. It's stuff from the past. Things that happened that I regret. Things I can't really change but they come back to me all the same. So when you see me and I'm not smiling, it might be that I'm thinking of things that hurt me inside or things I did that hurt other people."

"Are you glad you married Shawn?"

"He is the best thing in our lives, sweetie. A little too competitive when it comes to grilling and playing cornhole, but he's been a gift to both of us."

Courtney reached up and twirled Melissa's hair like she had done when she was little. "I like it when you laugh."

"Well, I'll try to laugh a little more."

"When can we talk about a horse?"

Melissa stood and turned out the light. "Go to sleep, Corty."

She walked toward her bedroom but stopped in the hallway. Birthday parties always reminded her of all she had missed in her son's life. What was he doing tonight? What kind of friends had he made? Did he have a girl-friend? How was he doing in school? Did he have dreams of college?

She could have told Courtney right then about her brother but she'd held back. How was she going to tell her?

She crawled into bed and patted Shawn's arm. He was reading a book but his eyes were already drooping. He yawned and gave her a hug.

"Surprised?" he said.

"Very. You shouldn't have gone to all that trouble."

"Celebrating you is no trouble. And finding people who agree with me was easy. I hope you had fun. You like your new four-wheeler?"

"You shouldn't have spent all that money."

"It was a selfish gift. I want to race you on the trails."

"Big mistake," she said.

"Why's that?"

"Because you're going to lose."

That December was unseasonably warm. Melissa deco-rated the house for Christmas but her heart wasn't in it. She bought Courtney a horse ornament as a stocking stuffer that she would open on Christmas Eve.

A few days before Christmas Shawn suggested they go for a ride on the trails near their house and Melissa got on her blue four-wheeler, taking the lead. The feeling of the wind in her hair and the racing motor and the twisting trail seemed to drown all the feelings inside. Shawn managed to stay close but on the way home, as they neared the barn where they had started, she veered left and took a shortcut. He kept going straight and she reached the finish and turned off her engine and waited.

When he pulled up beside her, he said, "I can't keep up with you today, babe."

Melissa stared at the tree line, wondering if she should share what was going on inside.

Sitting on his four-wheeler, Shawn was quiet. Whether he did it because he knew she was struggling or because he just didn't have much to say, she didn't know. Staying quiet was something that seemed to come naturally to him.

Finally he said, "You okay?"

"Today's David's eighteenth birthday."

"Oh, wow." Shawn stepped off the machine and turned to her. "Does that mean you guys can talk now?"

"Well, he's legally old enough to reach out to me if he wants to."

"Would he know how?"

"Shawn, I haven't updated my records since he was a baby. Then I moved. Married you."

"Do you want to talk to him?"

The question sent a shiver through her. To admit the longing inside was more difficult than harboring it. "I don't think he'd want to talk to me. He probably hates me for what I did."

Shawn always bobbed his head when he disagreed with something but didn't want to come out and say it. After a pause he said, "Well, there's only one way to find out."

"So you think I should call the law office?"

"I think you take it a step at a time. Call them and update your file so that when he wants to get in touch with you, he has the information."

"It's that simple for you? Just make a phone call?"

Shawn gave her his teddy bear look. It was a look that said he wasn't going to fight even if she wanted to. "It's not like you're inviting him to move in with us. All you're doing is updating the information in case he wants to reach out to you."

"And what if he doesn't want to?"

"Then you'll deal with that. We'll deal with that."

"But what if he does want to reach out?"

Teddy bear look again.

"Shawn, if he gets in touch, I'll need to tell Courtney."

"Okay."

"Don't give me that look. I hate it when you look at me like that."

Shawn rubbed his beard and pursed his lips. It was the same look he gave when he couldn't figure out why the grill wouldn't light. "Listen, I have enough faith to believe that if David never gets in touch with you, God's grace will be enough. He'll help you get through it. And if he does get in touch with you, I believe God will give you the ability to talk with him and begin a relationship you've never had. Either way, you're going to be good."

"And what about Courtney? She's going to hate me for giving her brother away. She's never even met him."

"I don't think she's going to hate you. Courtney loves you, Melissa. She may not fully understand, she may have some hard questions, but give her a chance."

"A chance to what?"

"To show you that no matter what you've done, you're still her mother. A chance to love you."

Melissa fought the tears. "But she's not ready."

"Are you sure?"

Melissa thought about the conversations she'd had with Courtney lately. She was growing up so fast and asking lots of questions about life, but Melissa wanted to protect her from all of that and she didn't want Courtney to think less of her.

"I can't tell her yet."

"Okay."

"I'll know the right time. And it's not now. Not yet."

Shawn put a hand on her arm. "I trust you. You'll know it when you're talking one day and it eases out. Now, come over here, I want to show you something."

She walked to the corner of the barn and when she turned, she realized Shawn wasn't beside her. He jumped on his four-wheeler, started the engine, and with a teddy bear smile said, "Race you back to the house!"

"The only way you'll beat me is to cheat!" she yelled as he zoomed away. She shook her head and realized she was laughing.

The next day, Melissa picked up the phone four times and put it down four times. It was only the law office, she wasn't calling her son, but the feeling was the same. Her mouth was dry as she paced the room. Finally she dialed and let it ring, closing her eyes and holding her breath until she heard a voice.

"You've reached the law offices of Kirsh and Clark. Our offices are closed for the holidays and will reopen for regular hours on January 2. If this is an emergency, please call—"

Melissa hung up. She'd finally gotten up the nerve and they were closed. She made a mental note to call them after the first of the year.

CHAPTER 18

✦ ✦ ✦

David sat down next to Nate just before the bell for history class. He gave Nate the stink eye.

"What's that for? Did I do something wrong?"

"You said you were coming to my birthday party. What happened?"

Nate put a palm to his face. "Okay, look. I've got an answer for that. It's not because I didn't want to be there. You have to hear what happened."

"I said you didn't have to bring a present."

"No, it's not that. I swear. I was getting my camera

ready to come over, you know, to take some shots of you blowing out the cake or whatever, and—"

The bell rang and their teacher, Mr. Russell, stood. He gave Nate a look.

"Okay, I'll tell you after class. You really have to hear this."

When class ended, David gathered his things and Nate shot out of his seat.

"Okay, so here's why I wasn't there."

"I don't want to hear it," David said.

"Dude, I swear I was gonna be there. But my sister got in this epic fight with her boyfriend, and I had to film it from the window. It was going on and on and I literally could not leave."

"You filmed it?"

"She doesn't know that. I was editing it for my channel."

David grabbed Nate by the arm. "No. You can't do that, Nate. What are you thinking?"

"Okay, I might let her see it, but dude, she was throwing bricks at his car. She hit it twice and he got out screaming at her and—"

"David, can I speak with you for a second?" Mr. Russell said as David neared the door.

"Sure." David stepped toward the teacher's desk and Nate followed.

"Just David. Nate, you can head to class."

Nate leaned in with a skeptical look. "Is it important? Because I kinda wanna hear about it."

Mr. Russell stared at Nate with a look that said everything.

"Okay, I'm good. But he's gonna tell me as soon as he leaves the room."

David shook his head as Nate left and he turned to his teacher. Mr. Russell was an African American man who loved to make history come alive for them. He had a way of teaching that made it feel like they weren't in school looking for test answers. History was about people and their struggles, the man said, and if you learn it and listen to it carefully, it will teach you lessons you can use in every aspect of life.

Mr. Russell narrowed his focus on David. "Look, I want you to think about something, all right? I'm overseeing the speech competition, and I think you should consider entering."

"Why? I mean, I'm not really good in front of crowds."

"Two reasons. Your classmates have a lot of respect for you. And I think you could speak on a theme that we've been given."

"What's that?"

Mr. Russell smiled. "The value of family."

David looked down and put both arms through his

backpack. "You mean, because I'm adopted." He said it with resignation, as if he'd been put into a different class of people.

"And that's an important perspective. So far, no one's focusing on that."

David shifted from one foot to the other and didn't make eye contact. He lowered his voice. "Yeah, but not a lot of people know that I'm adopted."

"I understand. I just believe that you could do a great job. There's even a cash prize."

"Yeah, I heard about that."

"Look, just think about it. Okay?"

"All right."

David hurried to his locker and found Nate talking with a classmate in the hall. He was giving her the address of his video channel. For Nate, everything was about videos.

As David opened his locker, Nate stepped over.

"Dude, I know I'm not supposed to know everything, but tell me everything."

"It was nothing. He was just talking about the speech competition." David closed his locker and stretched.

"Speech competition? Why would he want to talk to you about that? It's not like you're going to do it. You hate talking in front of crowds."

David reached for the back of his head and winced.

"Got another headache?" Nate said.

"Yeah, and I'm sick of them." David moved into the stream of students.

"Dude, I'm telling you, it's the science lab. It always smells like death on a cracker."

David noticed Elizabeth and smiled at her as she walked between him and Nate.

"Hey! What's up, Emily?" Nate said. "How's it going?"

Elizabeth was past them when David said, "That's Elizabeth."

"I was going to ask her to prom."

"You might want to learn her name first," David said.

Nate checked his watch and turned quickly, hurrying down the hall to get to his next class. David shook his head, then put his hand on his neck to try to stop the throbbing pain.

CHAPTER 19

✦ ✦ ✦

In late January, with the weather turning bitter cold, Melissa watched Courtney get off the school bus and trudge through the scattered snow. She slammed the front door behind her and kicked off her wet shoes, dropping her backpack and coat on the floor like they were sacks of rotten potatoes. She entered the kitchen without a word, grabbing cookies from the pantry and pouring a glass of milk before she sat at the table, her head down.

"Well, hello, sunshine," Melissa said. "How was school?"

Nothing but a shrug.

Melissa had heard something on the radio about

guiding your children through their preteen years and how important it was to connect with them each day. The psychologist had said that being available was the most important gift a parent could give a child, so instead of going back to what she was doing, Melissa pulled out a chair and sat.

Courtney looked up. "What?"

"Nothing. I'm just admiring the way you dunk your fudge-striped cookies. You seem to have it down to a science. All the way to the middle, then turn it and go to the middle again."

"Mom, stop." Courtney remained stone-faced and shifted in her seat.

"Now I get it," Melissa said, nodding and folding her arms.

"Get what?"

"How it feels when somebody you love doesn't smile."

Courtney stared at her and finally understood. She picked up another cookie and dunked it.

Melissa took a deep breath and waited, which was hard. She wanted to be in motion. Get something done. Maybe there was something here she could learn about Courtney. She thought of how Shawn had waited for her to talk at different times and how the silence had drawn her out.

She recalled a verse from Isaiah someone had posted on social media. The verse read, "In quietness and confidence is your strength." She wasn't sure what that meant exactly, or who the verse was written to, but it made her want to be still and let Courtney be the first to speak, if she spoke again at all.

Finally, after what seemed like a geological age, Courtney looked up at her. "In health class today they talked about how women have babies. The monthly cycle. Egg and sperm."

"Oh."

"I remembered what you told me. That God was the one who created sex and it's not dirty or anything. It just needs to be for people who are married."

"So you were paying attention when we had that little talk." Melissa gave her a smile. "What's wrong?"

"Somebody brought up abortion. And the teacher said that a woman has a right to choose, that it's in the Constitution. And Leslie said people who are against abortion just want to impose their religion on others. I wanted to say something, but I got scared."

"That's okay. Everybody gets scared when people disagree about important things like that."

"Yeah, but I should have said what I was thinking."

"What would you have said?"

"I don't know. That it's wrong to kill a baby. It was so sad, Mom. I don't get how people can look at a baby in the womb and not think it's a baby."

Melissa nodded, her mouth dry.

"Then at lunch, I got into a fight with Leslie about it."

"So you did say something."

"I thought I could talk with her and tell her what I thought. I mean, we've been friends since first grade. But she said her mom had two abortions and she was glad. And that nobody can take that right away. I didn't know what to say."

A knot formed in Melissa's stomach. It seemed like the perfect time to tell her story, but was Courtney ready?

No, that wasn't the question.

Am I ready to tell her the truth?

"I don't even want to go to health class anymore," Courtney said.

"I understand. Those kinds of conversations are hard. And if you believe that God formed us in the womb and calls all life sacred, you are going to be different than what a lot of people believe."

"I just don't get how anybody could want to do that to a little baby."

Melissa tried to think how best to steer the conversation, but before she could speak, Courtney stood.

"I'm going to do my homework before dinner."

"Okay," Melissa said, kicking herself for not taking advantage of the opportunity. It seemed like a never-ending cycle. She would hold back from saying something, then spend the rest of the day beating herself up for not saying it.

Later that evening, as the three of them sat to watch TV, Melissa pulled Shawn into the kitchen and explained what Courtney had said. "I feel like I blew it. I had the chance to say something and didn't."

Shawn cocked his head and smiled. "What is this thing with you about only getting one chance at everything?"

"What do you mean?"

"It's like you're putting so much pressure on yourself. You'd never tell Courtney that. Why do you put the bar so high for yourself?"

She didn't answer because she didn't know. But later, as she turned away from Shawn in bed and turned out the light, she wondered if perhaps it was because she didn't want to make another mistake that would haunt her.

CHAPTER 20

✦ ✦ ✦

Susan had been all for David trying different sports and activities. In her mind, the more the better. Try everything that interested you and you would be a more rounded person. She did give a sigh of relief when David decided against going out for the football team. He'd played in a flag football league in elementary school and looked cute in the uniform, but she'd heard about so many injuries through the years to students who played tackle football, some that were serious.

When David said he wanted to go out for the wrestling team, she didn't think much about it. To her, wrestling didn't have the dangers associated with other contact sports. It only took her one match to change her opinion. It was much more violent than she'd expected and even though they wrestled on a large mat, she was secretly unnerved and spent most of David's matches praying he would just survive.

But a funny thing had happened in David's sophomore year. He began to win his matches and actually dominate his weight class. His success made her learn more about the sport and become familiar with the terms and rules. Like in a chess match, she began to see when a competitor had the upper hand.

"You know more about this than I do," Jimmy said one day.

He was right. And the more she learned, the louder she cheered. She was there for every match through David's senior year. But of course, she also continued to pray for his safety.

In the match before district finals, David was up against a competitor he had never beaten. Their last match had been won by only one point and Jimmy had spent time with David going over the video replay. David was just getting over a bout with the flu in that previous match, and he had high hopes that he might make the finals, but Susan could tell he was nervous as he shook out his arms and legs and warmed up.

Jimmy yelled his support for David, and Nate was recording the match a few rows away. As the wrestlers met in the middle, the crowd got into it, yelling and screaming support. When David's opponent scored a takedown, Susan's heart sank.

"Don't worry," Jimmy said. "We talked about this. Just watch."

With his opponent trying the push him into the mat, David spun and rolled backward, pinning his opponent beneath him in one fluid move.

"That's it!" Jimmy yelled. "Pin him! Pin him!"

A few seconds of struggle and the referee slammed the mat. David rose and shook his opponent's hand and the referee raised his hand in victory.

"He did it!" Susan said.

"He's going to the finals!" Jimmy said.

When the event was over, Susan and Jimmy made their way onto the mat, where David's coach was high-fiving his wrestler.

"Get some rest," the coach said. "We'll see you Monday."

Susan hugged her sweaty son and didn't care. "Amazing!"

"You told me he was going to take you," Jimmy said.

"I've never beat him before," David said, still stunned.

"That was awesome!" Jimmy said.

Nate stood in front of David and put his phone out for a closeup. "So this is the best moment of your life so far."

"What do you say we go out to dinner?" Jimmy said. "You pick the place and we'll celebrate."

"I love dinner, great idea," Nate said.

"I'm so hungry," David said. "I mean literally, I could eat an entire cow."

"Wherever you want, honey," Susan said, putting a hand on his shoulder. It was such a moment of victory. She couldn't imagine anything clouding their joy that night.

Until David suddenly collapsed on the mat, falling with a sickening thud.

CHAPTER 21

✦ ✦ ✦

Susan saw David fall and then the whole world seemed
to blur. She crouched next to him on the mat, watching
him open and close his eyes as if he had no control over
them. She heard someone say the word *overheated* and then
Jimmy yelled for someone to call 911 while he leaned over
David. David's coach appeared and told everyone to move
back and not to touch David until the paramedics arrived.

Susan didn't obey. She had to stay as close to her son as
she could. What was wrong? He was so full of energy and
life during the match—how could he have collapsed?

"Please, God," she prayed. "Please." It was all she could
think to pray.

The next thing she knew, there were men in uniform next to David. Someone helped her up and she looked into Jimmy's eyes. He hugged her and she whispered, "What happened? What's wrong with him?"

"It's okay. They're going to help him," Jimmy said.

She saw the same fear in his eyes that she felt inside. That scared her as much as seeing her son lying lifeless on the wrestling mat. Jimmy had such a strong faith, such a belief that God was working in the good and the bad. But he was just as perplexed as she was.

Instead of driving to David's favorite restaurant, they followed the ambulance to the hospital, weaving in and out of traffic behind the vehicle with its lights on, siren blaring.

"What happened?" she said again in the car. "I don't understand."

"They'll figure it out," Jimmy said.

"What if they can't? What if he's gone? Jimmy, I can't lose my son."

He reached over and took her hand in his. "God gave us David, right? You believe that."

Susan nodded.

"He's been in this the whole time. And I think God is asking us again if we will trust Him. But we have to take this step together."

Susan looked up through her tears.

Jimmy's eyes were focused on the road ahead, the lights

of the ambulance flickering red and white on his face. "Just one step at a time. Let's trust that God has this, even though we're scared. Let's believe He will help us through whatever is ahead." He squeezed her hand and she saw the water in his eyes.

Susan looked away. She thought of the man in the Bible who brought his son to Jesus and she whispered, "'I do believe, but help me overcome my unbelief!'"

Once they arrived, Susan jumped from the car and hurried through the parking lot to the hospital entrance. She always had a warm feeling when she passed one. Their lives had changed for the better because of a hospital. Now, with the evening shadows falling, the building looked ominous.

Jimmy caught up to her at the emergency room door. She went directly to the front desk and asked where her son was but was told they'd have to wait in the lobby.

"I want to see him," Susan said.

"We're taking good care of him, Mrs. Colton. Let us work with him, okay?"

Relief flooded over Susan when she was finally able to see David in the exam room. He was dressed in a hospital gown, alert and propped up on pillows. He smiled when he saw them and she hugged him and sat next to the bed.

"How are you feeling?" Jimmy said.

"Okay, I guess," David said. "My head hurts."

"Do you remember anything that happened?" Susan said.

"I thought we were going to dinner and then everything went blank."

"It's okay," Susan said. "The doctors are going to help figure this out."

"Maybe it was dehydration or all the excitement of going to the finals," Jimmy said.

"There are a lot of people praying for you," Susan said. "We called Pastor Jeff. He's asked everyone to pray and he's on his way over."

"He shouldn't do that. He's probably busy."

"David," Susan said, "you're in trouble and he wants to be here. You're not bothering him."

A nurse walked in and checked David's pulse and other vital signs. "Dr. Patel is going over the tests. He should be in soon."

"Does he know what's wrong?" David said.

"I'm sure he'll be able to answer your questions."

Jimmy paced in the room until David suggested he sit down. "You're making me dizzy going back and forth, Dad."

"Sorry," Jimmy said. "I wonder what's taking the doctor so long."

"One step at a time," Susan said.

Jimmy glanced at her and saw a glint in her eyes. They had done this through the years, believed for each other, encouraged each other. When one became discouraged, the other would pick up the baton. Now, Jimmy was struggling to wait for news from the doctor, fearing what he might have found.

Dr. Vishal Patel walked in with a smile and a folder containing the medical report. He greeted them, then examined David. When he was finished, he moved to the end of the bed and looked at Jimmy.

"So do you have any medical conditions in your family history?"

"Well, David is adopted," Jimmy said.

"I see."

"And we don't have much medical information about them."

"I understand." The doctor paused and looked at David. He spoke matter-of-factly. "What we're dealing with here is excessive pressure on the brain. It's called a Chiari malformation, where part of the skull pushes on the brain and forces the tissue into the spinal canal. It's congenital. It develops as you grow. That's why your headaches have been getting worse."

Jimmy studied David's reaction as he tried to take in the information.

The doctor continued. "Really, what you need to know is that it won't go away unless we open it up and relieve the pressure."

"Open it up?" David said. He gave Jimmy a frightened glance.

Jimmy studied the doctor. "How much time do we have to make a decision?"

"I don't think we need to wait any longer. We have everything ready for surgery tomorrow morning."

Jimmy glanced at David, then took a tentative step toward the doctor. He lowered his voice. "What are the risks?"

"If I were you, I would do it before it gets any worse."

Jimmy put a hand on his son's shoulder and calmed his voice. His son suddenly looked so fragile. "David, you okay with surgery?"

"I mean . . . I can't take these headaches anymore."

"If all goes well, and I believe it will, then you won't have to," Dr. Patel said.

David gave him a timid nod and the doctor smiled.

"Good. I'll let my team know, then."

When the doctor was gone, Jimmy sat on the bed. "Hey, this is all going to work out. God knew this was going to happen."

"I know, but why is He letting this happen to me? I mean, Dad, my team is counting on me to compete in the finals. And what about college?"

"Honey, I'm so sorry," Susan said, her hand on David's chest. "If I could, I would make it all go away."

"I just don't understand."

"You know what?" Susan said. "I was angry with God for a long time after John and Michael died. But if that hadn't happened, I wouldn't have had you. And I cannot imagine my life without you."

"David, you're strong. And you're going to be fine with or without wrestling."

David looked at the ceiling and sighed.

Susan wandered into the hall and walked around the corner, nervously pulling her sweater sleeve over her hand. People walked past her, oblivious to her pain, and she felt so alone. She put her purse on the floor, then wrapped her sweater around her and crossed her arms, the emotion welling.

She had heard a phrase thrown around by well-meaning people, including once at a Bible study. Someone said to a friend who had just lost a job, "God doesn't give you more than you can handle." It had seemed cruel to her at the time, but the words seemed to buoy the newly unemployed friend, so Susan kept quiet.

Now, as she stood around the corner from the hospital room that held the son she loved more than life itself, she knew she had been given more than she could handle. And that was the point of every struggle, every trial—to admit her inability to handle life in her own strength, in her own power. This was an opportunity to lean on a power greater than her own.

I don't want to lose him, Lord, she prayed silently. *I don't want to see him go through this pain. I would rather have it myself. And I don't know if this surgery is the answer. The doctor thinks it is, but I'm scared.*

It felt like Gethsemane. And she knew she had to get to the point where it was not her will but His she chose.

"I know this is a chance to trust You and not myself. Not lean on my understanding. But I'm so scared. And I can't make sense of this. I can't understand what You're doing. Help me."

Jimmy was usually a step or two ahead of her emotions. He ran toward trust and faith and hope before she could catch up with him. She often felt like she had to carry a little more because he couldn't pick up his side of the emotional load. That feeling both comforted and frustrated her because she needed his strength but she also needed him to be human. When he walked around the corner, she tried to smile.

Jimmy rubbed her arms and she felt like she was going

to melt into the floor, the feelings were so strong. "I can't go home," she managed.

"I know," Jimmy said. "You stay here. I'll go home and get our stuff."

She looked into Jimmy's eyes and dared to ask the hardest question that came. "Are we doing the right thing?"

"Yes," he said quickly. "Yes."

"Okay," she said, hugging him tightly and letting her tears come. "Okay."

"He's going to be all right," Jimmy said into her ear.

She gathered herself and when she finally let go, she decided she would hold on to Jimmy's confidence, even if her own wavered. "Okay."

"I'll be right back," Jimmy said.

After he left, she dried her tears and put on her most hopeful face and walked back into the room. David protested and said she didn't have to stay, that she should go home and rest.

"Your dad and I are going to be here for you," she said.

The words and the way she said them seemed to comfort David. He grabbed the TV remote and flipped through channels, then turned it off.

"If the surgery is tomorrow morning," David said, "do you think I'll still be able to wrestle on Monday? I mean, it's the finals."

She patted his arm. "Let's just take this a step at a time, okay?"

David nodded. "Yeah. That's a good idea."

In the morning, after a night of trying to sleep in chairs and moving to the floor, Susan and Jimmy met with Pastor Jeff while the nurses prepped David for surgery. Their pastor had been there late the night before and prayed with them and was now back a few hours later. When did the man sleep?

Jeff opened his Bible to a passage in Isaiah, chapter 26. Susan knew verses 3 and 4 well. G had given her a handwritten card shortly after Michael's birth years earlier. She had that same worn card stuck to the mirror in her bathroom.

> *You will keep in perfect peace*
> *all who trust in you,*
> *all whose thoughts are fixed on you!*
> *Trust in the Lord always,*
> *for the Lord God is the eternal Rock.*

The nurse who was attending to David approached the little group. "We're about to move him into surgery as soon as the room opens up, but you can step in real quick." She paused and gave them a nervous smile. "And he's already responding to the anesthesia a bit, so congratulations, I'm going to be your daughter-in-law."

Susan glanced at Jimmy and Pastor Jeff and the two seemed as bewildered as she was.

With perfect comedic timing, the nurse said, "Just kidding. He did ask, but I said no."

She led them into the room and Susan saw immediately that David had become what she could only describe as loopy. She'd seen videos online—Nate had shown her several—of people on anesthesia who said wild and hysterical things. Now it was David's turn.

David was laughing at something when she walked in and when she said his name, he looked up, wide-eyed with surprise. "Aww, hey, guys, thank you for coming! Hey, come here, come here. I need to tell you something."

Susan and Jimmy leaned close. David's face was expectant, as if he were sharing a hidden secret that could save humanity.

Slowly, with a circular arm motion between them, he said, "We are family."

"Oh, my goodness," Susan said, standing straight as David began to sing the old Sister Sledge song, moving in the bed, bobbing his head as if he could hear the singers and the music at full volume.

Jimmy and Pastor Jeff watched and smiled. Susan leaned down. "David, I don't think this is the best time to sing."

"No, no, no, no, Mom. I'm going far in life. Farrrr."
He pulled his head back and pointed at her. "You're the
reason!" He looked at Jimmy. "You're the reason. All of
you are the reasons!"

David ran a finger over his lips and made a motorboat
noise she remembered from his childhood. Susan wondered if everyone reacted this way to the anesthesia.

Suddenly David noticed the third person in the room.
"Oh, hey, Pastor! I didn't know you worked here. Come
here, I got to tell you a secret." When Pastor Jeff leaned
close, David said, "I really like your sermons."

"Thank you," Jeff said.

"Especially the good ones," David said, and then he
broke into another round of laughter.

Thankfully the nurses arrived to take David to surgery.
Susan kissed him and David raised a hand and yelled, "All
right, let's do this, people! Let's kick this dog and make
him holler!"

Susan shook her head and walked into the hall, watching them roll David away. He was still talking when they
rounded the corner.

"And you're a reason, and you're a reason. There's a lot
of reasons around here."

"He's going to be okay," Jimmy said.

"I still want to pray," Susan said.

Jeff nodded. "Absolutely."

CHAPTER 22

✦ ✦ ✦

The first thing David saw when he opened his eyes was
the nurse with the pretty face and the kind voice. She was
studying the monitors beside his bed but noticed him
stirring.

"Hey, how are you feeling, David?"

"I'm not sure yet. Groggy."

"You did great in surgery. The doctor will tell you more.
He's been speaking with your parents. Are you hungry?
Thirsty?"

"I'm not sure."

The nurse smiled. "I'll get a tray for you and some water. You can eat when you feel ready."

"Okay, thank you," David said.

When he opened his eyes again, he heard a familiar voice. Nate came around the corner holding his phone up to capture the moment.

"There's the man. The legend. How do you feel, Captain America?"

"Hey, buddy, feeling pretty weak."

"You know, Cap was weak and puny before he was transformed. Actually, you're looking a little green. Do you know who else was green?"

"Don't say it."

"Dr. David Banner was weak before he turned green." Nate gasped. "Dr. David Colton Banner?"

David smiled.

Nate turned his attention to the untouched food on the tray at the foot of the bed. He found a container of Jell-O cubes and began scarfing them.

"How's our superhero doing?" the nurse asked as she walked through the door.

"I am no superhero," David said, his throat dry.

"Can I help you?" the nurse said to Nate.

"Oh yeah, can I get some more of this?" He pointed to the container he held.

"Are you family?" she said.

"I'm more than family."

David's mom and dad entered the room. David sighed, glad to see more familiar faces.

"Baby, you're awake," his mom said and kissed him on the forehead.

David's father stood next to Nate. "We've never seen this man in our entire life."

The nurse glared at Nate.

"Hey!" Nate said in protest.

"He's fine," his dad said, smiling. "Just keep security nearby."

"Well, David's doing fine," the nurse said. "I'll be back in a few minutes to change his meds."

"Hey, we brought pasta!" David's father said.

"Thank you, thank you, thank you," David said.

"Oh, I love pasta," Nate said.

✦ ✦ ✦

Susan took a seat in a chair near her son. Jimmy sat on the bed across from her. She studied David's face. He seemed a little pale but he was alert now and not singing or otherwise affected by the anesthesia.

"They haven't told me anything yet," David said.

Susan glanced at Jimmy. They had practiced what they would say in the hallway.

"Well, we talked to the doctor," Jimmy said. "They relieved the pressure, and he said that you shouldn't have any more headaches."

"Praise the Lord," David said.

"Yeah, a lot of people have been praying for you," Susan said. She and Jimmy exchanged glances and she could see the pain on her husband's face.

His eyes moistened as he turned to David. His voice was just above a whisper now. "Hey, the doctor also said . . ."

Jimmy paused and it was all Susan could do not to fill in the silence. But she didn't.

"No more wrestling."

"What?" David said, his voice like a child's. "Ever?"

"I'm so sorry, sweetheart," Susan whispered.

"God got you through this," Jimmy said. "That's not a little thing. I don't think we should take that for granted."

Susan leaned over and kissed David again. He was near tears. With a trembling voice she said, "I'm just so glad you're okay."

She was so focused on David and his struggle with the news they had given that she didn't realize Nate had moved closer. She glanced behind her and realized he had started recording them.

"This is so good, you guys," Nate said. "Can we just go back a few sentences and let me get that on here?"

"What?" Susan said.

"Just a few," Nate said. "Kiss him on the forehead again if you can and I'll get it."

"Dude, come on," David said. He waved a hand at Nate to get him to stop.

"Oh yeah," Nate said, catching himself as if he realized he was intruding on a private moment. "But I just thought it was magic. No one needs to see it. We're good." He smiled, acting as if everybody recorded the most intimate moments of their lives.

"Dad, can you get Mr. Spielberg to leave the building?"

"No, I promise, no more recording. I'm good."

Susan stood and put a hand on Nate's shoulder. "I think we just need a little alone time. You understand."

"I just thought the whole thing was so touching. It's a compliment for me to want to shoot this. You know that, right, David?"

"Nate," David said. "I love you, man. But go home."

Nate put his phone in his pocket. "Wait, what about the pasta?"

✦ ✦ ✦

Jimmy prepped a bowl of pasta for Nate and walked to the lobby with him. When he found out that Nate had been dropped off at the hospital and didn't have a ride, he waved him to the parking lot and drove him home. Nate

243

ate the pasta on the way because he said he didn't like it when it got cold.

Nate's house was twenty minutes away, and as they drove, Jimmy said, "You know, even though it can be a little much at times, the way you see the world through the camera is a real gift."

"That's not what David thinks."

"Sure he does. It's just that you have to be more sensitive. You know, get permission before you shoot the details of a person's life."

"That's what my sister said—not as kind as that, but, you know. I'll tell you, Mr. Colton, the best scenes are when people don't know you're shooting. You get gold when folks are just being themselves. That's what pops on the screen. I mean, I feel it when I see it. And the people who subscribe to my channel love when I capture the real stuff that happens."

"I get that," Jimmy said. "But flip it around. What if someone took video of you every moment of the day and posted it online?"

"I wouldn't have a problem with it."

"Really?"

"Well, I mean, for most of the day. Because most of the day I'm just taking video of other people." Nate thought a moment, then took another bite of pasta. "This is really good. The marinara sauce is to die for."

Jimmy pulled up to the house and saw a young woman pacing in the driveway and along the sidewalk, a phone to her ear. He turned off his headlights. "Wonder what that's about."

"That's my sister, Reese." Nate gave a heavy sigh. "You know, one of the reasons I was . . ." He stopped and waved a hand. "Well, I should just go."

"No, finish your thought," Jimmy said.

Nate put his empty bowl on the floorboard, his plastic fork clattering. "One of the reasons I like hanging with your family is because it's kind of different than mine. I mean, I love my mom and dad and I kind of like my sister, sometimes, you know? But your family, G and Paw Paw and Mrs. Colton . . . the way you guys talk and act and care for each other . . . My family cares but we don't always show it. At least, not like you guys. When I'm at your house, it's like I can feel it and taste it."

"Like the marinara sauce," Jimmy said.

"Exactly. So if I shoot too much, it's because I'm seeing something that feels real to me."

"That's a kind thing to say, Nate. I'm glad you feel that way. And we're always glad to have you."

"Except when I get kicked out of the hospital room." Nate waved a hand. "No, I get it. I kind of get carried away."

"Your love of video and filming, that's going to take

you somewhere. Don't give up on that. Just don't record everything."

Nate opened the door.

"And you can start by not recording her," Jimmy said, pointing to Reese, who walked in the opposite direction along the sidewalk.

"Oh, that's a sad story, Mr. Colton. Why do girls go for guys who hurt them? I don't understand it. She's either on the phone talking to him or talking with a friend about how bad he is. And then she keeps going back to him."

"That's tough," Jimmy said. "I've found that when people keep making bad choices, at some point they'll turn to the people who really care for them."

Nate thought a moment and nodded. "Thanks for the ride, Mr. Colton."

David was pushed out of the hospital in a wheelchair, something he thought was wildly unnecessary, but it was the hospital's policy. He sat in the back seat of the car and stared out the window, trying to process his disappointment. He was glad to awaken without a headache, but he was still bummed that his chance to wrestle in the finals had been taken away.

His coach had stopped by his room as they were finishing dinner the night before. He'd said some encouraging things and told David the team was just glad that he had come through the surgery and that the doctor had given a good report.

"That's the main thing," Coach Pruett said. "You gave it your all for four years. You came a long way from the first day you walked into practice. And your spirit, the one that didn't quit or stop learning and trying to get better, that was a real boost to the team. It's going to serve you well down the road."

"Yeah, but wrestling is not going to be part of the equation anymore."

His coach nodded. "Yeah, that's a bummer. And it can feel like God is rejecting your plan. But the way I look at it, it's not so much rejection as it is redirection. You're on a different path but you're still headed forward."

David had thanked his coach for coming and encouraging him, but the man's words troubled him. As David watched the scenery on the way home, he couldn't help thinking about the plan he'd mapped out for his life—the plan that was now gone. A wrestling scholarship would've meant that he could go to college on his own terms and not be dependent on his parents. As much as he loved them, he wanted to make his own way, to live his own life. Was there something wrong with that?

David had trophies and awards displayed in his room and he was proud of those. Was life all about how much he could win or accomplish? Was his life worth something only if he achieved things? Or achieved things on his own? That took him back to the day he was born. If he was a "mistake," he had to prove himself and overcome obstacles in order to feel worthy. Was that why this setback felt so bad?

David had been taught from early on that God was sovereign over his life. If that was true, why had this bad thing happened? Why couldn't God have allowed a doctor to see his condition when he was younger and treat him for it? Why had God taken away wrestling, something he loved so much?

That's what he was doing now—wrestling with life, struggling to not be pinned by his circumstances. And his parents seemed to want him to move on and embrace a new chapter in life before he could even process all the changes. He wanted to feel this fully, to let the disappointment linger as long as it needed, even though his headaches were gone.

As they neared home, his mom mentioned something about his upcoming wedding.

David leaned over and looked at her. "What are you talking about, my wedding?"

She laughed. "That's right, you don't remember. It's just something that happened when the nurse was prepping you for surgery."

"What did I say?"

"Trust me, I'm sure she's heard a lot of things like that," his dad said. "I wouldn't worry about it."

"Wait, did I ask her to marry me?"

They pulled into the garage and his mom told him what he had said to Pastor Jeff.

"You're lucky Nate wasn't there to record all of that," his dad said. His phone dinged with a message. "It would have gone viral by now."

David shook his head and grabbed his duffel bag and headed inside. "I think I need to apologize to a bunch of people."

"No, it's fine. It was just the anesthesia talking," his mom said.

"I don't remember saying any of that."

"And you weren't just talking. You were singing your heart out."

"No!" David said, incredulous.

"Yeah, ask Dad."

David turned to his father, who had his phone to his ear. "Dad, was I seriously singing?"

His dad seemed preoccupied and when he looked at them, David could tell something was up.

"Hey, I'd like you guys to listen to this." He held out his phone and pressed Play on the message.

"Hello, Mr. Colton. This is Abagail over at Kirsh and

Clark. I just wanted to call and inform you that Melissa
Cates, David's birth mother, has updated her records.
Now that David is of legal age, he has the right to contact
his birth parents if he is interested. You're welcome to call
back if you'd like more information. Feel free to let us
know, and have a great day."

David glanced at his mom during the message. Her
face was almost as bright as the yellow hoodie she wore.
And when she looked at him expectantly, he felt the
pressure again. Another adoptive mom might have felt
threatened, but it was almost as if his mom needed him to
be excited about the idea. But inside, the woman's words
stirred things he couldn't process.

"Wow, I forgot," his father said. "You're old enough
now."

David took a deep breath, closed his eyes, and slung
his duffel bag over his shoulder. "I don't know."

His mother followed him down the hall. "Well, we
should probably talk a little more about this, you know?
Do you think you might want to meet your birth mom?"

David whirled and snapped, "I don't know, Mom. It's
a lot to think about."

"Yeah, well, you don't have to do anything right now,
David," his dad said, trying to keep the peace. "It's okay."

David looked from his mother's pained face to his
father's. "I don't know if I want her back in my life.

I mean, I don't even know her. Is meeting her going to be—"

"I wasn't pushing you to do that," his mom said, interrupting him.

"No, there's no rush," his dad said. "We have plenty of time. We're not getting in the van to go meet her."

"That's right," his mom said. "But I was thinking, we might want to respond in some way?"

Her voice lilted up, ending in a question. Every time she did that, she expected him to have an answer. And he didn't have one and couldn't think of one and the pressure was reminding him of the headaches that were supposed to be gone from his life.

"Right?" she continued. "So maybe a letter for an update?"

David wanted the conversation to be over, so he said, "Okay. Fine. You can send her whatever you want." He turned and walked toward the stairs. "I'm going to shower and go to bed."

"Still no headaches, right?" his dad said.

"Still no headaches," David said. He trudged up the stairs.

✦ ✦ ✦

When David was gone, Jimmy turned to Susan. "We cannot rush him."

"I know. I'm sorry. But I got to thinking, wouldn't it be kind of cool for her to see him all grown up? She took a really big risk on us. She would be so proud of him."

"She would be."

"Yeah," Susan said and she got a look in her eyes that told Jimmy everything. She patted his arm and moved toward the kitchen. As she did, Jimmy got an idea. He walked into his room and found the box Susan had squirreled away. When he heard the shower stop upstairs, he gave David a couple of minutes to dress, then walked to his room and found him sitting on his bed. He knocked lightly on the wall and David looked up.

"Hey," Jimmy said. "Can I show you something?"

"Yeah, sure."

Jimmy sat next to him and handed his son a photo. "You remember asking to see that when you were about eight?"

David took the photo and studied the faces in the picture. "Dad, is that Brian and Melissa?"

"Yeah. We stopped for lunch after we came back from church. And you asked us, out of the blue, if you could meet your birth mother."

David nodded and seemed to recall the moment.

Jimmy continued. "And Mom said to you, 'Well, what would you say to her if you got to meet her?' And you said, 'I would say, "Hi, my name is David."'"

David laughed and kept staring at the picture.

"Then you asked us if we had a picture of them, so when we got home, I showed that to you. And you looked at it for a minute and you said, 'Wow, they look like nice people.' And you gave it back to me."

"How old were they?"

"I think she was eighteen and he was seventeen. She was pregnant when she graduated. Think about that. Imagine how scared she must have been. And then, deciding to place you for adoption. It must have been the hardest decision of her entire life. But I'm so glad she did."

David nodded, deep in thought, and Jimmy felt he could leave things right there, just let his son think about what he had said. But he felt compelled to share one more thing.

"David, God gave you to me and Mom as a gift. And you will always be our son."

David looked up at him and Jimmy gave him a loving pat on his knee. Then he stood and walked out of the room.

CHAPTER 23

✦ ✦ ✦

David rode with Nate to a burger joint in town they both liked. Nate wanted to know about his headaches and asked if he could see David's scar.

"No, I'm not showing you my scar."

"Why not?"

"Because you'll take a picture and put it online."

"What's wrong with that?" Nate said. "Just joking. Come on, let me see."

When David refused, Nate asked about David's wrestling career and how he felt about giving it up. It felt good to process with someone his own age instead of his parents. When the conversation turned to David's considering the speech tournament, Nate was all over it.

"Hey, listen, I didn't say I was going to do it. I'm just thinking about doing it."

"Dude, you totally should. That's five hundred bucks. That'll pay off my drone."

"Who says I'd give the money to you if I won?"

Nate put a cool french fry back on his plate. "Bro, look. I'm really proud of you. I know you love your family, but you've never really seemed okay with being adopted. You've basically tried to hide it."

"I have not tried to hide it."

"Yes, you have."

David lowered his voice and leaned forward. "Not talking about it doesn't mean I've tried to hide it."

Nate held up two fingers and pointed to his face. "Look at me. Are you okay with people knowing you're *adopted*?" He whispered the word for emphasis.

"Yes," David said. Then, like a deer in the headlights, he added, "Mostly." And after a second or two he changed that to "Not really."

"I don't know why. You have a great family. A family that loves you." Nate dipped a fry in David's ketchup. "People would kill to have a family like yours and mine."

"Nate!"

David looked up as Reese approached the table. David considered her one of the prettiest girls in school. She had long brown hair pulled back in a ponytail and today she wore jeans and a red shirt. David could tell she was not in a good mood the way she stomped to the table and stared her brother down.

"I didn't say you could take my car. I said that I would meet you at my car. Come on, give me my keys. I'm late for work!"

As Nate dug in the pockets of his jacket, Reese turned to David. Her face softened a little. "Hey, David."

David forced a smile. "Reese."

Nate finally found the keys and handed them to her. "Did Mom drive you?"

"Craig did," she said, grabbing for the keys.

Nate took them back. "Wait, you're back together with Craig?"

She grabbed the keys and lowered her voice. "Look, just mind your own business, okay?" She walked toward the door, then turned back. "And take that video down. Please? Before anybody else sees it."

As Reese left, David stared at Nate, dumbfounded. "You posted it?"

"We'll talk later, all right?" Nate said to Reese as she walked out the door. "Catch me up then!"

As Reese passed the window, Nate said, "I'm going to need a ride home."

"You drove me here," David said.

Nate's eyes darted. "That's not good."

Two days before the speech tournament, David found Mr. Russell in the hallway and walked beside him. He knew he was cutting things close, but he decided to risk it.

"Listen, I've been thinking more about that speech thing."

"Yeah, and?"

"I'm thinking I might try it."

"Really?" Mr. Russell said, stopping. "That's great. What made you change your mind?"

"I guess . . . I just needed some perspective."

Mr. Russell put a hand on David's shoulder. "I can certainly understand that. Well, I'll need you to fill out an entry form by the end of the day. There are a couple on my desk."

"Okay, I'll fill it out."

Melissa heard the rumble of the postal truck and walked to the end of the driveway to retrieve the mail. Courtney would be home from the bus soon and Melissa liked to look through the mail right away and pay any bills that came so they didn't hang over her. She'd learned that the hard way after a few were lost in the clutter of her desk. Shawn had been kind about the overdue penalties, but she'd made a mental note to be more on top of things.

Her life was, it seemed, all about overdue bills. Things she had done that she regretted and had squirreled away in her heart. She tried to forget the mistakes but they had a way of coming back and being delivered at the most inopportune times.

She looked through the junk mail and an envelope from a bank inviting her to open a line of credit. Halfway up the driveway she stopped and her jaw dropped when she saw an envelope with the return address of Jimmy and Susan Colton from Louisiana. She stared at it, her heart beating wildly, and willed herself to breathe.

Melissa had finally gotten through to the law firm and left her information, and she promptly forgot about it. She ripped the envelope open and saw a folded sheet of paper and hurried inside the house and unfolded it as she sat on the couch.

Inside was a high school senior picture of a young man with striking features. Dark-brown hair, spiked in the front, green eyes, a strong jaw, and a hint of a smile. He wore a necklace with a silver cross pendant, and she wondered if that was just a fashion statement or if it meant something more to him and he wanted others to know he identified with the cross.

Melissa held it up and the picture became blurry. She realized she was looking into that face again, the one she had seen in the hospital on that December day so many years ago. There had been a few pictures between then and now, but nothing like this, and her heart swelled with the vision before her.

She put the picture on the coffee table and spread out the handwritten letter. She wiped her eyes and read.

Dear Melissa,

We heard from the law office that you had updated your information. Thank you for that. Jimmy and I thought you would appreciate seeing what a handsome young man David has become. There is so much to tell you about him and if I get started, I won't be able to stop. I don't want to overstep, however. I want him to be able to tell you all that's happened when the time is right.

I'm enclosing his senior picture. He has been interested in wrestling for the last few years and had become quite good, even to the point of talk of a scholarship, but a medical procedure changed all of that. He's doing well now. See, I told you, if I get started, I won't be able to stop!

Jimmy and I wanted you to know what a gift you have given us. I told David not long ago that I don't know what we would have done without him in our lives. And my parents, G and Paw Paw, simply adore him and are his biggest cheerleaders in life.

We had gone through such loss before David came to us. I wasn't sure I even wanted to risk an adoption. But your phone call asking me about baiting my hook was the most surreal conversation I've ever had. And we've been true to our word about raising him—he can bait his own hook quite well.

David has a friend named Nate who has taken a lot of video of him over the last few years. I'll include the website where you can see some of that at the bottom of this page.

There's a verse from the Bible I prayed over David when we first brought him home from the hospital. I actually have it on a plaque that was over his crib. It's Jeremiah 29:11.

"'For I know the plans I have for you,' says the Lord. 'They are plans for good and not for disaster, to give you a future and a hope.'"

God has been faithful to us, even through significant trials. And I pray that you know that same hope.

Thank you, thank you, thank you, from the bottom of our hearts, for doing what you did more than

*eighteen years ago. I hope your heart swells with pride
as you look at what your sacrifice did for our family.
God bless you, Melissa.*

*Sincerely,
Susan Colton*

Melissa folded the page and slipped it back into the envelope. The door opened behind her and it startled her. She put the picture inside the envelope and put it on the coffee table. Courtney bounded in with her backpack, dropping it on the floor by the door.

"How was school, sweetie?"

Courtney headed for the kitchen, glancing at Melissa. She stopped and studied her face. "What's wrong?"

"What do you mean?" Melissa said, wiping her eyes with both hands.

"Your eyes are all puffy and your nose is red like you've been crying."

"Well, it's a good kind of cry."

"What do you mean?"

"Sometimes you cry when you're sad and sometimes you cry when you're happy. And this is a happy cry."

Courtney scrunched her face in thought. Then her eyes widened. "You mean like what might happen if I get a horse?"

Melissa couldn't hold back the laughter. "I suppose that's probably the best example of a happy cry."

"Does that mean I'm going to get one?"

"No, I didn't say that. You brought up the horse."

"You don't want me to have a good cry?"

Melissa shook her head. "Go get your snack, girl. You're something else, you know that?"

Courtney shrugged. "I can try, can't I?"

When Courtney went to the kitchen, Melissa felt like she could have used that moment to tell her about her brother. But it was too soon. She was still processing the photo she had just seen. She told herself to wait, that there would be a better opportunity.

Later, when Courtney went outside, Melissa typed David's name into her laptop and found a page of pictures. She touched the screen, as if she might be touching David's face. Then she typed in the website of the friend who had uploaded videos of David mugging for the camera and dribbling a basketball between his legs. There were birthday parties and an amazing video of David jumping from a rock cliff that nearly took Melissa's breath away. She had to turn away from the screen, it made her so nervous. Then she played it again and watched it all the way through. There were also videos of David wrestling and Melissa couldn't believe how adept he was. He glided over the mat. He really was good enough for a scholarship. She wondered what medical condition he had that would have ended his wrestling career.

The screen flickered and she saw an alert at the top of the page that a video was being livestreamed. She clicked on the link and saw a teen girl giving a speech in front of what looked like a large audience. Melissa nearly clicked away but stayed for a moment. The man at the podium was introducing the final speaker of the event, who was a senior and who had entered the speech contest only two days before.

"Please welcome David Colton," the man said.

Melissa froze as she watched David move to the lectern and prepare to speak. He wore a blue buttoned shirt and his hair wasn't as spiky as she'd seen in some of the pictures. He fumbled a bit at the start, and as he did, she found herself rubbing the palms of her hands on her jeans. It surprised her how nervous she was for him, just like a parent at a recital.

Finally he looked away from his notes straight at the audience and began.

"I've always wondered if my biological parents think about me. And I guess, maybe, it bothers me when people know that I am adopted. But it really shouldn't bother me. No matter the circumstances, I now have a family that chose to adopt me and loves me. And yet for some reason, I struggle to be content with that."

Melissa spoke to the computer. "I think of you every day."

David continued. "I guess maybe I didn't want to feel different or less valued. But I think a lot of those thoughts are only in my head and aren't actually reality. And when I step back and look at my life from a wider perspective, I see how much of a gift my parents are to me and that adoption has brought us together in a unique and beautiful way."

Melissa closed her eyes and tried to hold back the emotion but she couldn't. And she decided she didn't want to.

"Because," David said, "I'm absolutely sure that their lives would be a lot more boring without me around."

The audience laughed and so did Melissa. She couldn't believe she was watching her son speak to so many people.

"So the more I live my life," David said, "I believe that there's really no reason to feel different. We don't all take the same path. But I'm thankful for the family God's given me.

"When I think of my family, I think of home. And I wouldn't trade that for the world. Thank you."

Melissa put her head in her hands and tears streamed through her fingers. To see him—to actually hear his voice and watch him speak—touched her so deeply. But to hear him talk about his family made an even deeper impression.

The livestream continued with an award. The first place winner was a girl. Melissa couldn't imagine any better speech than the one David had given. Then the man moved to the lectern again.

"I may have read this in the wrong order. This year's runner-up, and a check for $250, goes to David Colton."

Melissa covered her mouth with both hands and squealed with delight. David shook the man's hand and took the check from him.

Melissa was so engrossed in what she saw on the screen that she didn't realize Courtney had come in and was standing behind the couch, looking at the computer screen.

"Who is that, Mom?"

Melissa turned, startled. She closed the laptop quickly. "Oh, it's a livestream of a school speech competition."

"Who was that David guy? Do you know him?"

Melissa sighed heavily. "Sit down, Corty. I have something I need to tell you."

CHAPTER 24

✦ ✦ ✦

David arrived late to the after-speech party that was held at Anna Reynolds's house. Her parents were the Reynolds Real Estate duo who had their faces on billboards around town and all over the Internet. It was no surprise to David that they had a nice house that was finely decorated. Music pulsed through the windows as he walked inside and he quickly spotted Nate, Sam, and Justin in the next room.

"David!" Nate yelled over the booming bass in the songs. "Swooping in and taking the win."

"Guys, I didn't expect to win anything."

"We didn't either," Sam said. "But you beat us."

"I'm sorry," David said.

"At least Anna didn't win again this year," Justin said. "I mean she always—"

Sam jabbed Justin below the ribs with an elbow just as Anna approached.

"Anna, hey!" Justin said. "Great job on your speech. Congrats."

Anna just sneered as she walked past Justin.

"That's rough," Nate said, tossing a cheese puff in the air. David caught it in his mouth and chewed.

"Hey, Dana and Lacy just walked in," Sam said, looking toward the door. "Let's go! Game time!"

Justin followed Sam. "Gentlemen, catch up with you later."

As Sam and Justin left, David's phone dinged. He pulled it from his pocket.

"Those goons," Nate said. "Hey, so get this. You know the graduation video, with the baby faces and all the information and stuff? I get to do it this year. Yeah, and I told them it was going to be five hundred bucks, and they went for it. Hashtag debt-free, know what I mean?"

David didn't catch much of what Nate said because he was glued to his phone. "Yeah, yeah. Good deal."

"What's up?"

"I just got a text from . . ."

"From who?" Nate said.

David studied the message and decided it was better to just hand the phone to his friend.

Nate took it and began reading aloud. "'David, this is Melissa. I don't care for social networking, so please forgive me. Please let your parents know that I'm reaching out to you. I'm willing to tell you anything you want. I don't want to hide anything. All I can say is, WOW, they raised the most wonderful boy I've ever laid eyes on.'" Nate handed the phone back. "Yech. Seems a bit much."

David put a hand on his head and tried to process what he'd just seen.

Nate studied his face, unaware. Then it dawned on him. "Dude, is this your birth mom?"

Dry mouth. Room spinning. "I'm going to go call my mom and dad."

"Yeah, step out, dude," Nate said.

Ever since their divorce, Brian Michaels had lived in fear that Melissa would one day reveal their secret. He had kept his family and friends and his new wife, Azure, in the dark about what had happened eighteen years earlier. As far as he was concerned, that chapter of their lives had been torn out and tossed away. And he wanted things to stay that way. There was only one problem—actually, two.

Melissa was the first problem. And then there was the baby. The infant who was now old enough to be drafted.

Brian liked to think that everything that had happened when he was a teenager was way back in the past. It was so far in the rearview that it could never affect the present. But there were times when he thought of mistakes he had made and ways he had treated others. In those moments a mix of emotions surfaced that he didn't want but couldn't deny.

The fear of the secret being exposed didn't strike him every hour of every day. It would hit at times out of the blue—at work or pushing his daughter on the swing or having a conversation with Azure. He would feel a pang of guilt that he'd never told her and imagine the fallout if she heard it from someone else. Still, he held back, believing that he could control news of the past by simply dismissing it.

He had a dream that kept returning, something unbidden from his subconscious, he guessed. He was in a big room with fancy tables filled with food, people holding fine china and drinking from tall crystal flutes. Everyone was dressed in tuxedos and formal gowns, like they'd just walked a red carpet. Everyone had perfect hair and bright smiles. And across the room he caught a reflection in a floor-length mirror that ran the entire wall. One person stood out amid all the finely dressed people. A tall man with mussed hair. When others moved, he noticed the man was only wearing underwear.

And the man in the mirror was him.

Frantically, he looked for a door but there was none. And the more frantic he became, the more people in the room backed away, whispering and tittering, and suddenly he was in the middle, alone, and the music stopped and people stared. Exposed and ashamed, he could do nothing but try to cover himself.

He awoke from that dream on many nights in a panic so great that he would roll out of bed and sit on the edge, rubbing his eyes and shaking. He wondered if others had that same kind of dream and what it meant. Did dreams mean anything?

Brian was standing by the firepit in the backyard of their house near Columbus, Indiana, watching his five-year-old daughter Presley giggle as she chased fireflies. His phone buzzed and he pulled it out and looked at the screen, then shook his head. Talking with Melissa was always a losing proposition. It dragged him into the past. He tried to avoid talking with her except for the times he had to—when they exchanged Courtney on the weekends, for instance. Sometimes he would have something he'd need to tell her about his schedule, but instead of calling, he'd wait until she phoned. Two birds with one call.

What could she want? Instead of waiting to hear the voice mail, he answered.

"Yeah, Melissa, what's up?"

A pause. Then in that dramatic voice, the voice that always sent him over the edge, she said, "I saw him."

"You saw who?"

"David. Our son."

A deep sigh. "What do you mean you saw him?"

"His parents sent me a picture. I updated my information like I said I would and Susan wrote a letter. Then I went online. Brian, he's amazing. He's smart and he's athletic—"

"I don't want to hear this," he said. "This doesn't concern me or you. Why can't you leave this alone? Nothing good can come from—"

"I told Courtney."

That stopped him in his tracks. He glanced at Presley frolicking around the backyard, going down the slide and climbing on the monkey bars dome he had bought and put together. He'd worked hard to get the dandelions from the yard and make the grass as soft and green as he could. She was barefoot and prancing like a pony.

"You did what?" he said.

"Brian, David is eighteen now. He deserves to know about where he came from and who—"

"Listen, Melissa, I know he is eighteen, but why now?"

"Why not now?" she said. "You think there's a perfect time to tell him?"

"No, I'm not trying to say there's a perfect time for something like this, I'm just . . ." He pulled the phone away and shook his head. Her voice touched that nerve, like ice water on a bad tooth. He put the phone back to his ear as she was in midsentence.

". . . and I think it would help me if I could see him and explain things. I'm not saying you have to. But I need this, Brian. Even though it scares me. And I wanted you to know."

"Yeah."

"I know you want it to be over. Just something we forget. But I can't. I'm not doing this to hurt you."

"No, I get it. I get it. And you are free to talk to him if that is what you want to do."

She was crying on the other end of the line. He hated to hear her cry. It brought back the car ride to Indianapolis and the parking lot circled by protesters. When he heard her cry, or any woman in his life, he felt out of control, like it was his fault.

"Okay. Yeah, listen, I've got to go. Thanks for the call."

He hung up before she could respond and stared at the fire as that day came back to him. Driving in silence. And then the noise of the people outside the fence. The people didn't sound angry so much as desperate, pleading for life. But what did those people know about their lives, their choice? What did they know of the corner the two of them were in?

And here he was in another corner because of the past. All because of their mistake.

Brian tried to ignore the storm inside and stay engaged during dinner, but the weight of his thoughts was too much. He couldn't hear much of what Azure said and she caught him staring off as they ate.

After dinner, he scraped the uneaten food from the plates and realized he'd hardly touched his own meal. He always had a big appetite but not tonight.

Azure had put Presley to bed and read her a story. He heard her reading in the singsong pattern of the book his daughter asked for every night.

"Well, she is a little ball of energy tonight," Azure said as she came back into the kitchen. As she loaded the dishwasher, she said, "I should have put her down at eight before she caught her second wind."

"Yeah," Brian said.

Azure had long blonde hair that fell over her shoulders. Her brown eyes had arrested him the first time he'd seen her. Her voice was soft and comforting, most of the time. Their relationship was so different from the one he'd had with Melissa. Azure was easy to talk with. She also seemed to know when Brian just needed to be alone and gave him space.

"Hey, what are you thinking about?" she said. "You've hardly said a word this entire night."

Brian stared at the dirty dishes, his back to his wife. How could he start the sentence that led to what he needed to tell her? There was emotion welling inside and he hated emotion.

"I . . . uh . . ." He sniffed and realized his nose was running along with the blur in his eyes. "There's something I need to tell you."

"Okay," Azure said nonchalantly, still stacking the dishwasher.

He turned and saw her and wanted to run, just like in his dream. But he knew he couldn't, not because he couldn't find a door, but because she deserved to know. So he mustered the courage, if that's what it was, and spoke.

"There's something I should have told you a long time ago, but, uh . . ."

Azure turned and faced him, and he looked at the floor. She leaned against the refrigerator. When she spoke, there was concern and a little fear in her voice. "Brian, what is it?"

He couldn't look at her. He didn't want to have her reaction seared into his memory. He spoke with his head down, as if the guilt of the secret was too heavy.

"I have a son," he said, and his voice sounded a million miles away.

Finally he looked at her. Azure's face said it all. Shock. Bewilderment. She took a breath. "A son?"

Brian nodded and looked down again, the pain on her face too much for him to bear.

"With . . ." She stopped and regained her composure. "With Melissa?"

"Yeah," he whispered.

Azure turned away and put a hand on the sink to steady herself. He waited for the barrage of questions about what had happened or why he hadn't told her, but she stayed quiet. And it was into the silence that he now spoke.

"I was still in high school. And . . . I just had a hard time telling anyone."

He looked up and saw Azure studying him intently. His goal had been to keep her from the hurt. But now he realized his concern hadn't been for Azure or anyone else—it had been for himself. He had held this in for nearly twenty years because he didn't want to hurt. And the secret had hurt him and everyone he cared about.

When she turned away, he whispered, "I am so sorry. I should have told you."

"Yeah," Azure said, her voice shaking.

Brian felt the emotion finally take control and he began to cry softly. He'd always thought that crying was the worst thing a man could do, but here he was, at the end of being able to control anything.

Azure turned and said, "Okay." Something in her voice gave him hope. She took a few steps toward him. "Look at me."

Brian looked into her eyes and saw his reflection. She didn't look away or even blink. She reached out and took his hands in hers. "I'm here for you . . . no matter what."

When she touched his face, he let go and wept, and she drew him into an embrace. Brian hugged her so tightly he didn't ever want to let go. And he felt something happen there in that kitchen that he'd never felt. He'd always looked at love as something you give once the other person earns it. But this was love in spite of his actions and his secrets. This was love without the strings.

They held on to each other for a long time before Azure let go and pulled out a chair at the table and sat. "I want you to tell me everything."

And he did.

CHAPTER 25

✦ ✦ ✦

David felt as if he had broken through some kind of space-time continuum that Nate would dream up, the past and present coalescing into a story that tied together people who had met each other on some distant planet. But this wasn't a make-believe story—it was real, and it was happening to him.

The events of the past few weeks were more than he could process. The loss of his wrestling career, the surgery, the message he received from his biological mother—it was too much to take in. And he knew that how he would respond, or even if he would respond at all, was not something anyone else could decide for him. He needed to make the decision of which path to take.

But which path was best?

He composed a message back to Melissa and deleted it. Then he composed another. He was on his fiftieth version when he asked his dad to review it. His father sat on the bed, David at his desk.

"Wait, I thought she didn't do social media," his dad said.

"I'm going to try this way. If she doesn't respond, I'll text her. So what do you think?" David said.

"I think it's a good first response, as long as you're sure you don't want it to go any further."

"But, Dad, I don't know how far I want this to go. I don't even know her. Besides, isn't this just like opening a whole other can of worms?"

"It's not like she wants anything from you, other than for you to know that she's willing to talk. And Mom did write to her."

"I know, and it's weird because part of me wants to know what it would have been like. Then there's another part of me that thinks it's better not to involve myself at all."

"I understand. For sure, it's safer to just leave it alone." Jimmy got up from the bed and sat closer to David.

"You know, just let her live her life. Then again, it could be really healing for Melissa. To hear from you and see what an amazing man you've become. Did you look up Brian?"

David turned to his computer. "Yeah, I did. But he never really posts anything."

"Well, maybe if you respond to Melissa, you could reach out to him, too. Either way, we'll support you."

An alert sounded on his computer and David read the message. "Nate is coming over later to interview me."

"He's going to interview you?"

"Yeah, he wants to film this whole thing and make a documentary. It's Nate, you know?"

Jimmy smiled. "Should be interesting. All right, David. Later."

As his dad left, David turned back to his computer and studied the message he wanted to send Melissa. He made a slight change and then hovered over the Send button. Finally he pressed it and took a deep breath. He'd done it. He'd finally responded. And that gave him the courage to find the page for Brian and his wife, Azure. David wondered, if he met his biological father, would people recognize him as Brian's son? David wasn't sure he wanted that, especially since his dad had done so much for him.

He had said they would support him whatever he decided. But didn't a little of his dad ache knowing that

David was interested in finding out more about Melissa and Brian?

✦ ✦ ✦

Brian tended the firepit, the flames flickering and sending sparks into the night. Azure held Presley in her lap as the girl looked at the night sky. It was just before nine and an hour past her bedtime, but they let her stay up to hear the crickets and enjoy the fire.

Though the evening was peaceful, there was still a storm inside Brian. He had gone from being grateful for Azure's support and understanding to frustrated with how Melissa just couldn't let go of the past.

"Maybe everything will settle down now," Azure said. "Maybe David won't want to reach out. I mean, think how his adoptive parents must feel about all of this."

"It's got to be hard for them," Brian said. "They're the ones who raised him."

"Exactly," Azure said.

"Who's David?" Presley said.

"Shhhh," Azure said. "Just let Dad and me talk."

"Maybe nothing will come of it and it'll just blow over," Brian said.

"And maybe something good will come of it. I can see how painful it is for you to even think about this. But what if walking through this together does something good? What if seeing him will bring the closure you never got to have?"

"I don't see what good could come of going back over the mistakes you make."

Azure hugged Presley tightly. "Are you saying he was a mistake?"

"No, but I pushed her to do something she didn't want. I drove her up there. I sold my radio to get the money. I really wanted her to take care of it. And we argued. So now, when I think about it . . . I don't want to think about it. Is that a crime? I just want to live my life and raise my family and do what I'm supposed to do without going back and digging through the trash."

He stoked the fire and Presley, oblivious to the conversation now, pointed out the stars and then spotted an airplane that passed overhead, its lights blinking.

Azure's phone dinged. She picked it up from the arm of the chair and read the message. After a moment she held it out to Brian. "Uh, you might want to look at this."

He took the phone. He and Azure had a joint social media account. He didn't pay much attention to it, letting her post photos and memes and animals and whatever else she wanted. Her phone alerted her to any messages.

On the screen he read, *David Colton wants to send you a message.*

He stared at the words and it felt like something

beneath him gave way, like he was falling and there was no way to stop. Finally he handed the phone back to Azure.

"I can respond if you want," she said.

Brian put another piece of firewood in the pit. He watched it catch and flame up.

David left Nate alone in his room to get it ready for the shoot. He was glad he had responded to Melissa and reached out to Brian, but there were so many unanswered questions. Even if both of them wanted to meet, he wasn't sure he could go through with it. Part of him wanted to, another part wanted to avoid any possible conflict. That made talking about all of this on camera even more difficult.

David returned to his room and saw the phone pointed at the chair and a lamp positioned toward his face.

"I just need to see if this is enough light before we start," Nate said.

"Look, I don't think I can do this," David said.

"Dude, you have to do this. It's going to be gold. Think about it. This could be—"

"Nate," David said. "This is not like jumping into the river because you want the shot to go viral. Okay? This is my life, not a social media post. I'm not your sister fighting with her boyfriend. You get it?"

Nate's jaw dropped. "You should say that. Seriously, that passion right there, the way you delivered that, was powerful. People need to see that side of you."

"You don't get it," David said. "All of this is not real to you. It's just something you capture on video. Life's not like that. You don't live it in front of a camera."

Nate held up both hands and backed away, closing the door. David sat on his bed and ran a hand through his hair as Nate leaned against the wall.

"We've been friends a long time," Nate said. "You know me better than my family does. Okay? And I'll admit I'm a video nut. It's in my blood. But ever since this came up with your birth mom, I've just had this sense that there's something bigger going on. This is not just about you and your adoption and your mom and dad. There's more to it than that."

"But it's my life, Nate. It's not a reality show."

Nate nodded. "I get that. I don't want it to be a reality show. But if I'm right, if there's more going on here than either of us understand, the best time to capture it is now, as it's happening."

"I can't be an actor in your play."

"See, that's just it. I don't want you to act. I want you to be yourself. Dude, you're the gift in all of this, don't you see? When your parents picked you up from the hospital that day, you didn't do anything to make them happy other than being you. Poopy diapers and all. Crying in the night, right?"

David stared at the floor.

"Think of it this way. If you're right and this recording thing is a bad idea, we stop, I delete the files, and that's it."

"You'd do that?"

"Yes. If that's what you wanted. But flip it around. What if there is something bigger going on than me interviewing you about your birth parents? What if this turns out to be something that, I don't know, somebody sees that helps them realize how valuable life really is?"

David thought a moment, then looked up at Nate. "You promise, if I ask you to delete the recordings, you'll do it?"

"A hundred percent."

David stood and sat in the chair Nate had set up at the foot of the bed.

Nate smoothed out the wrinkles on the bed and took his place behind the camera. "This looks fantastic. You ready?"

"What do you want me to talk about?"

"Just let it come from inside. Start with how you've felt about your adoption. Begin there. And look right in the lens, right here, okay?" Nate hit the Record button and pointed at David.

"I always wondered why they put me up for adoption.

I guess I put it out of my mind because I didn't want to be different."

"Wait, wait," Nate said. "Can you say that again? You didn't want to be an idiot?"

"I didn't want to be different. *Different.*"

"Okay, good," Nate said. "That's a lot better. Let's try that again but give me more, okay?"

"More what?"

"I don't know, more emotion? Look, I need to see it in your eyes. I need to feel it in your words." Nate gestured with his hands.

"What?" David said. He grabbed a tennis ball and tossed it in front of him.

"You have the emotion of a rock," Nate said. "I need you to pull me in a little bit. Okay? I need something else from you. Just talk about not fitting in but don't hold anything in. Put it all out there. All right? Don't hold anything back."

"Okay," David said, sitting up straight on the bed.

"And action," Nate said.

Suddenly David transformed, contorting his face and smacking himself. "I didn't want to be different! I just wanted to fit in!"

"Dude, are you kidding me?" Nate said, deadpan.

"What is wrong with me?" David said, his hands shaking with drama.

Nate stopped the recording. "That's a cut."

David laughed, then got back into character. "I'm so emotional right now . . ." Then he doubled over with laughter.

"You're such a diva," Nate said, moving to the other side of the room. "We'll take five."

David called downstairs, "Hey, do we have any ice cream in the freezer?"

"We do," his mom said. "I'll bring some up."

By the look on Nate's face, he was pleased with the idea. Behind him, David heard an alert and turned to his computer. He sat at his desk and found the message.

"It's Brian's wife. My birth father's wife."

Nate became animated and stood. "Okay, hold on, let me get this." He moved the tripod and set it up behind David, then told him he was rolling.

David read the message. "'This is a lot for Brian to process. He wants to take it slow. I'm sorry if this isn't what you were hoping for.'"

"How does that make you feel?" Nate said.

David sat back. "He doesn't want to talk."

Nate's shoulders slumped. "Dude?"

"Oh, sorry." David contorted his face. "He doesn't want to talk to me!"

"Are you serious? That was terrible."

"Well, we can go again if you want."

David's mom arrived with two bowls of ice cream. "Are you guys okay?"

"No, I'm trying to get some emotion out of this heart of stone," Nate said.

"Oh, bless you, honey," she said to Nate.

David took the bowl and turned back to the computer. Something caught his eye. "No way."

"What is it?" David's mom said.

"I just got a message back from Melissa."

"Just now?"

"Yeah."

"What did she say?"

"She wants to meet."

"Really?" his mom said.

"Yeah. Okay, wait, I didn't think we were going to meet in person."

"Well, does that make you feel uncomfortable?" his mom said.

David glanced at Nate and saw he had started the recording. His mom realized it at the same time. "Oh, sorry. I'll leave you guys to it."

"Bye, Mrs. C.," Nate said, his mouth full of ice cream. When she was gone, Nate said, "Let's take it from the top. I want to build off of what just happened here. That was a sweet moment. Can we try that? Take it from the top?"

✦ ✦ ✦

Susan dumped the clothes and linens on the bed in front
of her. Jimmy grabbed a towel and began folding it.

"I just wish he'd open up to me more," Susan said.

"Do you think you might be prying a little?"

"I'm not trying to pry. It's just that . . . is he even going
about this the right way?"

"Honey, do you think there is a certain way he should
be going about this?"

"No, sorry," she whispered. She sat on the bed. "You
know what it is? I've been picturing this moment ever
since he was a little guy. And now we're here. I just
thought that we'd take this journey together. Instead, he's
upstairs on his computer. Unless he tells me what he's
doing, I don't really know what he's doing."

"Honey, David's got to want to do this for himself.
He's not going to do it at all if he feels pushed."

Susan sighed and kept folding.

"You know what?" Jimmy said. "We haven't even
prayed about this like we should. Let's put these away
and do that."

Susan smiled as Jimmy took the pile into the next
room. When he was gone, she opened the dresser drawer
and pulled out a box of cookies.

"Hey, I had a thought," Jimmy said, coming back into
the room.

Wide-eyed, Susan looked up at him. Her cheek bulged with the uneaten cookie.

"Are you still hiding cookies?" Jimmy said.

"I need these," Susan said.

Jimmy paused as if wondering what to say next.

"Can we still pray?" she said.

Jimmy came around the foot of the bed, smiling. "Not until you share one of those."

Susan laughed and it felt like she was letting go of something as she did.

CHAPTER 26

✦ ✦ ✦

The lake was an hour away, the perfect distance for the family to feel like they were secluded but still close to home. Since he was little, David had loved coming here with his parents and grandparents and they had made some rich, warm memories. His grandmother, G, always made her signature fruit salad and they feasted on it throughout their stay. Then there were the fishing expeditions in their bass boat. And on this getaway, Paw Paw wound up catching most of the fish they would fry on the campfire that evening.

After dinner they gathered at the fire and listened

to Paw Paw tell his most-requested hunting and fishing stories from his childhood. David could recite several of them word for word, he had heard them so many times, but that was the thing about being around family. Their shared stories bonded them. And David hoped his story would do the same, that one day he might bring his own children to this spot and camp with them and tell them what it was like when he found his biological mom and dad.

"So, David, tell us the latest," G said. "Have you learned anything new about Melissa and Brian?"

"Well, they were married shortly after I was born and then divorced a few years later. Brian has a daughter now. He married a woman named Azure."

"Azure?" Paw Paw said. "That's a pretty name."

"Melissa married a man named Shawn Cates."

"Do they have children?" G said.

"I'm not sure. I guess I'll find out if we meet."

"If?" G said.

"I'm still thinking about it. All the ramifications. It didn't seem like Brian was ready to talk."

"Hmm," G said.

"Melissa said she and her husband, Shawn, actually don't live that far from Brian and Azure."

"Did Brian give a reason for not being ready to talk?" Susan said.

"No, he didn't. I guess it's just a lot for him to process."

"Who spends a lot to play chess?" Paw Paw said.

G repeated what David had said to Paw Paw a little louder and David saw his mother smile at the way she cared for him.

"How is Melissa?" G said.

"She's nice," David said. "She's a little paranoid of social media."

"I can understand that," his dad said. "I don't really like it either."

"We've written back and forth several times," David said. "And she still wants to meet."

"Do you know what you'd say to her?" his mom said.

David thought for a moment, warmed by the fire. He looked at his mother and said, "Thank you."

"I'd thank her too," Paw Paw said. "She gave us our grandson."

They ate the rest of the s'mores and talked until late in the night. Before Paw Paw went to his tent, he took David aside.

"Have you used those train tickets you got for your birthday?"

"No, I haven't decided where I want to go."

Paw Paw nodded and it looked like he had an idea.

"What?" David said. "Where do you think I ought to go?"

"Oh, that's tee-totally up to you. I was just thinking it would be nice for you to have a place you want to go instead of have to."

He patted David on the back. "Good night."

As David zipped up his tent, he looked through the net at the stars and the glowing remnants of campfires reflected on the lake. He appreciated Nate, but he was glad his friend hadn't come with them or the fishing and campfire would have turned into a Cecil B. DeMille production.

He lay back in his sleeping bag and wondered about Melissa and Brian. Was there conflict between them? Was he walking into something he might regret?

And then he recalled the story his mother often told about why Melissa had chosen her. She wanted someone who could bait a hook for herself, someone who could raise David well and teach him to fish. And his mother had done just that.

The joker card was nailed to an oak tree by the barn on Melissa and Shawn's property. It was Melissa's turn and the last two knives hit the card with a whack. Melissa raised her hands in triumph and yelled, "Beat you!"

Shawn, hands on hips and head turned in frustration, took the good-natured ribbing from his wife. He walked to the tree and removed the knives.

"You owe me a back rub," she said. "That's two out of three."

"I can count." Shawn returned to her and took aim. He hit the joker, but the knife didn't stick like Melissa's. It twisted in the card and fell to the ground and Melissa laughed.

"All right, what's the deal?" Shawn said.

She drew close. "You're throwing it like a baseball."

"Best three out of five," Shawn said.

"I knew you were going to say that! You can't change the rules. I won."

Shawn laughed as Melissa straightened the card and retrieved the knife.

"So how's David?" Shawn said.

A deep sigh. "I don't know. I mean, he's cordial. But I say a lot and he says a little."

"Oh, that can't be surprising to you."

"I know, I talk too much," she said, pulling the knife back to throw. It stuck in the card with a whack. Shawn shook his head. The next throw was dead center and Shawn stared with mouth open. "But I just . . . It would be nice to actually see him."

Melissa hit her third throw and as Shawn walked to the tree, he turned. "Why don't you ask God for it?"

"Oh, I have. Like a lot."

Shawn studied the knives in his hands as if he might

figure out the secret to her success. "And He hasn't responded?"

"You mean David?"

"No, God. You don't think He wants this to happen?"

"I guess He does. You know the whole thing about the three answers God can give. Yes, no, and not yet."

"Maybe we ask our study group to pray with us?" Shawn said.

"If I did that, I'd have to tell them the story."

"You don't think they could handle it? Those people care about you, Melissa."

"I know. But it's been a secret so long."

Shawn wound up and threw again. This time he not only missed the card, he missed the tree.

"Don't say it," he said.

"I didn't say anything," Melissa said, trying not to laugh.

"You know what I've heard about prayer? Sometimes we don't ask too much. We ask too little. We don't think God is powerful enough to grant our requests, so we hold back. Why don't you pray something big?"

"Like what?"

"I don't know. Ask God to work it out that David wants to meet soon. Like in the next couple of weeks."

She smiled again and shook her head. "I was looking on a map last night, trying to figure out the halfway point between here and Louisiana. Wouldn't it be something to pull up in front of their house one day—?"

"Hold up. You know what you should pray? That he'd want to come here."

"Here?"

"Why not? See where you live. Where he was born."

"That's way too much to . . ."

Shawn gave her a knowing look.

"I'd be happy if he'd let us drive to his house for just twenty minutes. I don't need him to come here."

"Well, if you don't want him to come here—"

"No, I do. It just feels like . . . presuming on God."

"Presuming to tell Him what you'd like? I don't think that's presuming at all. And if God says no, at least you were honest with Him."

The next evening, as Shawn grilled steaks, Melissa brought a bowl of marinated chicken pieces and asked if Shawn would grill them for dinner the next day. With tongs, she put the chicken on the grill and her phone rang.

"Just hit the speaker for me," Melissa said.

"Hello?" Shawn said.

"Hi, I'm looking for Melissa Cates."

"I'm here," Melissa said.

"This is Mandy from Kirsh and Clark. We've received a message from David Colton."

Melissa's mouth dropped and she glanced at Shawn.

"He said you guys have been talking over the Internet," Mandy continued, "and he's open to meeting in person. But, of course, that would have to be acceptable to both parties."

Melissa couldn't contain her joy. She gave Shawn a huge smile as she listened, stunned at the call. She couldn't help thinking of what Shawn had said about prayer.

"Oh yes! Yes, we are. We'd be happy to meet in person. Where do we need to go?"

"Well, apparently, he's willing to come to you."

Melissa stared at the phone. "He is?"

"Yes, ma'am. How would you like us to respond?"

Melissa covered her mouth with both hands. She buried her head in Shawn's chest and he held her.

"Ma'am?"

"She can't talk right now, Mandy," Shawn said. "But you can tell David that Melissa is overjoyed that he wants to come see her."

✦ ✦ ✦

David made the mistake of telling Nate about his plans for dinner with his family. Nate insisted on being there to shoot video for the documentary.

"We're just going to eat dinner and then I'm going to give them letters I wrote them. It's no big deal."

"What kind of letters?"

"Stuff that's hard to say. You know, how I feel about them. I want them to know that even though I'm going to see my birth mom, they'll always be my parents."

"Dude, that's like off-the-charts emotional."

"No, it's not. They're just going to read the letters."

"I have to be there. I won't let you say no. I will break into your house while your paw paw is saying grace if I have to."

David rolled his eyes. "Fine. But it's not going to be emotional."

On the afternoon of the dinner, David printed the letters and sealed them in envelopes, making sure each was labeled correctly. Nate followed him to the dining room, where his family waited. David sat and cleared his throat, his cheeks flushing red. Strange. His hands shook, just like they had at the speech tournament.

"Before Mom and Dad and I go to Indiana, I wanted to share a few things. When the idea of going to visit my birth mom first came up, I thought it would make things uncomfortable. But a part of me wanted to fill in this missing piece of the puzzle."

"Do you feel that something has been missing from your life?" G said.

"I guess I shouldn't say 'missing a piece of the puzzle.'"

"Who's missing a piece of the pizza?" Paw Paw said.

"Puzzle, dear," G said to Paw Paw.

"No, it's not that something's missing. It's more about asking the question of what my life would have been like. And just simply thanking Melissa for the choice she made."

"Honey, we want you to go on this journey," his mother said. "I mean, puzzles are a big part of life. And if you want to fill in a piece that you don't have, we're all for it."

"I think that this trip might be a discovery of how big that piece is," his father said. "And not just for you, but for all of us."

"I guess I just wanted to share something with the most significant people in my life." David grabbed the envelopes and gave them to the four around the table. Nate focused on David's mother and father, then on his grandparents.

David watched as one by one they opened the letters and began to read, glancing up at him, then back at the words.

To his grandparents he had written, *You are the most generous, beautiful, and amazing people I know; I am truly lucky to have both of you in my life in such important roles.*

His mother broke the silence and began to read hers aloud.

"'I'm not sure how either of you feels when you think about Melissa and Brian and how I'm not your birth son, and that bothers me sometimes. I hope the fact that they're my birth parents never deters you from realizing that the both of you are my true parents, and I hope that I never do anything to make it seem like I don't know that.'"

Hearing his own words read by his mother, spoken in the voice he loved, brought David to tears. He covered his mouth with a hand and couldn't hold back the emotion.

"Honey," his mom said, "that never bothers me a bit. It's irrelevant." She stood and came around the table and enveloped him in a hug. "David, I love you."

Through his tears he saw his father adjust his glasses and wipe his eyes. Even Nate reached out and patted him on the arm.

"Thank you," Paw Paw said, holding up his letter. "Thank you for sharing your heart. I'm going to treasure this."

"We both will," G said.

"I just don't want anyone to feel replaced," David said.

His dad beamed from the other end of the table. "I already know you love us." He held up the letter. "Now I just have proof."

CHAPTER 27

✦ ✦ ✦

Nate had been beside himself with excitement when David offered him the second train ticket. David's dad drove them to the station and the two jumped out and ran to the train with Nate shooting the entire flight from the car to the tracks.

David jumped onto the train car but Nate lingered outside, turning the phone toward himself and explaining the trip. David grabbed his backpack and pulled him up the steps.

"You don't have to film everything," David said as they walked through the first car.

"I'm not. Just almost everything. Now tell me what you're thinking."

"I'm thinking you don't have to film everything."

"Dude, this is why I came. Trust my genius. It's all part of the film *David Steps Out and Finds Himself Within*."

"What does that mean?"

"That's the title of the movie."

David couldn't help making a face. "That's dumb."

"Okay, what about *Journey of Uncertainty*?"

"That's worse."

"What about *Questie with My Bestie*?"

"Stop," David said, reaching the sleeping car and searching for his room.

"Fine. But you'll thank me one day. Hey, where are we meeting your parents?"

"At the hotel. I can't believe they decided to drive this far."

"That's commitment. Well, you're their only kid."

David opened the door to their compartment and Nate gasped behind him.

"Luxury! I got top bunk!"

+ + +

Melissa awoke entwined in the bedsheet, having rolled and changed positions through the night. She hadn't slept well, glancing at the glowing red numbers about every hour. She made breakfast for Shawn and her but didn't touch much of the eggs and bacon and hash browns. When she sat, she had to stand, and when she stood, she had to pace the room.

"You're going to wear a hole in the floor if you don't stop," Shawn said. "What was with you last night?"

"Nervous, I guess."

She sat and took out her phone and scrolled through the conversations she'd had with David. He was probably getting on the train at that very moment. And in about twenty-four hours, she would see him face-to-face. The thought thrilled her and frightened her at the same time.

The phone rang and it startled her. She picked up and heard Courtney's voice. "Can you believe he's going to be here tomorrow, Mom? I can't wait!"

Melissa found her favorite chair and sat. "Yeah, it's going to be great to see him, isn't it?"

"The best," Courtney said. "Do you think he'll want to stay with us after he meets us? Or maybe come to the house and stay over the summer? Can we ask him? We've got the extra room."

"I don't know, spider monkey. Let's try to keep our expectations low and see how it goes, okay?"

"Aww," Courtney said. "Can't you text and ask him?"

"Not now. Let's just meet first and then see what happens."

"Is Shawn coming to pick me up?"

"Yeah, he'll be there soon. He's finishing his breakfast."

"Okay. Mom, I'm so excited."

Melissa smiled. "See you soon, sweetie." She hung up, then rocked back and forth on the chair, clicking her nails against the back of the phone.

"So Brian and Azure know about David coming, right?" Shawn said.

"Yeah, I told him when I dropped Courtney off."

"What was his reaction?"

"You know Brian," she said. "I don't know what's going on in there. Or if anything's going on."

"Maybe Azure will help him see the value of reaching out."

"Maybe," she said.

Shawn grabbed his hat and opened the door. "Okay, I'm heading over there. We'll be back in an hour." He gave her a knowing look. "Melissa, you need to tell him before he gets here."

"I know," she said, looking away. She didn't need to ask who he meant.

Shawn stared at her without moving. That unnerved her.

"I know," she said again.

He closed the door and she sat with the phone in front

of her. She didn't know if David would accept his sister when they met. What if he stayed distant from Courtney and the two didn't click? What if he treated her like someone who didn't matter to him? The last thing Courtney needed was another disappointment in her life.

Then she had a flicker of a thought that felt like hope. What if instead of the worst, David accepted Courtney? What if he didn't reject or ignore her but showed kindness? What if he really became her older brother and took an interest in her? Would being raised by Susan and Jimmy provide that kind of thoughtfulness and grace? Was that too much to ask of an eighteen-year-old?

She didn't often have those kinds of thoughts because most of life was a worst-case scenario. She had spent her days thinking of all the things that might go wrong and choosing the worst because she thought the worst would probably come true. It was hard to break out of that mindset with the pain of her past.

And then she thought of Shawn and remembered what God had done in her life. She looked at the phone and decided not to let her fear guide her with David. She needed to believe that God was big enough to help them overcome anything that came between them. Faith instead of fear.

Just one step, she thought. *Just one text. Lord, help me.*

✦ ✦ ✦

David sat across a table from Nate in the dining car. The server had brought their drinks and sandwiches, and Nate was talking about an idea he had for a shot of David meeting Melissa for the first time. He wanted to shoot from above.

"I wish my drone was fixed—that would have been perfect."

"Don't overthink it," David said. "Just capturing the moment will be enough."

"Yeah, but I want anybody who watches it to feel what you and Melissa feel. That's how you hook people—you make them part of the experience."

"Then stay on the ground. Going up fifty feet in the air takes you away from what's happening."

Nate took a bite of his sandwich. "You might have a point there. Maybe I get an extreme close-up. You know, like in those 3D movies where it feels like you're inside the eyeball of the main character."

"No, you're not going to intrude like that, okay? That's why God created the zoom feature."

Nate laughed. "Good one. Okay, I won't get too close." He took another bite and sat back. "So what do you think it'll be like? For you, I mean. When you see her the first time."

David glanced at a mother at a table in the corner with

two children. Where were they going? What were they talking about as the miles rolled past?

"I'm not sure how I'll feel," David said. "It all feels surreal right now. Like it's happening to somebody else."

"That's good," Nate said. "You need to say that on camera."

David reached out and stopped Nate. "No, no camera right now. Just eat your lunch."

A message arrived and David picked up his phone. A single-word text was on the screen.

Hey.

"Oh, wow," David said.

"What?" Nate said.

"It's Melissa." Three dots under the text meant she was writing something. When it came, David read it to Nate.

"'I need to tell you something that I haven't mentioned yet.'"

Nate leaned over the table. "Well, what is it?"

"I don't know. It says she's still typing."

Nate's face brightened. "Dude, what if she won the lottery? And she's loaded?"

David gave him a skeptical glance.

"She won the lottery and she's loaded," Nate continued, "and when we get there, there's going to be like a massive house."

"No," David said. "I don't think so."

"Okay, well, maybe she feels bad that she's loaded and she didn't tell you. So when you get there, she's going to give you a portion and then you're going to be loaded too!"

David was glued to the phone, waiting. The little dots on the screen disappeared. "She stopped typing."

"Okay, look. The minute she texts you back, I need you to read it out and give me a big reaction, okay?"

This was the problem with having Nate along. David couldn't simply react, he had to filter it through Nate's cinematic mind.

What could it be? he thought. What had Melissa failed to tell him about herself? Had some doctor given her a bad diagnosis? Was she going through chemo and had lost her hair?

Nate had his camera up, focused on David's face, but he seemed to squirm for some reason.

"You good?" David said. "What's going on?"

"What's she say?" Nate said.

"She's still typing," David said.

Nate groaned, his eyes darting. He bounced on his chair, still trying to hold his phone to catch David's reaction.

"What's wrong?" David said. Then he spotted Nate's empty glass of soda.

"I've got to go to the bathroom!"

"Then go."

"I can't miss your reaction." Nate looked behind him

as if searching frantically for the nearest restroom. David knew it was in the next car.

Finally Nate could stand it no longer. "All right, don't read that until I get back, okay?" He pushed his chair back and hurried away.

David turned his attention to his phone again. He felt a rising tide of anxiety. He took a deep breath and rubbed his hands on his jeans.

Melissa looked at the words she'd written, the secret that wouldn't be a secret any longer. There was something about sending a text like this that felt like releasing birds. Where would they fly? When she hit Send, she would lose control.

Father, I don't know how David will react to this. But I pray that this would be welcome news to him and not something that turns his heart away from me. I trust in You to do something good in our lives.

As she said *amen*, she hit the Send button and waited.

David ran through more scenarios of what Melissa might want to tell him. His thoughts were interrupted by the phone alert showing he'd received another message. He grabbed it and read the words. Then he stood as if he couldn't sit and read the text.

"Oh, wow," he said, and emotion began to flood. "Oh, wow!"

Nate returned, wide-eyed. "Dude, did she respond? Did you read it?"

David handed Nate the phone. He read the text and looked up at David, clearly shocked. "You have a sister?" Then in a voice the whole train could hear, Nate yelled, "You have a sister! Dude, this is crazy! This is like, 'Luke, I am your father.'"

David sat and tried to bring Nate's tone down. "I'm pretty sure it's not the same thing."

"This is huge!" Nate yelled. Then it became clear to him how many people were staring at them and he sat. "What's her name? Is it Leia?" When David didn't answer, he lowered his voice as if he'd figured out the mystery. "Is it Rey?"

A new message came. David smiled as he said, "Her name is Courtney and she's twelve."

Nate seemed just as moved as David. "Princess Courtney. This is incredible!" He snapped out of his reverie and pulled up the camera on his phone. "Okay, this is good. Let's do this. Really focus in on me. Give me a good reaction, like you just got the text for the first time. You ready? Okay. And go."

It wasn't hard for David to act surprised. He was still reeling from the text. He spoke to himself and pondered the words as he did.

"I have a sister."

Nate looked at David. "Tears? Can you pull tears? Maybe that's too much."

Nate gave him more direction, but he finally said, "Cut."

"Okay, now put that down," David said. "Why would she wait so long to tell me that?"

"Dude, you think your sister will be there tomorrow?"

"She has to be. I want to see her."

"Wow, this story just keeps getting better."

"I should take her something."

"What do you mean, like a present?"

"Yeah, you know, just something I can give her since I've missed all her birthdays. What would a twelve-year-old—?"

"What about flowers?"

"Do girls that age like flowers?" David said.

Nate pulled up the screen on his phone. "I know exactly who to ask."

Nate dialed Reese as they walked to their sleeping car. Then he put her on speakerphone.

"Nate, why are you asking me this? You're so obtuse."

"I know, but I'm trying to lose weight," Nate said, winking at David. He whispered, "Listen to this."

"I said *obtuse*, not *obese*. I'm hanging up."

"No, no, don't, Reese. David is here. You know we're going to see his birth mom, right?"

"Whatever."

"She just texted him and said he has a full-blooded sister that he has never known about. And I was thinking it would be good for him to bring her something. What did you like when you were twelve?"

"How am I supposed to know what she likes?" Reese said. "Text her mom back and ask her."

"Just humor me," Nate said. "Think back a few years. What did you like to do when you were that age?"

"I don't know, maybe a stuffed animal. You can't go wrong with a stuffed animal."

The line went silent for a moment.

"Is that it?" Nate said. "Got anything else?"

"No. I mean, maybe. I was just thinking of the present Dad got me on my birthday that year."

"What was it?" Nate said.

David listened as Reese's voice changed. It was like she was reliving her childhood as she described the present. And when Reese was finished telling the story, David leaned forward and spoke into the phone.

"Reese, this is David. Thank you for that. I know exactly what I'm going to get her."

"Well, good luck meeting your sister," Reese said, her voice devoid of emotion. "I hope she's nothing like my little brother."

"Oh, so kind of you, big sister," Nate said.

✦ ✦ ✦

Brian had placed Courtney's backpack by the front door so she could leave as soon as Shawn arrived. She was playing a video game with Presley and Azure in the family room.

When he heard the rumble of Shawn's Jeep in the driveway, he yelled, "Courtney, time to go."

"Just a minute!" Courtney called. "I have to finish this game."

Brian took a deep breath and watched Shawn come up the sidewalk. He didn't have much contact with the man other than saying hello when he picked Courtney up from her court-ordered visit. He grabbed Courtney's backpack and opened the door and yelled behind him, "Make it quick!"

Shawn stood at the bottom of the steps and Brian handed him the backpack. Shawn took it to the Jeep and put it in the back, then turned around.

"She's finishing up some game with Presley. You want me to go get her?"

"No, that's fine," Shawn said with a wave. "I'm in no hurry."

"All right," Brian said, turning to go back inside.

"Hey, could I talk with you about something?" Shawn said.

"I guess." Reluctantly Brian walked down the steps and leaned against the handrail.

Shawn shoved his hands in his pockets. "Look, I know it's none of my business. This whole thing with David."

"Oh, that."

Shawn dipped his head. "I mean, if it were me, I wouldn't want anybody sticking their nose into—"

"No, go ahead. Say what you need to."

"I've been watching some of the videos of him. He looks a lot like you. Tall. Athletic."

"Handsome?" Brian said with a smirk.

Shawn laughed and it seemed to put both of them a little more at ease. "When I look at the videos, there's something in his eyes. He's been given a lot of love. You can tell that. But there's almost a question you can see on his face. Maybe I'm reading too much into it."

"I haven't seen any videos. Just a few pictures. I think Azure saw him wrestling and jumping into the water or something like that."

Shawn nodded and flicked a rock off the concrete with the toe of his shoe. "Meeting him is something Melissa has dreamed about. Having him come up here has her over the moon. That he would come all this way. But she's scared at the same time, you know?"

"What's she got to be scared of?"

"What David will think of her. She still hasn't told him about Courtney. But I keep coming back to the fact that there's a young man in Louisiana who's coming up here who has always wondered about where he came from. About his biological mother and father. Circumstances being what they were, maybe he's asking the question."

"What question is that?"

"Is he a mistake?"

Brian looked out at the lawn he had mowed the day before and noticed a spot he'd missed. Finally he said, "He ain't no mistake."

"Maybe it would help him to hear that from you," Shawn said.

The door banged open and Courtney bounded out like a colt released in a pasture. "Where's my backpack?"

"It's in the car, Courtney," Shawn said. "Give your dad a hug."

She hugged him and he patted her back.

"Bye, Dad. See you next time."

"All right," Brian said.

She turned before she reached the Jeep. "Are you going to see David when he comes to the house? I can't wait!"

Brian glanced at Shawn. "We'll see."

Brian watched them pull out of the driveway. Shawn looked at him one more time and nodded. Brian stood on the porch until they drove away, then went to the back and brought the mower to the front and cut the spot he had missed.

CHAPTER 28

✦ ✦ ✦

The train pulled into the station as shadows fell on the Indiana countryside. David's parents weren't set to arrive for a couple of hours, so David and Nate used a ride-sharing service to get to the hotel. As the driver approached the hotel, David spotted a shopping mall a few blocks away.

"Are you thinking what I'm thinking?" Nate said. "Dinner and a toy store?"

They checked into their room, then walked toward the mall and the restaurants situated nearby.

"Listen, can you keep your camera in your pocket for an hour?" David said. "I just need a little break."

"No problem. Except for the toy store. I mean, you've got to let me shoot you picking it out."

"Okay, but that's it. Promise?"

"Cross my heart and hope to get food poisoning."

"Don't say that," David said.

Susan and Jimmy arrived at the hotel later than they expected. She texted David and told him they were exhausted and going straight to their room for the night. Though she could barely fall into bed, it took her a while to wind down. The anticipation of the day ahead and Jimmy's deep breathing made sleep more difficult.

She kept going over what Melissa's home would be like, how her husband would react to David, and David's text about his biological sister. That news had made her gasp as Jimmy drove. There were so many dynamics going on that would culminate in that one moment when they would meet again. And secretly, though she never wanted to communicate it, Susan wondered if the relationship between her and David might change.

Susan awoke to the smell of coffee and fresh oatmeal. Jimmy had brought it from the breakfast bar in the lobby.

"Thought you could use a few more minutes of rest before we get going," he said.

"You were out like a light last night."

"I thought you would be too."

"I wanted to. There's just so much going on inside."

She ate and dressed and Jimmy pulled the car to the front of the hotel while she went to David's room.

Nate answered and gave her a big smile. "Hey, what's up, Mrs. C.?"

"Is David ready?"

Nate glanced toward the bathroom. "He's still powdering his nose."

"No, I'm not," David yelled. He came to the door and smiled. "Hey, Mom."

"Hey," she said, noticing his new shirt. "Oh, that's nice. I like that." She stepped back, still in the hallway, more questions running through her mind. "So did you ever hear from Brian or Azure?"

"Nope. And at this point I'm not really expecting to."

"Did you have enough breakfast this morning?"

"Yeah, I'm good. You know, I'm a little nervous, but I'm okay."

The conversation felt stiff to her and she wanted to relieve some of David's stress with her words or her presence, but as they looked at each other, she realized how nervous she was.

"You all right?" David said.

"Oh yeah. I'm good. I'm real good." She paused and the silence felt awkward. Finally she said, "So Dad's down in the lobby and I'm going to go meet him and you just come down in like ten minutes?"

"Perfect," David said.

Deep breath. She walked toward the elevator but David called for her. He stepped into the hallway as she turned.

"Look, I know I don't say it enough, but I love you."

Susan's heart melted and all the stress and anxiety seemed to float away as David drew closer.

"You are and always will be my mom."

She put a hand on his shoulder. "David, thank you. I think I really needed to hear that today."

They hugged and Susan said, "I love you."

"I love you."

She pulled back and looked him in the face and with determination said, "Let's go meet Melissa."

✦ ✦ ✦

Jimmy had printed step-by-step directions to Melissa's house. Both David and Nate poked fun at him for not using the GPS on his phone, but Jimmy told them he preferred the old-fashioned way.

"If you let your phone tell you where to go, you never use your brain." He tapped his forehead.

As they drove past cornfields and then through the small town, Susan pointed out the quaint streets and stores with awnings.

"Dude, you could have grown up on the set of *It's a Wonderful Life*," Nate said.

Jimmy took a wrong turn and pretended to be sight-seeing, which only added to the stress in the car and the call to use the GPS. Nate had been shooting video from the time he came down the elevator and seemed intent on getting all the material he could.

When they turned onto the road where Melissa and Shawn's home was, Jimmy looked in the rearview. "David, what makes you most nervous?"

"To see what they're like. To see what traits I may have gotten from them."

"Environment plays a very big part," Susan said.

"But hey, I need to know where my good looks came from."

Nate laughed. "What good looks?"

"I'll give them your good looks, but that's about it," Susan said.

Jimmy checked the sheet. "Okay, it looks like we're almost there."

The home came into view. It was green and white and set in a wooded lot. It seemed to fit perfectly with its surroundings. Jimmy turned onto the gravel drive and slowly pulled forward.

"It's really happening," Nate said, training his camera on the home.

✦ ✦ ✦

Inside, Melissa continued to pace. Shawn and Courtney had left her alone and moved to the kitchen to work on a puzzle.

Melissa had changed her outfit three times before she settled on her jeans and her red blouse and, of course, the cross necklace Shawn had given her after they were married. She wasn't sure if she should try to cover a few of her tattoos, but she had come to the conclusion that she was done hiding things about herself. She was who she was with all of the scars and experiences, mistakes and hurt.

She was glad to be alone in the living room, watching through the window blinds for any sign of the Coltons. Her heart beat wildly with any car that passed. Then a blue minivan slowed and turned in to the driveway.

She couldn't speak, couldn't breathe. She managed to open the front door and then retreated from it. Shaking, she went back to the window and watched as the car came to a stop and a side door opened. A young man in shorts got out and studied the house.

Is that my son? she thought. *Could that be him?*

Melissa walked to the screen door and pushed it open and began weeping with her first steps. She put a hand to her mouth and tried to hold herself together, but her feet were running now and she couldn't hold back the motion or the emotion. It felt like she was being drawn to him by some heavenly magnet.

David met her in a hug and all of the feelings she had held for eighteen years came gushing like a flood. She hugged David with one arm and covered her face with the other hand and sobbed.

All of the questions, all of the fear melted like wax and Melissa was simply there with her son. Instead of looking down at him in that hospital room so long ago, with David wrapped snugly in a blanket and Melissa holding the baby who didn't have a name, she was looking up at him and he was holding her tightly as they stood in the driveway. The son she had placed in another's arms had returned.

"It's good to meet you," David said.

She couldn't answer. Tears were all she had.

✦ ✦ ✦

Susan stood by Jimmy as they watched David and Melissa. It was as if Melissa melted when she reached him. Susan could only think of how grateful she was that such a reunion could take place.

Jimmy put his arm around Susan and neither could take their eyes from the scene. After a few moments, Susan couldn't wait any longer. She approached the two and said, "Can I have a hug too?"

David stepped back and Susan hugged Melissa tightly and said over and over, "I love you, I love you."

Then it was Jimmy's turn. "Melissa, it's good to see you," he said as he hugged her. His was a more careful, tentative hug, but genuine.

✦ ✦ ✦

Spent with emotion, Melissa retreated to David and stood in front of him, looking at him through blurry eyes. She had been overjoyed to see pictures. She was amazed at the videos. But having him here, standing in front of her, was beyond her wildest dreams.

When she could finally speak, she said, "I want you to meet someone."

✦ ✦ ✦

David had watched his mom and dad hug Melissa and felt as moved by their meeting as he had by his own embrace with her. When Melissa turned back to the house, David remembered his sister was waiting too. Having grown up as only child, discovering he had a full-blooded sister was stunning. But instead of that being simply information, he turned to the house and saw a girl in a pink T-shirt with her hair in ponytails.

Courtney walked tentatively through the door onto

the porch and David met her there. Fighting tears himself, he said, "Hi, Courtney. Nice to meet you."

With a shaking voice, Courtney said, "Nice to meet you, too."

She pulled back and looked down at him, as if she were looking for something in his eyes, some way to prove this fairy tale was actually real.

A man with a beard came down the steps and introduced himself. "Shawn Cates. Good to meet you, David." Shawn smiled broadly and it was then that David fully felt like he wasn't an intruder in their lives. He was among people who wanted him to be there.

Shawn shook David's dad's hand and met his mom and Nate.

After an awkward moment of not knowing what to do next, David turned back to Courtney, who hadn't taken her eyes off him. "Can you believe this?" he whispered.

Courtney shook her head, and the smile she gave him looked just like his own.

"Well, everybody come inside," Melissa said.

David followed Courtney and sat next to Melissa on the couch.

"Happy tears," his mom said to Melissa.

"I know," Melissa said. "I've been crying all day. I'm sorry. I'll calm down soon."

"You don't have to calm down," David's mom said. "Don't apologize. Let's just talk."

Melissa put her face in her hands again. "I can't believe you're here." She paused and studied David's face. "I want to say so much. I don't even know where to start."

"No, I'll start," David said, and the room got quiet. "First off, I just want to say thank you. Thank you for making the choice that you did, almost nineteen years ago, to let me be adopted. I mean, you allowed me to have the life that I have now." David looked at his mom and dad and Courtney, then back at Melissa. "Without you I wouldn't have all this. So thank you for that. I'm pretty sure their lives would be pretty boring without me around."

Everyone in the room laughed through their tears.

"But I was wondering if I could hear your story," David said. "And how you made the decision."

Melissa wiped a tear away and nodded. "Okay. Well, it was a confusing time. Scary. Your adoption was hard and easy all at the same time. I mean, going through those 'Dear Mother' letters was . . . overwhelming."

"How many letters did you go through?"

"I don't even know. A lot. But I just knew—when I got your parents' letter, I knew."

"It was because of the hook," David's mom said.

Melissa laughed. "Yeah, I wanted your mom to be down-to-earth. Basically, someone like me." Her voice softened and she said a little sadly, "What I could have been. To do the things I wanted to do with you, but I knew I couldn't. I wanted you to have a mom to be there for you. And she couldn't be afraid to get her hands dirty."

"So any one of those letters could have been my parents."

"Yeah, I guess."

"Do you remember calling me?" David's mom said.

"I do. I do."

"My hands were shaking. I didn't know what to expect."

"When I was getting further into your story—" Melissa turned to David—"into your parents' story, it just grabbed me. Your parents seemed to be genuine. They seemed to have genuine faith, and they didn't use religion as a bargaining chip. Jesus is my Savior now. Jesus is my Lord. It's because of Him all this is happening."

David had wanted to ask about her faith at some point but didn't know how to bring it up. That she had volunteered this important part of her story warmed his heart.

"So what did Brian think about all of this? Me coming back?"

Melissa's voice changed. It lowered and she looked somber. "I'll let him speak for himself."

"Okay, sure." David studied the carpet, wondering if he'd ever get the chance for Brian to speak for himself. Before he could recover, Melissa spoke in a tiny voice, like a child reaching for a hand.

"So were you mad at me?"

David looked up and saw Melissa's tortured face. "Never."

Tears came to her eyes again. "Did you ever think that I didn't want you?"

David rubbed his hands together and leaned back. "Umm . . ."

"I would understand if you did."

"No. I think I just wondered if you ever thought about me. That was my only concern."

Melissa seemed to drink in the words but she didn't say anything. After a moment David said, "Listen. I'm so grateful for my life. But I had a hard time telling people that I was adopted because I hadn't really realized what that meant yet."

David looked around the room at his mom and dad and Courtney. Shawn was there and Nate was busy with his camera. He turned back to Melissa. "But I'm glad that I'm adopted."

Melissa looked him in the eyes. "I thought about you every day."

Another flood of warmth spread through David and he said, "I'm not mad at you. If anything, I'm thankful."

More tears from Melissa and she tried to contain them but couldn't. When she could speak, she turned to David's mom and said, "When you know your baby's not coming

home with you . . . I'd be lying if I said I wasn't jealous.
There's about every emotion you could feel." She looked
back at David. "But I knew you were going to the right
place."

Melissa put a hand to her face and her shoulders shook.
David drew close and put an arm around her. "Thank you.
I've had a great life."

"I know you have," Melissa said through her sobs.

"It's because of you. You gave that to me."

Melissa pulled back. "Thank you," she said quietly.
She looked at Courtney, whose eyes were rimmed with
tears.

His dad's phone rang and he looked at the screen and
stood. "I'm going to take this outside."

Brian had gotten the Coltons' contact information from
Shawn but hadn't figured he'd use it. Now his hand shook
as he heard the ring on the other end. On the third ring
he almost hit the red button to hang up, but then he
heard the voice of a man he assumed was Jimmy Colton.

"Hello?"

"Mr. Colton?"

"Yes?"

"This is Brian Michaels. I was wondering if you could
bring your son over to meet me."

"Oh . . . um, yes. Yes, we can do that."

"I don't know if he still wants to . . ."

"He would like that very much."

"All right. How about tomorrow afternoon?"

"Uh, tomorrow works."

"Melissa can give you our address."

"Okay, great."

"We'll look forward to it."

"Great, I'll tell him."

"All right," Brian said. "See you then."

"Hey," Jimmy Colton said, "thank you for calling."

David watched his father leave and the room grew quiet. He glanced at Nate, still holding the camera. Nate raised his eyebrows, signaling David. David shrugged and Nate tilted his head toward Courtney. When David still didn't get the hint, Nate blew his lips like a horse.

"Oh, I almost forgot," David said. He looked at Courtney. "I've missed a lot of your birthdays. So I have some catching up to do."

"No, you don't," Courtney said, her hands placed tightly between her knees, shoulders hunched forward.

"I've got something in the car I want you to see."

"Let me get it," Nate said. "But you can't look out the window. And you have to wait until I come in to see it because I need to get your reaction to it, okay? No pressure, I just want to make sure I don't miss anything—"

"Nate," David's mom said, "I'll get it."

"Good idea," Nate said.

"Now, if you don't like it, you can return it for something else," David said. "I kept the receipt."

Courtney looked at her mother, her eyes wide.

Susan stepped onto the porch and found Jimmy staring at the front yard. When he turned, his mouth was open as if he'd just heard earth-shattering news.

"You're not going to believe this," he said.

"Hang on. I need to get something from the car."

Jimmy grabbed her arm. "It was him."

"What?"

"On the phone. That was Brian who called me. He wants David to come to his house tomorrow."

Susan's mouth dropped. She hugged Jimmy and turned back to the screen door and pulled him inside. "Tell them," she said. "You have to tell them now."

Jimmy was not used to being the center of attention. He put his phone in his pocket and looked up and saw all eyes in the room on him. Nate had his phone trained on Jimmy's face.

"Who was it, Dad?" David said.

"It was Brian."

"What?" David said.

Shawn took a step forward. "What did he say?"

"He's agreed to meet with David. With us, I guess. He's available tomorrow. Said he wants you to come to his house. Melissa, you have his address."

Shawn smiled broadly, his eyes crinkling. "I'll write the address down for you. I know a shortcut."

✦   ✦   ✦

David could hardly believe it. After the messages back and forth with Azure and all the talk of Brian "processing" things, he'd assumed they wouldn't meet.

"Wow, talk about two birds with one stone," Nate said. "I mean, two parents with one train trip."

Courtney touched David on his arm and he looked down at her.

"Sorry, Courtney. Let's just go out to the car together."

"Wait, let me get in front of you," Nate said. When he was outside near the car, he yelled, "Action!"

David shook his head and opened the door and ushered Courtney to the driveway. They stood at the back of the minivan and Courtney tried to see inside.

"No, no, she has to close her eyes and keep them closed until you show her," Nate said.

"He's the director," David said. "Okay, close your eyes. Dad, can you pop the back door?"

The latch clicked open and David reached inside to pull out his present. He looked at Melissa and there was something about her face he couldn't read. She was crying now and whispered through her tears, "How did you know?"

David shrugged and knelt in front of Courtney. "Keep them closed, Courtney. Before you open them, like I said, I've missed a lot of birthdays and I don't know if you'll like this or not, but . . ."

Courtney's knees knocked and she couldn't contain her smile or her excitement, her body shaking in anticipation.

"I guess you can open them now," David said.

She took her hands away and opened her eyes. David put the horse on the ground in front her. A big stuffed stallion with a flowing mane. Reese, Nate's sister, had suggested it because she had loved playing with horses when she was Courtney's age.

Courtney looked up at David, then at Melissa, and burst into tears. Huge, racking sobs that surprised him and made him think he had done something wrong, something unkind. Melissa knelt on the driveway and hugged her, and David stood and moved back a few steps.

"Didn't expect that," Nate whispered. "Maybe you should have gone with the jump rope."

"It's okay, honey," David's mom said, kneeling beside Courtney and Melissa and trying to comfort the girl.

Shawn came up to David and put an arm around him. He whispered, "She's been asking us to get her a horse. Did you know that?"

David shrugged. "I had no idea."

Shawn shook his head. "Best present ever."

CHAPTER 29

✦ ✦ ✦

David played a boxing video game with Courtney and
everybody laughed when she knocked him out on-screen.
Shawn grilled burgers and they ate and laughed together.
David watched Nate eat as he gathered more video
footage—scarfing french fries as he held the phone,
the ultimate multitasker.

Courtney put the horse on her bed and ate beside
David and followed him all afternoon. They played
another video game, and this time David had no mercy
for his little sister—and she still beat him! As the afternoon continued, Courtney pulled him into her room and
showed him some of the drawings she had made.

"These are fantastic, Courtney. You really have a lot of talent at this. I hope you keep up with it."

She didn't seem to hear the compliment. She left the room and he found her on the couch and sat by her.

"What's with the long face?" he said.

"I don't want you to leave. I just got my big brother."

"Hey, it's so awesome to finally meet you. I still can't believe I have a sister." David looked into her eyes and saw the hurt there and wasn't sure of everything Courtney had been through. Suddenly he got an idea. "I want you to have something." He unclasped his necklace with the cross on it. Courtney moved her ponytails and he put it around her neck and fastened it. She held up the cross and looked at it, then turned to David with a smile. Then she hugged him and put her head on his shoulder.

Melissa and Shawn walked into the room, trailed by Nate with his camera.

"Hey, David," Melissa said. "I wanted to ask you something."

"Yeah, sure, what's up?"

Nate stepped forward for a better shot, and Shawn turned and glared at him.

"Oh, don't mind me, I'm just filming everything," Nate said with a nervous laugh. "By the way, this is gold." He put an arm around Shawn and whispered, "Pure gold."

Shawn gave a reluctant nod and stepped away.

"So I'm kind of a tomboy," Melissa said. "And I like a little adventure. Shawn does, too, as long as it doesn't include heights. I've seen your cliff-jumping videos, and I wondered if you would do something with me."

"Yeah, what's up?"

"Would you go skydiving with me while you're here? No one will go with me."

It felt like something came alive inside David at that moment. "What? Are you kidding? I've always wanted to go! No one will ever take me." He looked at his parents.

His dad smiled and said, "We'll watch from the ground."

Shawn smiled. "No, intentionally jumping out of a perfectly good airplane just doesn't seem like a good idea to me."

"I'm in," David said to Melissa.

"Really? Yes!"

David gave Melissa a high five. After that there were about a million hugs from Courtney, who didn't want him to leave. David knelt before her. "Look, I'll see you again, okay?"

"You promise?" Courtney said.

"You got it, little sister."

In the van, David turned to Nate as he buckled. "Did you get some good stuff?"

"Incredible. This is the best day I've ever photographed."

David clicked his seat belt and thought a moment. "You know, I guess since you're the official videographer that means you have to, like, film everything, right?"

"Yeah," Nate said, changing a setting on his phone.

"Good. Then you're coming skydiving with us."

Nate laughed hard. "No, no, no. Nate is not jumping. That won't happen. Never. Ever!"

David shook his head as Nate struggled with the instructor he was harnessed to and became more agitated in the plane. When they got to altitude and the door opened, Nate began clawing like a scared cat being tossed into a lake. Though he protested and his eyes grew wide, David knew when they got to the ground, he would have great video he could include in the documentary.

After Nate jumped, Melissa and her instructor took their place at the door. She gave David a thumbs-up and yelled, "Let's do it! See you there!"

David watched as Melissa jumped through the door. Then it was his turn. He had jumped from the rocks by the river, but this was in another league. But in a sense, his whole life had become one jump after another, falling into some scary new experience.

"You ready?" his instructor said.

"Yeah, let's do it!"

✦ ✦ ✦

On the ground, Susan sat in a lawn chair, her sunglasses pushed up, unable to look at the plane overhead. Jimmy and Shawn sat next to her with their eyes glued to the sky.

"Melissa's got a little adventure in her," Jimmy said.

As relaxed as anyone could be, Shawn said, "She sure does."

Susan put her hands together in front of her, her knuckles white.

"David seems to be pretty even-keeled," Shawn said.

Susan put her head in her hands now, praying, begging God to just let them make it to the ground safely.

"This Nate fellow," Shawn said. "Is he . . . okay?"

"Depends on what you mean by okay," Jimmy said.

"He seems to be pretty dramatic," Shawn said.

"Are they out of the plane?" Susan said, still unable to look.

"They're out," Jimmy said. "And the chutes are up."

"Looks like they're almost ready to land," Shawn said.

Finally Susan got up the nerve to look. One glimpse of David's face, even from this distance, eased her fears. He was smiling from ear to ear.

✦ ✦ ✦

As Melissa came in for a landing, she couldn't stop yelling. The feeling of jumping and falling and then being caught by the wind and settling to the ground so gently made her heart race.

Her instructor unhooked her and she ran to David, who had just touched down. "Wasn't that a rush?"

"That was so worth it," David said, hugging Melissa.

"We did it," she said.

"That was amazing."

She laughed and pointed at Nate. He had jumped first and was landing last, probably because he wanted the parachute pulled early, she guessed.

Nate yelled and moved his legs wildly, like a cartoon character, and though the instructor tried to help, he landed on his rear and toppled, the instructor falling on him.

As Nate struggled to get to his feet, David yelled, "Hey, did you survive over there?"

Nate pulled his helmet off, gasping for breath. "So not worth it! So not worth it!" He knelt and leaned forward, kissing the grass again and again.

Melissa laughed as they watched the instructor help Nate to his feet. Then she turned to her son with one more idea. She knew he had train tickets for the return ride, but there was one other place she wanted to go.

"Hey, I don't know how much time you have before you leave, but after you meet with Brian, could I show you one more thing?"

"Yeah, sure. How about Saturday morning?"

Melissa smiled. "Perfect."

✦ ✦ ✦

Brian Michaels was a ball of nerves all day. He got home from work and started a fire in the firepit he'd made in the backyard. Back here was his oasis, where he could escape the pressures of life.

But the one thing he couldn't escape was David. And now that Azure knew his secret and had encouraged him to reach out to his son, Brian felt a little of the stress lifting. A little guilt and shame and whatever else it was that had festered inside through the years was ebbing from him. Still, he was nervous, standing and walking to the front of the house and looking up and down the road.

Finally he decided he would just sit there until something happened and not jump up at every passing car.

"Big day," Azure said, sitting beside him.

"Yeah," Brian said, glancing at Presley as she played in the yard.

"She's been looking forward to this all day," Azure said. "Keeps saying she can't wait to see 'Javid.' Guess we need work on her *d*'s."

Brian stared at the fire and the torches that were there to keep the mosquitoes away. He rubbed his hands together and watched Presley pick a dandelion he'd missed.

"What are you feeling?" Azure said.

"I've been trying my whole life not to feel anything. It's hard to put into words. But it does seem like I'm going through a situation here that has me on the outside looking in."

"What do you mean?"

"Like everything's happening to me and I don't have a say in it. Just like all those years ago."

"You could call them and tell them you've changed your mind."

"No, that would be worse. Part of me just wants to get it over with, meeting him and all."

"What does the other part of you want?"

"The other part's curious. I wonder if he's as good-looking as I am."

Azure laughed. "And humble?"

Brian smiled and poked at the fire. "Yeah."

"Why did Courtney call you earlier?"

"She wanted to tell me about meeting him. She sounded kind of sad, to be honest. She wanted to come over here and join us, but I didn't think that was a good idea."

"This is a big shock for all of us," Azure said. "But in the end, I think it'll be good. Maybe meeting David will help you. You're not hiding that part of your past anymore."

Brian nodded. He heard a car pull up at the front

of the house. Then a couple of doors slammed. He had texted Jimmy to just come around the back when they arrived.

Brian stood and walked a few steps away from the fire, and around the corner came a redheaded kid holding up a phone. And then Brian saw him. Almost as tall as he was. Brown hair like an ocean wave. And his walk—the amble was just like his own. It was like looking in a mirror.

Brian reached out a hand and David shook it and came closer, hugging him with his other arm.

"What's up, Brian? Nice to meet you," David said.

"Nice to meet you," Brian said. He looked David in the face, then got sidetracked by the redheaded kid with the phone. Who was he and what was doing here?

"Don't let the camera guy weird you out," David said. "This is Nate, my best friend. He wanted to help us remember all of this."

Nate held out a fist and Brian bumped it.

"Nice to meet you," Nate said.

"Yeah, well, I'll do my best to ignore you," Brian said. "And the camera." He gave a quick smile and Nate laughed. "Well, come on and sit."

Azure shook hands with Jimmy and Susan. She was a lot better with this kind of thing than he was. When they were finally seated, David took the lead and Brian was glad of it.

"I just wanted to say thank you for letting us stop by. Very kind of you."

Brian studied David's face, his warm smile, the way he was able to communicate so easily. "Yeah, you're welcome."

There was an uneasy silence then, and Brian wasn't sure if he should say something or stay quiet. Azure sat next to him and he could tell from the way she looked at the ground that she was going to let him do this on his own and not take over. With his mouth dry, he took a breath and started.

"You know, I've been carrying this secret with me for almost two decades now. I didn't tell my wife until a couple of weeks ago. That was a relief."

Brian looked at Azure and she touched him on the shoulder, encouraging him on. When he found the words, he spoke again. "My mom was adopted. Her mom couldn't raise her and she hated her for it. So I always figured that you'd hate me too."

"No, I don't hate you at all."

Brian looked into the face of his son as if he could see deep into his soul, and he believed David was telling the truth. He felt moisture come to his eyes and tried to shake it off but couldn't. He looked at the fire and smiled. "That's good to hear." Then he looked away and nobody said anything, and it felt like all the words had left the world.

He lifted a hand and Azure took it. When he spoke, his voice trembled. "You know, that's why I had such a hard time choosing adoption, because of that. But now that I look back at it, the other option that we considered was worse. Much worse. And I'm sorry. It was kind of foolish when I think about it now."

"I actually wanted to thank you. You're part of the reason I have all of this." David looked at his parents. "Thank you."

"You know, there were times when I thought, what if we would have kept you? But I look at you and I see your parents, and I realize that it was the right call."

David couldn't help staring at Brian, his mannerisms, the way he seemed to process life. When they walked inside, he saw Brian's gait and recognized his own walk, the way he held his hands to his sides and took long strides.

When Brian said he had made "the right call" on letting David be adopted, something stirred inside. Their lives would have been a lot easier if they had simply gone for an abortion. That thought led him down a different trail altogether and it was not a trail he cared to travel. Maybe there was more to his story than they had told him. He wanted to ask Brian, but he didn't feel like this was the time or the place.

Azure asked David to come to Presley's room and he felt bad when he realized he hadn't brought her a gift. His sister wanted him to see her collection of toys and books. David followed them and Presley showed him every stuffed animal she had in her closet and told him what each was named.

"She can't say her *d*'s too well, so you're Javid to her," Azure said.

"Javid's fine with me."

Presley handed him a book from her nightstand and asked David to read it.

"No, honey," Azure said. "David needs to go talk with Daddy."

Presley gave her mother a quizzical look.

"I know what," David said. "Let me tell you a different story. It's one about a family of geese my dad told me a long time ago. Want to hear it?"

Jimmy watched Susan break the ice with the Michaels family. She was so good at smiling and making others feel comfortable, even with Nate following everyone around the house with his phone. David went into one of the back rooms with Azure and Presley, then they came to the living room and Presley had to show David all the pictures in their photo album.

Brian wandered into the kitchen and Jimmy approached him. "So Presley is five years old?"

Brian handed him a can of soda and leaned back against the sink, shoulder to shoulder with Jimmy. "Yeah. I guess she would be David's half sister."

A silence followed and Jimmy took a breath. He had planned to talk with Brian and say what was on his heart at some point, but he wasn't sure Brian was ready for anything but small talk. Finally he launched in.

"Hey, thank you for having us over. It really means a lot to David that he got to meet you."

Brian turned and looked at Jimmy, then looked at the floor. "I'm just sorry it took so long."

His words were filled with regret and his face showed shame.

"I understand," Jimmy said.

Brian kept his eyes on David and Presley and leaned forward as if he were trying to gain momentum to get something out, like digging at a splinter jammed deep in his soul. Finally he turned to Jimmy with a furrowed brow. "Thank you for raising him in a way that I know I never could. I'm certain that he's going to go much farther than I ever did."

Brian reached out a hand and Jimmy shook it, and something was exchanged between them, a strength for strength. Jimmy couldn't help feeling that he might be taking some of the pain and regret from Brian in that handshake.

"You gave him that," Brian said. And that was it. He turned and walked into the living room.

Stunned at what had just happened, at the depth of Brian's words and what they meant, Jimmy stood in the kitchen, unable to move. He had always felt blessed by David's presence in their home. He was a gift to them, and as David liked to say, he kept their lives from being boring. But perhaps for the first time, he considered what he had given David—not just a roof and a room and support to launch into life with a strong faith and confidence in himself, but also a knowledge that he was loved unconditionally. He had always tried to treat David so he knew his father's love wasn't about how he performed but because he was a beloved son and always would be.

From the living room, Jimmy heard Presley say, "Daddy!" Brian picked her up and lifted her high.

Jimmy turned toward the wall and put his soda on the counter and tried to take in what he had heard and what was happening in that house. When he looked up, David was walking into the kitchen. The sight made Jimmy's heart swell.

"I love you, Dad," David said, moving toward him and giving him a hug that Jimmy knew he would never forget.

Jimmy patted David on the back and they embraced until Susan came in the kitchen. She didn't ask anything, just joined them in the hug.

CHAPTER 30

✦ ✦ ✦

On the drive to the hotel that night, David talked about what he had discovered about Brian and some of the questions he still had about grandparents and extended family.

"Brian is not the most talkative person," Nate said.

"Yeah, but I felt like he was really glad to see David," David's dad said.

His mother turned in her seat. "Azure told me that from her perspective, this whole thing has done something to Brian."

"What do you mean?" David said.

"She told me he cried when he told her about what happened. She said Brian never cries about anything."

"I can believe that," Nate said.

"Just before we left," his mother continued, "she pointed out how Brian was holding Presley and hugging her. She said she hasn't seen him do that in a long time. Almost like he's free of something that was holding him back."

Nate turned to David. "What do you think Melissa wants to show you tomorrow?"

David shrugged. "She wouldn't say."

Back in the hotel, David called dibs on the shower. He felt emotionally wrung out. Nate found something on the TV he wanted to watch and David spent a half hour under the flow of hot water, the emotion rising about all he had experienced the past few days. He shook his head at the mysteries of the past that were solved and the ones that weren't.

He dressed and opened the bathroom door to let some of the steam out, expecting to hear the blare of the TV with some action film Nate was watching. Instead, he heard silence. Then he realized Nate was talking on the phone with someone. His voice was low and instead of his joking and fast-talking ways, he sounded upset.

"No, no, Reese, you can't. You have to tell them."
A pause. "No, they won't. You don't know what they're
going to say." Another pause and it sounded like Nate was
choked up. "I know, I know. Just don't do anything, okay?
Just don't do anything, just wait. I'm going to be home
soon and we're going to . . ." Nate grew silent again, then
with more emotion said, "Yeah, okay. Well, I love you.
Yeah, I'll talk to you later."

David had never heard that from Nate before and he
felt bad he had overheard the conversation. He walked
out and noticed Nate with his back turned, the phone on
the bed as if Nate had tossed it there.

David dried his hair with a towel and moved toward
the bed. He touched Nate on the back. "Hey, you good,
man?"

"No, I'm not," Nate said.

Nate turned and David saw the pain on his face.

"Hey, dude," David said, concerned. "What's up?"

Nate sat on the couch and rubbed his chin. When he
spoke, his voice was choked with emotion and his eyes
rimmed with tears. "My sister, she got back with her idiot
boyfriend." A long pause. "And she's pregnant."

David froze. He didn't know what to say. He shook his
head and sighed. "Oh, dude."

"You can't tell anybody, all right?" Nate said.

"No, I won't."

Nate sniffed. "Why? She said she was done with him. I just don't know what to do."

David sat on the edge of the bed. He had known Nate a long time and had never seen him this concerned and upset. "Does it strike you as odd that we would be making a video of my life right now? And then your sister calls and tells you she's going through the same thing Melissa went through?"

"I thought about that," Nate said. "But I don't think she would listen to Melissa or anybody right now. I think she's going to do something she'll regret."

"I get it. But instead of what she might do, look at what she did."

Nate looked up, bewildered. "What do you mean?"

"She called you. She trusted you with that news. That says a lot, don't you think?"

Nate looked away and something sparked in his eyes. "Yeah, you're right. She did call me."

"That tells me she's open," David said. "She wants to at least consider choosing life."

"You really think so? But you don't know her boyfriend. This Craig is such a loser."

"I think Brian pressed Melissa pretty hard. But she stayed strong. She made the right decision."

"I hope Reese can do that."

"I'm going to be praying for her tonight."

"Yeah, you and me both," Nate said. "But do you think that really works? I mean, sometimes it just feels like I pray stuff and it bounces off the ceiling."

"My mom says prayer is pouring out your heart to God. And when you give Him the things that are troubling you, something happens inside. You find peace by giving God the things that wrap you up. If you trust Him to take control, He can do that."

"Would you pray for Reese?"

"I'll do better than that. I'll pray for her and her baby."

The next day Melissa drove to the corner of Parker Avenue and Thirteenth Street near Indianapolis. She parked and stood at the iron gate in front of the building with a heavy heart. She hadn't been here in years and had no real reason to visit now except to remember and meet with David. The railing around the parking lot was the same as she remembered, and when she closed her eyes, she could hear the voices and see the nurses walking toward her with a blanket and the radios.

She shook off the memory and walked around the block, noticing houses and trees. How many lives had been taken here? How many futures altered forever? Her own future had been changed with a decision made inside the redbrick building. She recalled Brian driving to the clinic in silence and parking, then handing her money, as if he didn't trust her enough to give it to her before they arrived.

The vivid images she recalled surprised her. Just the sense of the place was enough to awaken memories that had been dormant for nearly two decades.

The Coltons' minivan pulled up and parked along the street. Melissa stood by the fence and watched David get out first. Nate was busy with his phone, capturing the walk of the family along the sidewalk.

"Hey, thanks for meeting me here," Melissa said, hugging David.

"Of course. So where are we?"

"Nineteen years ago, when I found out that I was pregnant, Brian and I drove here together. This fence was lined with protesters." The emotion snuck up on her and she faced the fence. "I came here to have an abortion."

She glanced at David and he was clearly shocked at what he was hearing. She turned back to the fence. "When I got out, they put a blanket over my head and a radio beside each ear to drown out all the noise. But as I was walking in, I could still hear their voices. I heard this woman say, 'Your baby has ten fingers and ten toes. Please don't kill it!'

"So we get inside, and they make you pay immediately. So I go back, I have my gown on, I sat down on a cold table, and there was a tray with all these tools on it. And the door opens and the doctor walks in, washes his hands, puts on a pair of gloves, sits down on a little silver chair and scoots across the room. He told me to put my feet in the stirrups. I lay back and turned my head, and I heard the words, *Get up! There's still time.*

"Right as he went to touch me, I said, 'I can't do this.' He just backed up, ripped his gloves off, threw them in the trash, and left. He didn't say a word to me. They don't protect you when you leave. They protect you when you come in. So all those people thought I did it.'"

Melissa closed her eyes, trying to push back the emotion overwhelming her. She locked eyes with David. "Those few seconds . . . You wouldn't be standing here. I would have killed you."

The pain of the story was written on David's face. His chin quavered and tears came. Melissa had told him abortion was something she and Brian had considered, but she could tell he hadn't understood how close he had come to being a statistic.

"I'm so sorry," she cried and she put her arms around him and David hugged her, holding her neck with his hand. They were both holding on to each other in a grateful embrace of regret and love and hope.

"Don't be sorry," David said. "You let me live. There's nothing to be sorry for."

Melissa spoke into his shoulder. "I thought you might hate me."

"No." David pulled back and looked at her. "I don't hate you at all. I'm so grateful."

Susan approached and it was clear she had heard the conversation. With a smile in her voice, she said, "My turn." She hugged Melissa tightly, and there was a mixture of sadness and forgiveness and joy in the laughter Melissa felt at that moment.

"Thank you for choosing life," Susan whispered in her ear.

Melissa pulled back and took Susan's face in her hands. With determination she said, "I know what happened all those years ago."

"What?" Susan said.

"I had to be the mom who let go so you could be the mom who won't. Thank you for being there for him."

They held each other and cried. Melissa said, "I couldn't let you go home without knowing all of it."

"I'm glad you told him," Susan said.

A few minutes later, Melissa noticed David and Nate in a conversation. The quirky redheaded kid who was so enamored of being behind the camera had put it in his pocket and was wiping away tears. Had her story done that to him or was something else going on?

✦ ✦ ✦

On the train ride home, David watched the countryside pass as if it were his life. All the decisions made and people who had led him to this point passed like a blur as he considered what was ahead. Nate sat across from him going through video he had shot at the former abortion clinic.

"You need to get that in there somehow, in the final video," David said.

"Get what in there?"

"That the abortion clinic was eventually closed. It's a county health facility now."

"I can put text on the screen at the end or you can do a voice-over," Nate said absently. "The bigger question is, what do we call this? I mean, we can have the most gripping story in the world but if we don't have a good title . . ."

"What about *I Chose Life*?"

"Too on the nose," Nate said. "It explains what happens. And if you're right and people see this who are trying to make a decision like Melissa did . . ." He thought a moment. "You want something artistic, something that draws you in but doesn't give it away."

"Like what?" David said.

"Like . . ." Nate dropped his phone on the table between them. "I don't know."

Nate wasn't his hyper self. He wasn't thinking of the

next shot he could get or next location to shoot. There was a letdown for both of them from the events of the past few days. David had found answers to so many questions, and more questions had surfaced. For Nate, it had been an intense time of gathering video he could use for the documentary, and David could see his mind spinning with how he would cut things together and pull viewers in. Nate talked about the kind of music he wanted to use to make things even more dramatic and emotional. But the situation with Reese seemed to occupy him more than any of that.

Finally Nate picked up the phone again and spoke as he stared at the screen. "I don't know what I'm going to tell her."

"Tell who?"

"Reese. I know she's probably thinking the same thing Melissa did." Nate looked at David. "Her baby could be somebody's best friend someday."

David listened to the clack of the wheels on the track and felt the vibration of the train. A thought came to him. "Hey, could I talk to her?"

Nate gave a slight nod. "Maybe. She's pretty stubborn, dude."

Nate held the phone up and switched videos. He leaned a little closer to the screen. "Hey, what about Parker Avenue?" He looked up as if seeing a theater marquee above him and lifted a hand. "*I Almost Died on Parker Avenue.*"

"Whoa, that's a little morbid." David looked out the window at the trees, the hillsides exploding with green. "How about *I Lived on Parker Avenue?*"

Nate nodded. "All right, okay. I like it. I might use it. Maybe."

CHAPTER 31

✦ ✦ ✦

David thought about writing a note to Reese and having
Nate slip it under her door. She spent most of her time in
her room these days. But in the end, they decided against
it. Better to let the conversation happen naturally.

David spent time at Nate's house watching the footage and the initial cutting of the video and audio for the
documentary, but he couldn't help walking into the hallway and looking at Reese's door just a few steps away. And
he prayed for her as he looked.

He had begun to pray not only for Reese but also for
her boyfriend, Craig, that God would open their eyes to

see what was really happening. He prayed for an opportunity to talk with her. And then he prayed for the baby. A real, living human was being formed in Reese's womb, and David prayed the child would not only survive but be able to thrive in the world.

Use me, use my story, use Melissa or Brian in this, Lord. I don't know how You're going to do it, but I trust that You can because you care more for Reese and this baby than anyone.

David was engrossed in the footage of the skydiving, arguing with Nate about what to include, when he heard the door open behind them. Reese stood there in a cranberry sweat suit, both pants and shirt. She moved her head left as if telling David to follow her, then closed the door.

David put a hand on Nate's shoulder. "Did you tell her I wanted to talk?"

"No, I haven't seen her out of her room."

As David walked out the door, Nate said, "No pressure, but this might be your only shot."

"Thanks a lot," David said.

Nate's house had a wraparound porch and Reese stood at the railing with her arms crossed. David put his back against the wall by the door, giving her space.

"Heard you had quite a trip," Reese said.

How had she heard that? "Yeah, it was amazing and scary and emotional and really good. All at the same time. But really hard, too. I learned a lot."

"What was hard about it?"

"I don't know, hearing the truth. The pain Melissa went through. Brian, too. When I got up there, he didn't want to meet. He said—"

"I heard," Reese said coldly, interrupting him.

"How?" David said.

"Nate keeps his speakers turned up to jet engine level. It's not hard to put two and two together."

"Yeah, I suppose not," David said, trying to smile. "And I need to thank you. You know, the idea you gave Nate about Courtney. The horse."

"It was a hit with her?"

"I wish you could have seen her face. I mean, you can see it through the camera, but being there was . . . It was like those videos of pets that get lost and then make their way back to their owners. Courtney just hugged that thing and put it on her bed and kept staring at it."

Reese didn't respond. She began to pace the porch.

"Reese, she is the cutest kid. It's so bizarre to see someone that you've never met, that you never even knew existed, and they look so similar to you."

"So now you have a full sister and a half sister?" Reese said, her voice sounding unconvinced of David's excitement.

"Yeah."

"Isn't that kind of weird?"

"It is weird. But you know, it's also kind of awesome. I just assumed I was an only child."

Birds sang in the trees and provided the soundtrack that filled in the pauses of their conversation.

"So what now? Will you still see your biological family?"

"The Coltons are my family. But if everyone's okay with it, we'll definitely keep up with each other."

Reese put her back against one of the columns and thought a moment. David didn't want to come on too strong and scare her away, but he also didn't want to shrink back from the truth of his story. He breathed a quick prayer.

"I'm not sure it's always like that," Reese said. She turned and sat on the top step and crossed her arms again.

What to say? He had no idea what she was going through inside. And yet he did. There was another life growing there. And he remembered his prayer for the baby.

"Yeah, maybe not," he said, sitting on the top step too. "But I can tell you that I'm so glad she got off that table. I'm so glad that I'm here. Reese, I was at that abortion clinic nineteen years ago, in her womb. And she let me live. You know, I can only thank God for that. There's already so much death. You could give life. Life that is already inside of you."

Reese glanced at David. She rocked back and forth as

if in pain, and her brow furrowed as if he couldn't understand the turmoil inside.

After a moment, David sighed. "Listen, if you and Craig aren't ready, there are many, many men and women out there who are ready to be parents. Just like mine."

Reese looked away.

"Look, I don't mean to pressure you, but would you at least think about it?"

Reese didn't respond. She seemed to be struggling, like a person walking a tightrope and trying hard not to fall.

"You asked me if it was weird having two sisters now," David said. "I think life is what it is. It's weird and it's surprising and it's scary and wonderful and unpredictable. Weird's okay if you embrace it, you know?"

Reese pursed her lips and made a fist with her hand. Then she got up from the steps and crossed her arms again and shook her head as if she didn't want to hear any more. She hurried to the sidewalk and David watched her walk away.

He couldn't help feeling that he had failed. Maybe he had even made things worse. But he had tried.

He hung his head and closed his eyes. *God, You know what's going on inside Reese. You know how much Nate and his parents care for her. Would You use my story for good? Help her choose life. Give her hope, I pray. And I trust You to do it.*

CHAPTER 32

✦ ✦ ✦

TEN MONTHS LATER

The sky was overcast and dark clouds threatened rain at the March for Life rally. There were only about a hundred people gathered on the plaza steps, but David felt like he would have had just as many butterflies in his stomach if ten thousand had been there.

His father straightened his tie. "You nervous?"

"Just a little," David said, holding up his hand to show how much he was shaking.

"You're going to be great. Just tell your story, right?"

"That's all I can do," David said. "And hope someone is here who needs to hear it."

His mother handed him a bottle of water. "Guess who's here? Melissa drove down to see you. I saw her a minute ago."

"Wow," David said. "Doesn't Courtney have a game today?"

"Shawn is with her. Melissa said she wouldn't miss this for the world."

One of the organizers walked up to David. "The director is going to make some introductory remarks and then introduce you. You ready?"

"Let's do it," David said.

When he was introduced, there was polite applause and he took his place behind the podium. As he looked out over the crowd, he noticed Melissa and she smiled and clapped her hands and mouthed, *"You can do this."*

Suddenly, with his mother and father watching, and other friends and strangers as well, David felt at peace with himself and his story. His dad had been right. All he had was his story and he just needed to be faithful to tell it.

"Melissa and Brian lived in Indiana," he said. "They were eighteen years old, seniors in high school, not married, and had no money saved. But Melissa was pregnant. So they decided that abortion was their solution. They went to the abortion clinic, ready to abort their child. But to get into the clinic, they had to pass the pro-life protesters praying for them, trying to get them to change their minds. As Melissa was walking in, she heard one woman tell her that her baby had ten fingers and ten toes.

"As she sat on the table, ready to abort her child, she remembered what that woman had told her. And she realized that her baby was special, and that her baby was real.

"So she left the abortion clinic and choose adoption. And that's how I'm here. I was that baby nineteen years ago."

✦ ✦ ✦

When David finished, the organizer introduced another speaker. David walked into the crowd and Melissa found him and gave him a huge hug.

"That was just awesome," she said. "I don't know how you speak in front of people and stay so calm like you do."

"Believe me, I was nervous. But every time I tell my story, it gets a little easier. I mean, I don't want to get up in front of a lot of people and talk, but when I do, I think of you."

"What do you mean?"

"It took such courage for you to get up and walk away from that clinic. So I just draw on the courage you had and I tell my story."

Melissa hugged him again. Then she hugged his parents and they moved away from the crowd to talk.

Reese walked up to him, holding her baby and smiling at David.

"How's little Jackson doing?" David said.

"He's doing well. Nate was his first babysitter, did he tell you?"

"Of course," David said. "I have no memory left on my phone because of this little guy. Nate's taking pictures and sending them every day."

Reese looked down at Jackson. "Did you know that his middle name is David?"

David nodded.

"I'm going to kill Nate—he promised he wouldn't tell you."

"Thank you," David said. "It's an honor for him to have my name."

Reese looked up at him and tears rimmed her eyes. "I don't think he'd be here if you hadn't told me your story."

"I wasn't sure you were even listening that day when we talked," David said.

"I heard you. I was just trying not to. And then I snuck into Nate's room while he was gone one night and pulled up the video he's been working on. It was different watching it than just listening to the audio through the wall. I cried when you and Melissa met for the first time."

"We're hoping a lot of people see that video."

"When I look back, I don't know how I could have considered making that choice," Reese said. "When you're in the middle of it, it seems like a good idea. It seems like it will solve things." She held Jackson close. "But I'm grateful that I made this choice. Forever grateful."

"One day Jackson is going to look at you and tell you he's proud of you for doing what you've done."

Reese walked away and David breathed a prayer of thanks for the little life she held in her arms.

A woman approached him followed by a teenage boy. She reached out a hand and shook David's.

"I am so glad you are telling your story, young man," the woman said. She pulled her son in front of her. "I brought Damien with me today to hear what the speakers would say."

"Well, I'm glad you could be here," David said.

"You see, your story is Damien's story too. I was being pressured to have an abortion. Even my family said I was crazy for having my child. But I want you to look into his eyes and tell me if I was crazy or not."

Damien rolled his eyes. "Aw, Mom. Stop."

"God has His hand on you, young man," the woman said to David. "You be faithful to tell how good He's been to you."

"I will do that," David said. He looked at Damien. "And you can be thankful for a mom who loves you enough to brag on you."

She patted Damien's chest and the boy smiled. "Is it true you're going to law school?"

"LSU."

"Then you go out there and be the best lawyer you can be for the Lord, you hear me?"

David smiled. "I'll do that."

CHAPTER 33

✦ ✦ ✦

The owners of the Orpheum Theater unrolled a red carpet that was closer to orange, but to David it felt like he was living a dream he'd never dreamed. The premiere of the short film Nate had created was being shown to family, friends, and invited guests in the town.

Courtney insisted she sit by her big brother and no one on the front row would deny her. Brian and Azure sat behind them with Presley, and Melissa and Shawn were next to Courtney. There was an empty seat for Nate to David's right—he was onstage shooting video of the event. Then came David's parents, and beside them were Paw Paw and G.

Finally, as the moment arrived for the showing, Nate hurried to his seat—then left again, returning with a tub of popcorn big enough to feed a small village.

"Dude, you're going to get butter on your tux," David said.

"I have napkins," he said. "Courtney, want popcorn?"

David's mom leaned forward to say something. Then she shook her head and smiled at Nate.

David had seen the film in its various stages, with and without music. There were cuts that Nate had made on advice of an industry professional who had caught wind of the project. The woman had edited some major films and was as committed to life as David and Nate. She believed in the message and suggested a few ideas, which Nate took.

From the moment the lights went down, the audience quieted and seemed captured by the fast-moving drama on the screen. The tension crescendoed until the moment David stood in front of Melissa's house and she ran toward him and embraced him, sobbing uncontrollably. David turned his head and saw men and women with hands over their mouths, some visibly weeping, unashamed of their tears.

"Gets me every time," Nate whispered, buttery popcorn on his breath.

Courtney hung on to David's arm when she came on

the screen, then with both hands covered her eyes. David put an arm around her and whispered, "You were fantastic, little sister. Awesome!"

The crowd laughed when David and Melissa jumped from the plane. Nate raised his eyebrows and smiled at the footage because he had cut himself completely out of the jump.

When the credits rolled, the audience stood and applauded and a microphone was brought to center stage.

David was the first to speak. "Thank you all for coming. I know many of you have seen some of the film before, but we want to share it now with as many as we can online. The story is not just about me and my birth parents and my adoptive parents. I really believe it's bigger than that.

"Our stories are given to us to steward. And we can decide to keep them hidden or release them into the world. A lot of our lives we want to keep to ourselves. The mistakes. The things we regret. Things we're ashamed of. But somehow God uses all of that to showcase His grace and how much He really loves us. And I hope that comes through every time people see this film."

Melissa stepped to the microphone. "I look at myself up there and it's almost like I'm looking at another person. I never wanted to tell that story. But seeing it again tonight helps me remember all those years ago and the scared teenager I was.

"David was an answer to a prayer I hadn't prayed," she continued. "I didn't know God back then. And I couldn't see Him in the pain and the struggle. How do you reach out to hold a hand you can't see? You can't do it. But tonight, I give God thanks that He saw me and that He was there for me when I didn't even know it. He was holding me even though I thought I was alone.

"We've already heard from some people who have seen this little film. It's making an impact on hearts. It's giving women and men the courage to say yes to life. To say yes to ten little fingers and ten little toes. You'll never regret embracing life, even if it's painful."

David's mom and dad said a few words. Brian and Azure just waved to the crowd and nodded when they were mentioned.

Finally Nate stepped forward. "I've known David since the first grade and I have to say he's put up with a lot from me. His whole family has. When I heard about his adoption and that he might get to meet Brian and Melissa, I thought it would be a good story to capture. I kind of made a nuisance of myself at David's house and on the trip to Melissa's. But I don't regret any of it. I'm glad I was part of it.

"What you don't know is that someone I love a lot went through this same story, right as we were shooting this. And when she saw what had happened to David, even though she just wanted her problems to go away, she had the courage to say yes to life, like Melissa did."

Nate's voice began to tremble and he looked down at the microphone. "David's right. This is a lot bigger than just a film about his life and his adoptive parents and birth parents. This is really about all of us. Nobody in this room, nobody who watches this film is a mistake. The love that the Coltons showed David came from somewhere deep inside, even beyond them. It's always been a picture of God's love for us. And I hope you feel that as you think about the film, that God has a bigger plan for the pain and struggle you're going through."

David's heart swelled because he had never seen Nate speak so slowly and with such conviction. Usually he was talking fast and making points and gesturing with his hands, but now his words came deliberately and with emotion.

"Dude, where did that come from?" David said when Nate stepped back.

Nate shrugged, then pointed to his heart. David hugged him.

Susan was getting ready for David's departure again. He was heading back to school, and every goodbye was hard. Sure, she could text him and call and email, but there was something about how fast he was growing up that made her scared she was losing him.

She knew that wasn't true, and she prayed for a tranquil heart and a willingness to let him be who God wanted him to be. But there was still an element of, "Lord, I believe. Help my unbelief."

After breakfast, David asked if the two of them would come with him on a drive before he left for school and they agreed.

"Where are we going?" Jimmy said.

"You'll see," David said.

On the way, David talked about his favorite professor, a former judge who David discovered had signed the legal papers to finalize his adoption. "It's crazy that he would come back into my life after all these years," he said. "He's a real friend and mentor to me now."

Susan smiled and watched the familiar scenery. When David made the turn into the cemetery, her heart fluttered. She and Jimmy got out, and David opened the trunk and pulled out two arrangements of yellow lilies and baby's breath, giving one to her and one to Jimmy.

They walked to the stones of her sons and she knelt and placed the bouquet by John's grave. Jimmy placed the flowers by Michael's.

David knelt with them. "You know, you said something to me when I was in the hospital waiting for surgery. Do you remember?"

Those few days were etched in her mind, but she wasn't sure what she had said.

"You said you were angry with God for a long time after John and Michael died. But you realized that all of that loss made a place in your heart and your home for me. You said you couldn't imagine life without me."

Susan nodded and hugged David. "That was true. It still is. I can't imagine it."

"Neither of us can," Jimmy said.

"I just wanted to come here before I head back and thank God for my brothers. Nate said the film shows that every life is precious, and theirs were too, even though they didn't live long."

"David, that's so sweet that you would remember two little babies you never even met."

"God has used their lives in mine. I want to remember their stories." He put a hand on the ground and stood. "You've taught me that you can't pick and choose what's part of your story. It's all there for a purpose. I have two brothers and two sisters now."

David reached into his pocket and pulled out two fishing lures and placed one in front of John's grave and the other in front of Michael's. "I can't wait to meet you two," he said, patting the stones. "I promise we'll go fishing one day in heaven."

"I want to be there for that," Jimmy said.

Susan walked back to the car and Jimmy caught up with her and slipped a hand into hers.

When they got home, David said goodbye and got in his car and began to drive away, then stopped and leaned out the window.

"Almost forgot," he said. "I left something for the two of you in the kitchen. Paw Paw and G told me I ought to do it."

Susan looked at Jimmy with a blank stare. They waved at David and hurried to the kitchen. On the counter was a note that said, *No fighting over these*. Underneath was an unopened box of Girl Scout cookies.

Susan laughed and Jimmy held her until her laughter turned to tears and then back to laughter again.

DISCUSSION QUESTIONS

1. When Susan and Jimmy lose their infant sons, Susan at first struggles with the belief that she is "carrying more than her fair share of the grief." How does she come to understand Jimmy's grieving process? Was there a time when you processed a loss or another difficult situation differently from someone you loved? How did that affect your relationship?

2. What did you think of Jimmy's decision to resubmit the adoption application? Was he right to do that without telling Susan? How would you have advised them to move forward when they felt differently about trying again for an adoption?

3. Do you think Susan and Jimmy tell David about his adoption at the right time, in the right way? How would you have suggested they broach the subject, if they'd come to you for advice?

4. Melissa thinks about David constantly, wondering about his life and how he's growing up, while Brian tries not to think about their son and wants to move on. Did you understand both reactions? Whose perspective did you sympathize with more?

5. David also struggles when his wrestling career is interrupted. When you've faced disappointment, have you been more inclined to sit with it for a long time or to quickly put it behind you? How do you balance disappointment with the desire to move forward? What does trusting God look like after a loss?

6. Melissa tells Brian, "You can't keep secrets all your life. They'll eat you up inside. They'll tear other people apart too." Do you believe there's ever a reason to keep secrets? How are the characters in this story affected by secrets?

7. As David grows, Susan and Jimmy face the fear of losing him in a number of different ways. How do they respond to each of these instances? How do you think you would respond in their place?

8. Shawn tells Melissa, "You know what I've heard about prayer? Sometimes we don't ask too much. We ask too little. We don't think God is powerful enough to grant our requests, so we hold back. Why

don't you pray something big?" Do you agree with
his perspective on prayer? Was there a time in your
own life when you found yourself asking God for too
little? Or when you risked praying something big?
What happened?

9. David's experience gives him the opportunity to talk
to Reese and influence a critical decision in her life.
What pieces of your own story, even if painful, might
be used to help or strengthen or inspire others?

10. Has adoption touched your life in any way? Tell the
story.

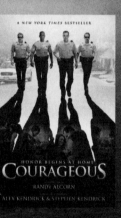

OVERCOMER

✦ ✦ ✦

Barbara Scott felt defeated every time she looked at Hannah. She didn't want to, but she did. For weeks she had inquired about getting the girl into a new school, but doors closed. Hannah had a reputation she couldn't shake. Barbara inquired at private schools in the area, but when she heard the cost per semester, she politely thanked them and hung up the phone.

In late July, as the enrollment period was coming to an end, a woman named Shelly Hundley left a message. She said she was in the financial office of Brookshire Christian School and wanted to speak about Hannah. On her break at work, Barbara returned the call.

"Thank you for calling me back, Ms. Scott. I was told you were interested in Hannah attending here?" The woman spoke in crisp tones. She sounded like she had her life together. Not a care in the world.

"I did inquire there, but when I heard the cost, I knew I couldn't make it work. But thank you for—"

"I understand, Ms. Scott. And you're right—Brookshire isn't cheap. But we think our school is worth the investment. There are some great people here who really care about our students."

Barbara couldn't believe the sales pitch. "I'm sure they do, ma'am. But I can't afford it."

"I understand. But there may still be a way," Shelly said quickly, before Barbara could hang up.

"What way is that?"

"Why don't you and Hannah come by the office tomorrow afternoon?"

Barbara wanted to say, *What's the point?* Instead, she said, "I work until six."

"How about in the morning, before you go to work?"

"I work two jobs to make ends meet. I start at five tomorrow morning and I'm not done until six in the evening."

"I see," Shelly said, pausing. "What if we met tomorrow night at seven thirty? That would give you time to get home, have dinner with your granddaughter, and then bring her here."

Barbara shook her head. This woman wasn't giving up. And how did she know Hannah was her granddaughter?

All of that swirled in her brain until Barbara had enough. "Look, I appreciate you offering to stay late, but I don't see a reason to trouble you. Even if you cut the rate in half, I can't afford it."

"Please. Just bring Hannah to the school tomorrow evening. I promise it will be worth the effort."

Barbara reluctantly agreed, though she doubted the woman's words. Everybody had an angle. Everybody was looking for something from somebody and if you trusted them, at best you'd get hurt and at worst you'd have your heart broken. Many times over, as Barbara had learned. What if she took Hannah there and she actually liked this school? Why get the child's hopes up when there was no chance?

But Barbara had exhausted every other option already. And a hopeless possibility was still better than no possibility at all. The next evening, after a quick dinner, Barbara and Hannah headed to Brookshire.

"I don't understand why we're going there if we can't afford it," Hannah said.

"You and me both, baby. Somebody wants you to see the school. And I'm guessing they want you to see it and like it enough to get me to pay. It's not gonna happen. Not in a million years. But at least we can hear the woman out."

Hannah put her earbuds in and Barbara motioned for her to wait. "Don't get too attached to this place. Act coy. Do you know what *coy* is?"

"Not really."

"It means . . . don't get excited. And if you do, don't let her know. Play it cool."

"Okay."

Barbara hated to admit that every time she looked at Hannah, her stomach churned. Every time she saw those deep-brown eyes, she saw her daughter's face. She saw the way Janet had squandered her life. She saw Hannah making bad choices and mistakes that would follow her, maybe for the rest of her life. Hannah was running for something just out of her reach.

The problem, Barbara knew, was that when she looked at Hannah and saw Janet, she also saw herself. Three generations along the very same path, though making very different kinds of mistakes along the way. Life for Barbara had become a nonstop loop where she worked all day and came home to her little house by the bend in the river. She had scraped up the down payment and moved in only to be too tired to enjoy the accomplishment. On so many levels her life was one step forward and one step back down a flight of stairs. Here she was again at the bottom landing trying to pick herself up.

Her marriage had been like that. She'd found a man she thought could make her happy. The outcome wasn't good. At first, the marriage had gone well. Everything *seemed* fine. She called him "honey" and he called her "love." The trouble came when she discovered she wasn't his only love.

Barbara had inklings something wasn't right from their first date. He made her feel warm and cherished and cared for, unlike other men who didn't open car doors or act gentlemanly. But something was off. Something didn't quite fit. It was just a hint of a question mark, a twinge of doubt, that Barbara pushed down. Strangely, the doubt about him became a doubt about herself. Every time she had the feeling that something was off, she kicked herself and heard an accusing voice: *What are you thinking? He's a good man. He'll be a good provider. A real catch. Why are you sabotaging your chance at a good marriage?*

She heard that in her head as she walked the aisle and said, "I do." And she did. She pushed all the questions and doubt away and plunged in.

And then, one summer day five years after the wedding, things fell apart. It happened, strangely enough, with the idea of cleaning her house, top to bottom. While Janet was content in her playpen, Barbara rolled up her sleeves and chose to start with the spare room upstairs. She opened the closet and removed clothes she didn't even know she had. In ten minutes she had her first load ready for Goodwill and felt she was making progress.

She took everything from the shelf above the clothes—photo albums, magazines, a strongbox with birth certificates and important papers, and mementos collected from their honeymoon. With everything clear, she noticed a square piece of wood in the ceiling slightly askew, probably the entry to the attic crawl space. The panel sat funny, revealing a hole, like it had been recently moved. She tried to reach it, but even on tiptoes she couldn't. She carried the crooked, paint-scarred stepladder from the garage, checking on Janet. She climbed the ladder and pushed at the board, but instead of aligning it, she became curious. What was up there? She took another step up and peeked over the edge of the opening.

What Barbara saw sent her life into a spiral. Videos. Magazines. Those were bad enough. What took her breath away were pictures in a plastic bag. She opened them and looked through them. These were not old pictures but recent. As she stared at them, all the doubt she had felt while dating and in the last five years rose like a mushroom cloud. The man she thought she had married, the one who called her "love," was not who she thought he was. He wore a mask. And the pictures showed the face behind it.

Standing on that ladder, seeing the truth, had crushed Barbara. But she also resolved then and there that she would never be taken in by anyone. She would never let someone convince her they were something they weren't. She had learned the hard way you couldn't trust anybody. If you did, they'd let you down.

Now, driving to Brookshire, seeing Hannah in her peripheral vision, she felt like she was on some rickety ladder. She had gone through unimaginable hurt and pain with Janet, who sneaked around with T-bone, who lied about where she was going and what she was doing. All she had left of her daughter was a photo album and a gravestone.

The summer sun was still up when they arrived at Brookshire. The school grounds were immaculately trimmed.

"Sure looks different than Franklin High," Hannah said.

Shelly met them at the front door and insisted on giving a guided tour. They walked through the halls and into the gymnasium. She showed them the track and other athletic fields. Sports seemed to be a big deal, though the recent closing of the steel plant had caused a diaspora.

That's it, Barbara thought. *Enrollment is down and the school is desperate to get new students.*

Shelly took them to a beautiful library, a media center, the cafeteria, and an auditorium that looked amazing. Barbara wanted the tour to stop, but she followed the woman through the halls. After a half hour, Shelly led them to her office. The room was furnished nicely but wasn't over-the-top.

"So what did you think, Hannah?" Shelly said, smiling and folding her hands on her desk.

Hannah glanced at Barbara, then back at the woman. "It's nice."

"How would you like to go to school here?"

Barbara leaned forward. "Ma'am, I told you there is no way I can afford—"

Shelly raised a hand and opened a folder on the desk. "There's a friend of the school who heard of Hannah's situation and wanted to help."

"Friend?" Barbara said. "Who?"

"A person who wishes to remain anonymous," Shelly said. "Hannah's tuition has been paid. For the entire year."

"What?" Hannah said, glancing at Barbara with eyes as wide as saucers. She put a hand over her mouth as she stared at her grandmother.

Barbara's jaw dropped, too. Tears came to her eyes. *Who would do such a thing?*

"I don't know what to say," Barbara finally said.

Shelly looked at the folder. "Now, there is the situation of the expulsions at the former schools. There's a code of conduct we ask our students and their parents or guardians to sign. You'll see the dress code, as well. I have a welcome packet that explains all of that. So if you agree, you simply sign the forms and return them."

"We can sign that now," Barbara said quickly.

Shelly smiled. "It's another month before school starts. Take the packet, read it carefully so you know the rules and what's acceptable and not acceptable."

"I can assure you Hannah will abide by all the rules," Barbara said. "That trouble she had, that's over and done with. Right, Hannah?"

"Yes, ma'am," Hannah said, her voice a little too soft for Barbara's liking.

"We are grateful for this opportunity, Ms. Hundley. And you can trust that Hannah will be on her best behavior."

Shelly looked at Hannah. "I think you're going to find the teachers and staff here warm and welcoming. The students all want to learn. We have a great athletic program, though to be honest, we're not sure which sports will be available in the fall. What are your interests outside of the classroom?"

Hannah seemed confused by the question.

"She ran track last year," Barbara said.

"Cross-country," Hannah said, correcting her.

Shelly nodded. "That's great. You should go out for the team."

As they left, Barbara paused in front of the school and studied the list of names on a plaque. That's when it came together. That's when she realized what had happened.

In the car, Hannah stared out the windshield, dumbfounded. "Did that really happen?"

"I can hardly believe it myself, but it really did, baby."

"I wonder who gave the scholarship."

Barbara swallowed hard and stared at the road. "That's not important. What is important is for you to study hard, work hard, and avoid any of the trouble you got into at Franklin High. You understand me?"

"Yes, ma'am."

Barbara drove toward home and a memory jumped out of nowhere. She and her daughter would celebrate when something positive happened. If Barbara got a raise or if Janet got a good grade on a test or a part in the school play, Janet would pull out the same song and play it over and over. At home, she turned up the speakers and danced around the house. The memory made Barbara smile.

Instead of turning left as they neared their house, she took a right.

"Where are you going?" Hannah said.

"'Celebrate good times, come on,'" Barbara sang, dipping her head and snapping her fingers.

"What are you talking about?"

"It's something your mother used to sing. Anything good happened and she'd play that song and dance. And we'd go to Anna Banana for ice cream."

Hannah smiled and seemed to enjoy the sight of her grandmother singing and dancing behind the wheel. Barbara thought it was a breakthrough. Things were beginning to turn around.

ABOUT THE AUTHORS

Chris Fabry is an award-winning author and radio personality who hosts the daily program *Chris Fabry Live* on Moody Radio. He is also heard on *Love Worth Finding*, *Building Relationships with Dr. Gary Chapman*, and other radio programs. In 2020, he was inducted into the Marshall University School of Journalism and Mass Communications Hall of Fame. A native of West Virginia, Chris and his wife, Andrea, now live in Arizona and are the parents of nine children.

Chris's novels, which include *Dogwood*, *June Bug*, *Almost Heaven*, *The Promise of Jesse Woods*, and *A Piece of the Moon*, have won five Christy Awards, an ECPA Christian Book Award, and two Awards of Merit from *Christianity Today*. He was inducted into the Christy Award Hall of Fame in 2018. His books include movie novelizations, such as *War Room* and *Overcomer*, and novels for children and young adults. He coauthored the Left Behind: The Kids series with Jerry B. Jenkins and Tim LaHaye, as well as the Red Rock Mysteries and the Wormling series with Jerry B. Jenkins. He encourages those who dream of writing with his website heyyoucanwrite.com. Find out more about his books at chrisfabry.com.

Alex Kendrick is an award-winning author gifted at telling stories of hope and redemption. He is best known as an actor, writer, and director of the films *Overcomer*, *War Room*, *Courageous*, *Fireproof*, and *Facing the Giants* and coauthor of the *New York Times* bestselling books *The Love Dare*, *The Resolution for Men*, and *The Battle Plan for Prayer*. Alex has received more than thirty awards for his work, including best screenplay, best actor, and best feature film. Alex has spoken to churches, universities, and conferences all across America and in other countries. He has been featured on FOX News, CNN, *ABC World News Tonight*, *CBS Evening News*, *Time* magazine, and many other media outlets. He is a graduate of Kennesaw State University and attended seminary before being ordained into ministry. Alex and his wife, Christina, live in Albany, Georgia, with their six children. They are active members of Sherwood Church.

Stephen Kendrick is a speaker, film producer, and author with a ministry passion for prayer and discipleship. He is a cowriter and producer of the movies *Overcomer*, *War Room*, *Courageous*, *Fireproof*, and *Facing the Giants* and cowriter of the *New York Times* bestsellers *The Battle Plan for Prayer*, *The Resolution for Men*, and *The Love Dare*. *The Love Dare* quickly became a number one *New York Times* bestseller and stayed on the list for more than two years. Stephen has spoken at churches, conferences, and seminars around the nation and has been interviewed by *Fox & Friends*, CNN, *ABC World News Tonight*, the *Washington Post*, and other media outlets. He is a cofounder and board member of the Fatherhood Commission. He graduated from Kennesaw State University and attended seminary before being ordained into ministry. Stephen and his wife, Jill, live in Albany, Georgia, where they homeschool their six children. They are active members of Sherwood Church in Albany.

kendrickbrothers.com

TYNDALE HOUSE PUBLISHERS IS CRAZY4FICTION!

Fiction that entertains and inspires

Get to know us! Become a member of the Crazy4Fiction community. Whether you read our blog, like us on Facebook, follow us on Twitter, or receive our e-newsletter, you're sure to get the latest news on the best in Christian fiction. You might even win something along the way!

JOIN IN THE FUN TODAY.

 crazy4fiction.com

 Crazy4Fiction

 crazy4fiction

 @Crazy4Fiction